SAHARA'S REVENGE

THE SILESIA CHRONICLES BOOK ONE

SHANNON BLAKE

*For Frank
and for my children*

True love isn't just for fairy tales.

ONE

Something was wrong with Sahara's vision. Everything was a blur of hazy shadows and refracted light. She could only just make out the line of prisoners in front of her, their arms pinioned to the walls of their cages by chains. Dead? It was impossible to tell.

She squeezed her eyes shut and opened them again. This was wrong. All wrong. They'd sedated her for the transfer from her home-world of Amaryl to the prison moon of K'ilenfir. She should still be in stasis, like the rest of the prisoners, who were...asleep?

Not asleep. Dead.

The ship shuddered and she heard a low rumble from some-where in the engineering decks below her. For a sickening moment, she was weightless, and then she crashed to the floor, dragging against the chains holding her arms. Her cry of pain came out as a dry croak. She felt heavier than she'd ever been in her life.

She squeezed her hands open and shut, trying to coax blood back into them. The chains bit into her wrists. She tried to stand on tiptoe to relive the pressure, but her body was heavy. So heavy.

"Help!" she squawked before she could stop herself.

It was ridiculous to shout for help. The Drakkin didn't give a damn about her. This was a prisoner transport, not a pleasure cruise —and she was lucky they'd kept her alive after what she'd done. And anyway, she thought grimly, she didn't need her arms to be a divining wand in those mines.

She squinted at the limp bodies in front of her. None of them looked like her team—Rilla and Ivy and the twins.

For a split second, her heart lurched in hope. That's why there were no guards. There'd been an uprising and her team had taken the ship. As soon as they cleared the bridge, they'd come for her.

"Rilla!" she shouted, her voice still a pathetic croak. "Ivy! I'm over here! I'm alive! I'm—"

The ship shuddered again. The bodies in front of her lurched and swung weirdly, like the half-gutted corpses of pigs and chickens she'd seen hanging in the back of the butcher's stall back on Amaryl. She wanted to vomit.

She dragged against her chains as that head-spinning dizziness of partial-G swept over her.

What if she was wrong?

What if they're all dead?

She had no idea where they were. What if she hung here for days? She shuddered. With her body out of stasis, she'd starve or die of thirst—unless the ship crashed first.

Waves of panic overwhelmed whatever was left of the heavy narcotic in her blood.

"Ivy!" she shouted. "Kris!"

A crawling feeling along her spine made her shudder again. Something was horribly wrong. The hyper-instinct that had made her the Chrysalis—and the only one to make it through the Shift—was screaming at her.

A strange, acrid smell slowly filled her cell.

What is that?

Her muddled brain struggled with recognition until she dragged in a deep breath and choked.

Smoke.

She couldn't see any sign of fire anywhere near her. It could be coming from anywhere.

The ship lurched again, suspending her in free fall for a few hideous seconds. She crashed against her chains, harder this time, and the link connected to the bracelet around her right wrist snapped. The heavy fetter banged against the side of the ship. Sahara doubled over, clutching her numb arm to her chest.

A wave smoke poured through the deck, burning Sahara's lungs. She buried her face in her right elbow and tried to breathe. From somewhere ahead of her, she heard a vague klaxon. As she struggled to see through smoke-bleared eyes, the cold white lights in the corridor flickered and died, replaced by strobing red.

The klaxon sounded louder now, and a horrible grinding noise from somewhere in the bowels of the ship brought Sahara's full consciousness back with a vicious surge of adrenaline.

Focus, she told herself as her mind plunged in a thousand different directions. *Solve the problem.*

The ship was going to blow—she knew that for certain. But there had to be an escape pod somewhere, maybe even more than one. If she could get out of this damn cage, maybe she could find her friends and they could get off the ship.

She braced her feet against the inner wall of the cell and hauled against the chain holding her left hand. It fought her and she swore viciously. She gripped the chain and leveraged all her weight against it. As her palms grated down the metal links, blood slicked them and she gritted her teeth in pain. She wrenched the chain back and forth with a guttural roar.

It was no use. She dropped the chain, panting a little and curling her fingers against the burning pain in her palms.

Suddenly, a roaring sound filled the deck, and the ship shuddered like it would shake itself to pieces. It plummeted, and the artificial gravity systems went offline. Sahara floated upward, and the blood from her arm drifted past her face in tiny beads.

Then something exploded.

Shock waves rolled along the ship, flinging her against the back of the cage. She slammed her head against the metal, and the chain that held her left arm broke. Smoke billowed down the length of the ship, and every alarm was now blaring. Red and yellow lights strobed in the haze.

Another explosion rippled through the ship, this one even closer to her than the last. The ten cages in front of her warped like string and a blast of heat almost knocked her senseless.

She had to get out. She plunged forward and grabbed the door of her cage. The metal was warped so severely that the lock was jammed, but there was just enough space for her to squeeze between the bars and the cage frame. The metal tore her flimsy shirt, and she gasped in pain as it snagged her side and ripped the skin.

I will show neither pain nor fear.

The Shell mantra echoed in her mind as she propelled herself up the corridor using the bars of the cages. The ship spun around her, and she tumbled wildly from side to side. The haze was so thick that she could barely see, but she paused at every cage and stared at the prisoners' faces. All men...and all dead.

They've got to be here somewhere.

She reached the front of the deck. The blast door had been blown out, and she pulled herself through the opening into a wide corridor. She pushed off and floated forward. Just ahead, she saw a series of viewports, but they were all shielded. Beyond those, a narrow set of stairs led to the lower decks.

"I'm coming," she said under her breath. "Just hang on..."

As she reached the viewports, the ship pitched again and Sahara went with it, spinning crazily as she slammed into the ceiling, the walls, the floor. She scrabbled to grab hold of something—anything—to stabilize herself. She finally caught some kind of handle near the ceiling, but it moved with her. It was the release for the viewport shields.

As the shields retracted, any hope Sahara had that she'd survive this died inside her. Re-entry flames gnawed the sides of the ship.

They were hurtling toward the barren surface of a desert planet—but there was no way to know which planet it was.

She launched herself toward the stairs, but as her hand touched the railing, the ship crashed into the sands. The impact flung her into the wall and she hit her head again. She crashed onto the steps and tumbled down into the darkness of the hold below. Smoke choked her, and she heard glass shattering and then the sound of ripping metal. Sahara curled herself into a fetal position, trying to protect her head and neck.

And then the ship exploded. The blast of heat scorched her skin as pipes and metal showered down around her. She only knew she was screaming because of the burning ache in her throat and lungs.

Just as soon as the inferno began, it was over. For a long time, Sahara didn't dare to move. The seconds dragged into minutes, and the ship groaned around her like a living thing. Somewhere nearby, she heard the sharp clang of more metal falling. She had to get out before the hull collapsed.

Get up.

Slowly, Sahara uncurled herself and got to her hands and knees. She was shaking so badly that she could barely control her muscles, and the taste of blood filled her mouth. She tried to spit, but it did no good.

Get. Up.

She struggled to control her breathing, but she choked on the smoke. With an almost superhuman effort, she got to her feet. Above her, she could see light, but the deck where she stood was utterly dark. She took a step forward and tripped over something. She caught herself against the wall and stood there, shuddering.

Anything could be down here.

Anything...including her friends. She pressed her forehead against the wall, coughing as smoke billowed around her again.

For an agonizing moment, she battled her panic and her fear. But the thought of her friends trapped down here in the suffocating darkness propelled her forward. She groped her way along, shoving metal and pipes and wiring out of the way with her feet. Sparks showered down around her and, for an instant, she could see.

The hold ahead of her had completely collapsed and a wall of twisted metal blocked her path. There was no way through. She turned around, determined to find another way around the wreckage.

I'm coming. Just hang on.

She took a step, steadied herself. And then she heard a vague roaring sound that grew louder by the second. Heat shimmered around her, but it wasn't until she saw the wall of fire heading down the corridor that she registered what was happening.

She sprang toward what was left of the stairs. It was a mess of wreckage, and she clambered wildly, slipping and cutting her hands, her legs, her feet in her desperation to get out before she was burned alive.

She reached the upper deck and sprinted for the blown-out windows. For a single instant, she hesitated, staring down at the sands below.

As the fire raced up behind her, she jumped.

TWO

Sahara hit the sand a dozen feet below her, rolled head over heels, and then slid to a stop at the bottom of the massive dune created by the crash.

For a long time, she lay there, shaking and numb. She had no sense of time, no sense of place. The heat of sand and sun surrounded her and cradled her like a mother's embrace.

But she couldn't stay here. Already, she could feel her skin burning, even through her shirt. She pushed herself to her feet and looked around.

Shimmering sand stretched away in every direction to the horizon line. She'd never seen such emptiness in her life. Her homeworld of Amaryl had been green, full of the softness of evening rains and the glittering morning dew that nourished all the growing things. It was a world of water, and of life.

Her mouth tightened into a bitter line. *It was until they showed up.*

As she clambered up to the top of the artificial dune, she wondered if maybe that was this world's story too. Maybe all of this was the fault of the Drakkin.

As she reached the top of the dune, she confronted the ruins of the ship Even if she'd wanted to attempt it, there was no way back inside. Flames slithered from the shattered viewports to lick the sides of the ship, and ugly black smoke billowed into the sky.

Her escape was nothing short of a miracle. But as she swept her gaze once more across the burning and deserted sands, she choked on a laugh and a sob.

A miracle...or some kind of cruel joke.

While she was still in training with the Shell all those many months ago, Marsyas had reprimanded her for putting the mission first and her team second. And when it actually mattered, when the fate of her homeworld hung in the balance, she'd done exactly that.

She'd led her team straight into a trap, and now they were all dead.

They were dead, and the mission had failed.

Sahara closed her eyes and drew a deep, shuddering breath. They shouldn't have had a pyre like this. To drift away in the embrace of the waves, with tiny bobbing lights to guide you...that was the way of her people.

Or it least, it used to be. She pushed the memory of her mother's cold, silent burial out of her mind. It had been a long time since they had been allowed the comfort of their rituals.

And maybe it's different for the Shell. Maybe this is how we all end—buried in smoke and flames and sand on some nameless planet.

She wrapped her arms tightly around herself, as if she could hold her friends close to her heart one last time, and then she turned away from the wreckage and faced the crushing loneliness of the desert.

I don't even know what planet I'm on.

She couldn't solve that problem at the moment, so she thrust it aside. She was still alive, and she intended to stay that way. Without water or shelter in this heat, she knew she would die of exposure. And she also knew that as soon as the transport ship failed to arrive at the labor camp on Silesia, the Drakkin would track it down.

She allowed herself a smug smile. *They'll want to be sure I'm dead.*

But for whatever reason, the Power that kept the wheels of the universe in motion had spared her. So now the Power needed to give her a hand.

At first, nothing happened.

But then, slowly, she felt the tug of the Sight deep within herself. She fought it at first, but then a thought knifed through her mind.

What other hope do I have?

Taking a deep breath, she lowered her gaze once more to the sands.

Vague shapes shimmered up from the surface, like the watery silver forms of illusion. But as she focused on them, they grew until they swallowed the sun and the sky and the sands in darkness.

She tried to pull back. This wasn't the Sight—this was something else. Panic seared through her and she tried to break away, but it was as if something had her in its grasp.

And then the darkness lifted—and her vision opened onto what seemed like another world.

A shadowy colonnade. Bright blue sky. The murmur of water. Two intense, silvered eyes beneath a shock of dark hair. A man's face— strong jaw, dark stubble. He looked up, like he was looking straight at her.

For a moment, his face registered total shock. And then he recovered himself enough to say, "Head for the dunes. East."

The vision shattered and Sahara dropped to her knees.

The pain in her head was so severe that it nearly made her vomit. She pressed her forehead against the heat of the sands.

Who was that?

Whoever it was, he'd given her directions. To what, she didn't know—but anything was better than waiting around here to die.

When the pounding in her head lessened enough for her to stand, she got to her feet and turned slowly around.

There.

In the direction that must be east of her position, a ribbon of dunes stretched away toward the horizon line.

She glanced back at the ship, bidding Rilla and Ivy and the twins one last farewell. Then she started walking.

Within ten minutes, her head was pounding again—but this time from the scorching heat. She tried to lick her dry lips, but she had barely enough saliva to swallow. And even when she could muster up enough moisture to wet them, the sun desiccated them again anyway.

As she dragged her feet through the sand, she realized how crazy it was to follow the directions of some kind of hallucination. As if on cue, she stumbled and fell.

"I'm going crazy," she muttered, picking herself up. "Probably hallucinating from the drugs. Or hitting my head—how many times did I hit my head?"

Too many to count.

She glanced back over her shoulder at the transport, black against the glaring silver-blue of the sky. The smoke still spiraled its way into the sky like a beacon of death and destruction. As she watched, it seemed to form a shape.

She shuddered. She'd seen that sign before, darkening the sacred sands of the Divining, when her father had forced her to use the Sight.

They're coming.

And she knew, with the deep certainty that the Sight gave her, that they weren't just coming for her.

The sight of the dragon sign had come too late for her to save Amaryl. But maybe it wasn't too late this time.

Sahara picked up her pace as much as she could. She couldn't finish what she'd started if she was dead.

She had no idea how long she walked—the endless sands and sun made time seem to stand still. But when she glanced over her shoulder again, she couldn't see the wreckage of the ship.

The sun was already getting lower in the sky, and that meant night was coming on. Night...and the Power only knew what things came out of the sands at night.

She staggered forward a few more steps and twisted her ankle. She croaked in pain as she sprawled flat in the dazzling golden sands. The tiny grains were like so many stones tearing at the skin of her face, hands, and arms—skin that was already raw from the crash and the hours in the burning sun.

Gingerly, she probed her ankle joint and winced. Not broken, thank the Power. She flexed it gingerly and then pushed herself to her feet. As soon as she put her weight on it, pain stabbed through it and she almost collapsed again. Gritting her teeth and blowing out her breath in a slow hiss, she tried again. One step. Then two. It hurt like all hell, but she could make it.

The sun hung low on the horizon like a bloody disc when she finally reached the line of dunes. She clambered up the side on all fours and then straightened up as she reached the summit.

There was no one here.

THREE

"Serves me right for trusting a damn vision," she rasped aloud.

Her voice sounded like a strange buzzing and her lips hurt when she moved them. She forced her tongue over them, but the more she licked them the worse they felt. They were so badly chapped from the sun and the desert wind that they felt three times their normal size.

There was nothing to do now but keep going. She couldn't sit here in the sand and wait here for help that was never going to come.

She started cautiously down the slope. It was such rough going that she couldn't think about anything but keeping her footing. But she hadn't gone more than two feet before the sands shifted beneath her and she tumbled all the way to the bottom. With a grunt, she slammed into the sands.

She cursed as she pushed herself upright.

Pain. That's what comes from trusting the Sight. Just a hell of a lot of pain.

A small sliver of shade from the dune cut across the blinding ocean of sand, and she scooted into it to rest for a while. The shade was like a long drink of water, and she leaned against the slope at her back. The chill of the sands after the scorching heat made her shiver.

Her flimsy shoes were in shreds, so she pulled them off and threw them aside, wincing as she tweaked her injured ankle. The soles of her feet burned like they were on fire, so she dug her toes into the sand, trying to comfort them in the gritty coolness.

Rilla and the others...they'd want her to keep going. Marsyas had always said that life was hope, and while she might be low on hope, she was still breathing.

"Time to go," she mumbled, and pushed herself to her feet.

Her muscles were stiff now and her body felt so heavy. She didn't make it ten paces before she fell again. Her legs wouldn't hold her upright, so she crawled, dragging herself along for what felt like ages.

Finally, she collapsed, utterly spent from dehydration and heat exhaustion.

I'm sorry, Rilla. I can't. Ivy, I can't. Marsyas...

She could almost see his face, frowning at her, telling her to get up, to show neither pain nor fear.

But she didn't feel pain or fear. She felt numb, and she wondered if this was dying.

Small swirls of sand, red with the glow of the setting sun, began to dance around her and she watched them blankly. They were mesmerizing, those little whirlwinds. But as she watched, the swirling became a frenzy, throwing sand in her face and blinding her.

She turned her head to the side, trying to protect her eyes, and she croaked in surprise. Planted not six inches from her face were heavy leather boots, almost the color of the sand that swirled around them. She pushed herself over onto her side and looked up.

A man stood over her. He wore sand-colored clothes, goggles over his eyes, and a loosely-wound scarf the same color as his clothes covered his mouth and nose.

She squeezed her eyes shut and shook her head. It was another cruel illusion, trying to trap her.

But when she opened her eyes again, he was crouched beside her, and she could see the ornate ivory hilt of a sword peeking just over his left shoulder.

He removed his goggles, and his eyes glimmered silver over the folds of the scarf.

Sahara couldn't breathe as she stared at him. Cold fear and wild hope clashed in the pit of her stomach.

She knew those eyes.

But just to be sure, she tentatively reached out and tugged the cloth down from his face, revealing his angular jaw dark with stubble.

"Why didn't you wait for me at the dunes, *xenali?*" he asked. Even the voice was familiar, and Sahara began to tremble all over. He gestured at the sand devils. "The harbingers almost erased your tracks...and if they had, I never would have found you in time."

"Who are you?" she whispered hoarsely. She tried to lick her cracked lips. "How did you know I was here?" And then, "What planet is this?"

He grinned at her rapid-fire interrogation. "Drink first, questions later."

He helped her to sit up and then pulled a small flask from his thigh pocket and held it to her lips.

A thin trickle of liquid ran into her mouth. She took it eagerly enough, but it wasn't water. It burned all the way down her throat and she shoved his hand away, coughing violently.

"What the hell was that?" she demanded.

"Rapid hydration fluid."

He crooked his hand under her elbow and hauled her to her feet. Sahara bent double as a wave of dizziness flooded through her. Whatever he'd given her to drink had been nasty stuff, but once her head stopped spinning, she felt some of her strength returning. She angled to look up at him.

"What planet is this?" she repeated. "And how did you know I was here."

"This is Silesia, the last surviving human outpost in the quadrant.

And I found you because—" He hesitated for a fraction of a second, then shrugged. "I knew where to look, I guess."

"Silesia. Where the Drakkin labor camps are?"

His eyes narrowed. "Yes."

If today was any indicator of what life would have been like in the camps, she offered a silent prayer of thanksgiving to the Power that she'd been spared.

"I saw you," she said. "In that—vision or whatever it was." She peered at him curiously. "Did you see me too?"

He didn't answer, but tugged his scarf up over his mouth and nose and put his goggles back on. Then he pulled another scarf and pair of goggles out of his pack and handed them to her.

"Put these on. In about five minutes, you won't be able to breathe."

When she put on the goggles, the bands automatically tightened around her head, making a snug seal around her eyes. She found the cloth harder to manage, and he finally had to wrap it for her.

"I don't have anything here to dress your other wounds," he said, his voice muffled. "But when we get to Albadir, you'll be well looked after. I promise."

That name sounded familiar. Why was it familiar? She wished she could remember.

"Don't worry about me. I'll manage," she said stiffly. He swung away from her, but she caught his arm. "Wait. Before I follow you into this hellscape, I need to know your name."

"Jared Alareth." He gripped her hand firmly. "Let's go. Storm's coming."

FOUR

Sahara could barely keep up with Jared's pace through the rising sandstorm. His grip on Sahara's hand tightened as the visibility dropped, and soon the feel of his hand was the only thing that connected them. The howling wind battered her already bruised body, and she could hardly keep her footing in the sliding sands.

And then came the darkness. She didn't think the winds could get any more brutal, but as soon as the last light faded, they whipped across the sands with a gale force. She wondered how Jared even knew where they were going, and as she stumbled and almost fell, she wondered why they didn't just lie down and let the sands take them.

Just before the last of her strength gave out, Jared stopped. Sahara staggered into him and slammed her bare toe against stone. She bit down on a curse.

"Careful," Jared said, his voice husky from the sand and the long walk. "This is stone now, not sand. We're in the foothills just west of the city." He lifted her hand and pressed it against the stone.

Sahara said nothing. Her toe throbbed and she huddled against the wall of rock, seeking some reprieve from the brutal weather.

"Don't move," Jared said. "I'll be right back."

"Wait—where are you going?" Sahara asked.

She put her other hand out, blindly feeling for him in the darkness, but he was already gone. The metallic tang of panic filled her mouth. Surrounded by the dark and the wailing sands, she hadn't felt this alone since the Shift.

Marsyas had taught her to focus on breath in moments like this. *Breath is life. Life is hope.*

She repeated it over and over again, until her heart slowed its mad racing.

And then, somehow, she knew he was back. Something in the air felt charged, or there was some warmth about him that made the darkness seem less intense.

"This way," he said, taking her hand again.

He led her a few paces along the rock, and then she heard the sound of stone grinding on stone. Cool, slightly musty air gushed over her. She guessed there was some kind of opening in the rock in front of them, and she hoped there would be water. She had never felt so thirsty. Her tongue stuck to the roof of her mouth and she could barely swallow.

Letting go of her hand, Jared left her alone again. She heard a soft noise, and a moment later light from a torch just inside the door pushed away the darkness. Jared pocketed a small silver lighter and then beckoned her inside. She stumbled forward and he slid the door shut behind her.

It wasn't just bare stone, this little hole in the foothills. Lush rugs, in hues of red and gold that reminded her of her own homeworld's rich wines, covered the floor. Gorgeously carved wooden chests squatted against the back wall, and a few stone jars huddled along the wall on her left. Next to these were baskets heaped with flat bread and dried fruits. On her right was a low couch made from carefully arranged embroidered cushions.

Jared pulled off his goggles and face cloth in a small shower of sand, and she did the same. He piled their gear next to one of the stone jars, and then he began ladling water into two stone cups.

"What is this place?" she asked, her voice croaking in the quiet of the cave.

"An outpost," he answered. He brought her a cup and handed it to her. "Drink slowly," he cautioned as she raised it to her lips.

She tried, but as soon as the cold, clear water slid past her lips, she guzzled greedily. Her head pounded and she staggered forward to the couch and collapsed on the cushions. They were softer than she had expected, and she realized just how exhausted she was.

He filled a basin with water and drew a soft cloth from one of the baskets. As he crouched in front of her, she realized that his eyes, which had been silver out in the desert, were as dark as shadow now. The intensity of his gaze made her stomach tighten. It wasn't just kind attention—it was suspicion.

"How did you end up all the way out here, *xenali*?" he asked.

"Why do you keep calling me that?"

"*Xenali*? It's our word for stranger. Outworlder. You didn't give me your name, so I've got nothing else to call you."

He dipped the cloth in the basin and handed it to her. She dabbed gingerly at her face.

"It's Sahara—" She stopped. That tugging certainty of the Sight warned her to be careful. "Just Sahara."

"Sahara." He repeated it slowly, as if tasting the syllables as they rolled off his tongue. "No last name?"

Still that look of suspicion. She wished she could remember why Albadir was so familiar.

"None that matters."

She pressed the cloth to the throbbing cut on her forehead but it hurt too much. She sucked in her breath through her teeth and he lifted her hair away from the gash.

"That's a nasty cut," he said. "How'd you get that?"

She clenched her jaw. "I fell."

He took the cloth and rinsed it out in the basin, and then swabbed at the cut gently. She stiffened under his touch.

"I'm sorry," he said. "But if I don't clean it—"

"It doesn't hurt," she lied.

He arched an eyebrow and continued his work in silence. As soon as he was satisfied, he retrieved a small jar from another chest and opened it carefully. It held a pale green ointment that smelled sweet and clean. Jared carefully scooped some onto his fingertip and daubed it on her forehead. She clenched her teeth. It might smell nice, but it stung like hell.

"That's the best I can do for now," he said.

He returned the ointment to its chest and then piled two wooden trenchers with bread and dried meat and fruit. He handed one to her and sat down cross-legged on a cushion across from her.

"Eat," he said. "Restore your strength."

Sahara nibbled on a piece of bread. "You said you knew where to find me. Did someone send you?"

His mouth quirked in a smile. "Yeah. You did."

Sahara stopped, the bread halfway to her mouth. "So you did see me."

"I was heading to breakfast, minding my own business, and then out of nowhere, everything faded away. I watched your ship fall out of the sky. And I saw you, standing there on that hill, lost and alone."

"Has it happened before? Visions like that?"

He shook his head. "Not like that. It was like—the weirdest fever-dream I've ever had. But I knew that if I didn't find you, you'd die, so I told you to meet me at the dunes. And here we are." He grinned at her. "I guess it's a good thing you listened."

She pushed the trencher away and hugged her knees to her chest. Her whole body felt like it was on fire, but she shivered uncontrollably.

"Hey," he said, his voice suddenly so gently that it almost brought her to tears. "You're okay. We're safe here for tonight."

"Not afraid," she chattered. "Fever."

Her head throbbed so much that she couldn't keep her eyes open. She curled up on the cushions, but she couldn't stop shaking. Jared laid a hand across her forehead.

"It's the heat," he said.

He set his trencher aside and rummaged in one of the chests, pulling out a soft, dark blanket. He draped it over her and she nestled under it, feeling like a child again. The blanket was softer than anything she had felt in a long time. Her shivering melted away under its warmth, but her body still ached with fever.

Jared busied himself with what looked like some sort of burner. It was beaten copper, rectangular in shape, and the surface begin to glow with heat. He set a mug of water on it, and as soon as it was steaming, he sprinkled a dark red powder into it. Then he shut off the burner, swirled the liquid twice, and brought it to her.

"Here." He slipped an arm around her shoulders and raised her head so that she could drink. "This will ease the fever and the pain. Then you should sleep."

Sahara hesitated for an instant, hazily remembering the pungent drink he had given her earlier. But he pressed the cup against her lips and tipped it, and as the warm liquid slid into her mouth, she swallowed. It was slightly sweet and its warmth seeped into her. She drank the rest and let him settle her back onto the cushions.

"Sleep," he told her with a smile.

Sahara closed her eyes and slipped into a dreamless sleep.

FIVE

Jared watched her for a moment, and as soon as he was satisfied that she was actually asleep, he got himself a blanket and retreated to the rug on the other side of the cave. He unbuckled the sword and leaned it against the wall, then wrapped himself in the blanket and lay down.

Listening to her soft breathing, he turned their conversation over in his mind. She hadn't answered his question about where she'd come from. And that strange flash of a vision that had led him to her hadn't told him anything much either, except that the hulking black transport ship belonged to the Drakkin.

He'd only seen one other ship like that. Six months ago, he'd been sent to gather intel on the Drakkin labor camp located somewhere in the northern mountains. He hadn't been able to find it, but he'd seen one of those ships on approach.

That must have been where she was headed. A deep foreboding spread through him. *What could she possibly have done to deserve a sentence like that?*

Jared rolled over onto his back and stared up at the ceiling of the cave.

What would his people say when he brought her into the city tomorrow? And what would happen if he told them that she was the sole survivor of the crash of a Drakkin prison ship?

They would probably dump her right back where I found her.

There were those in Albadir who would see her as an omen. They would take her and wrap her in ritual. He didn't know much about her, but he had a hard time believing that she would appreciate being made into some kind of Chosen One.

And then there were those who would drag her back out into the desert to die of exposure. They desired at all costs to avoid attracting Drakkin attention, and harboring an escaped convict had no place in that plan.

They had a point. If the Drakkin somehow inventoried the bodies in the wreckage and discovered that she was missing, they might very well come to Albadir looking for her—and that would mean the end of their fragile existence.

He pressed his palms into his eyes and tried to silence the next thought, but it was already formed in his mind.

Maybe I should just leave her here.

There was food enough for a week on limited rations, and he could resupply her whenever he was out this way. But she would essentially be a prisoner here.

He studied her face as she slept, and he knew that even if he left her here, she would never stay put for long.

Even as he returned to the puzzle of what she must have done to merit the labor camps, another thought loomed up in his mind.

The Drakkin had kept her alive.

Either that meant she was so insignificant that they didn't care about working her to death—or she was too valuable to execute, and she was being sent to the camps for some other reason.

He couldn't fathom what that reason might be—but if he was right, they were going to want her back.

SIX

Some hours later, a soft noise somewhere in the cave startled Jared awake. The torches had almost guttered out, and in the deep shadows he could just make out Sahara sitting against the wall. She was watching him intently, and he pushed himself up on his elbow.

"Feeling better?" he asked.

"It's been a long time since I've slept without being drugged," she said. "I had nightmares."

"I know."

She didn't seem to appreciate that, so Jared avoided her stony glare by opening the door of the cave. The violent night winds had stilled into a gentle breathing and the eastern horizon trembled with light. To the west, the last of the night stars were ending their dance, drowning in the glow that was spreading across the sky. He inhaled deeply as the dawn breeze stirred his hair, and then he turned.

"We'll make it to the city today," he said. "But we need to start soon or we'll get caught in the heat. And that wouldn't be good for you."

She still said nothing, and Jared wondered what she was thinking. He drew two cups of water and brought one to her. As he handed it to her, he glanced down at her leg, which was stretched out in front of her. Her ankle was swollen and the outer tendons were black and blue. He set his cup aside and took her foot gently in his hands. He heard her sharp little gasp and glanced up at her. Her jaw was clenched against pain, and there was a fierceness in her eyes that surprised him.

"I'll wrap it as best as I can," he said. "Are you hungry?"

"No."

"You should eat something anyway," he told her. "You're going to need your strength."

"I've been thinking. It would probably be better for you—for all of you—if you left me here. There's food, water, shelter—"

"Are you telling me you'd actually stay here if I left you?" She didn't answer. "Do you honestly think you'd survive out there on your own again?"

"Maybe."

"Not an option. I'm not the type who abandons people."

"You're not abandoning me. I'm choosing to stay."

"And do what? Live here like a hermit?" She lifted her chin and he laughed. "I've known you for less than a day, but I know you're not the type to retreat."

He busied himself with breakfast, piling a handful of dried fruits, some nuts, and a long strip of dried meat on a piece of flatbread. She took the food mutely but didn't touch it. He took a piece of cloth from one of the chests and ripped it into long strips. She watched him with that unnerving gaze.

"And anyway, whether you stay here or not, they'll find you eventually."

"Probably."

She picked up one of the dried fruits and rolled it between her fingers. He could feel the struggle inside her. Something was pushing her toward despair.

He sat down across from her and took her ankle once more in his hands. "I have a friend back home. Incredible fighter. He was the one everyone looked to when things went sideways because even if he didn't know what to do, he somehow pulled it out. And then..."

He stopped and glanced up. She was leaning ever so slightly toward him, as if his voice were a lifeline.

"What happened?" she asked.

"He lost the one person he was supposed to protect."

The sudden flash of pain in her eyes felt like it went straight through his heart. He hated that he'd been right about her, and he almost wished he could take back everything he'd just said.

"And what happened to him after that?" she asked, very quietly.

He finished wrapping her ankle. "I guess what I'm trying to say is —maybe if you feel like there's nothing left to live for, you could find something you'd die for...and try that instead."

He met her gaze with a kind of shrug, but the expression on her face was so intense that it made his breath catch in his chest.

"We need to go." He gestured to her trencher. "Eat."

By the time they left the cave and stepped out into the desert, the sun was rimming the horizon and the sands glowed like molten gold. Jared set an easy pace, following the rim of the foothills into the rising sun, but they hadn't gone far before Sahara began to lag behind. She glared at him when he turned to check on her, so he pushed forward, figuring she'd tell him if she needed to stop.

As they approached the final ridge of dunes, he turned and saw her sitting on the sand. He jogged back and crouched beside her.

"Is it your ankle?" he asked. She didn't answer. "Let me help you."

"I'm fine."

She pushed herself to her feet again, favoring her leg, and limped away. Jared caught up to her and fell into step beside her. They followed the line of dunes in silence until the heat began to shimmer on the sands. Under the merciless sun, Sahara's pace slowed again, and Jared had to keep circling back to her side. She wouldn't speak to him and would hardly look at him, and even though he knew she needed his help, he was afraid to get near her.

As they reached the last ridge of dunes, he stopped to let her catch up. The high towers and walls of the city of Albadir glimmered in the distance, and he'd never been so happy to see them.

"What's that green stuff over there?" Sahara croaked from behind him.

"Orchards," Jared answered. "There's a river—the city is built around an oasis. Come on. It's not far."

He tried to keep the pace as quick as he thought she could bear. He jogged up the last rise, his boots sinking ankle-deep in the drifting sand. Below him, a wide plain opened out, transected by a river that glinted like fire in the sun. When Jared turned to point it out to Sahara, he saw her lying motionless in the sand at the bottom of the ridge.

"Sahara!" he shouted. He half-ran, half-jumped back down the slope. "Sahara!"

She didn't move. Jared slid down beside her in a shower of sand and laid a hand on her back. Her shirt was damp with sweat, but her lips and skin were dry as parchment. She stirred slightly at his touch and he blew out his breath in relief.

"You can make it," he said. "It's just over this ridge. Come on, Sahara. We're almost there."

"Why don't you just leave me here to die," she croaked.

It cut through Jared like a knife-stroke. "We're home. You can't quit on me now."

"Why not?"

He brushed the hair out of her eyes and smiled. "You can do this. You have to try."

That fierceness was back in her eyes. "I should be dead. Just like my friends."

Jared caught himself. "No. They would want you to live," he said. And without waiting for her to protest, he lifted her in his arms.

He powered back up the slope and set out across the last stretch of sand. By the time he reached the city gates, she was unconscious.

SEVEN

WHEN JARED LIFTED HER UP OUT OF THE SANDS, SHE WAS TOO weak to fight him. She hated feeling helpless, but he carried her as if it were the most natural thing in the world, and secretly she was grateful.

The gentle rocking motion of his stride and the warmth of his body lulled her into sleep before they reached the top of the dunes, but it was a sleep filled with nightmares.

"You will show neither pain nor fear," Marsyas said, pausing in front of her. She stared straight into his eyes.

And then they weren't the same eyes—they were silvered, as if they were powered by some internal energy source.

"Why not? What's wrong with showing fear?" It was Jared's voice, arguing with Marsyas over her head.

"You don't know the Shell. You don't know what she was made for. She is the Chrysalis, and she is marked."

And then the eyes were Marsyas's eyes again, staring directly at her as if they could read her soul.

"Have you forgotten, or have we all died for nothing?"

"I haven't forgotten!" she shouted, struggling up out of the darkness.

Vaguely, in a dizzying arc over her head, she saw high arches, a colonnade of windows. A man's face fuzzed in and out of focus as she struggled to sit up against some gentle resistance. She reached out and grabbed him, her fingers spasming.

"Marsyas!" she gasped. "I haven't forgotten! I saw the dragon in the sands...I saw it!"

"Hush," said a woman's voice.

Sahara came to herself with a gasp.

A willowy woman pried Sahara's fingers from the man's arm and forced her to lie back. Sahara fought her, but the woman had far more strength than Sahara would have guessed.

"Let me go!" she shrieked. "Marsyas!"

The man laid a hand against her cheek and she grabbed it, clinging to it as the tears came.

"I'm so sorry," she sobbed. "I tried. I tried to save them. There was too much smoke...too much...I shouldn't be here. It should have been me. It should have been me."

"*The balance has been disturbed,*" Marsyas said. "*The Order of the Drakkin will be reborn.*"

"*How?*" she sobbed. "*I killed him.*"

"*The Taken will fill the void.*"

The Taken.

Her fevered mind cast about frantically for a meaning and landed on a memory.

A black shape, with something pale and thrashing slung over its shoulder, glided across the grass toward the trees.

Her brother's upturned face was an agony of fear and a boy's fury. He was pounding on the Drakkin's back with his fists, kicking his pudgy legs like he was swimming.

She fought ferociously against the hands that held her down. "NO! Deor!" she shouted. "Let me go! You have to let me go!"

Strong arms wrapped around her and stilled her frantic movements. She writhed a moment longer, until utter exhaustion overwhelmed everything else. A cup was pressed against her lips and a cool liquid slid into her mouth. She swallowed, and the world around her spiraled into a dark and dreamless void.

Minutes or days passed, she couldn't tell. But when the darkness finally lessened, she heard two quiet voices speaking over her.

"Has she said anything else?" a woman's voice asked. It was soft and sweet, like her mother's voice used to be.

"Nothing for two days."

Sahara felt a hand on her cheek—small and cool and gentle. "The fever is finally lessened."

"It broke just before you came." A pause. "You look worried. What is it?"

And now, vaguely, Sahara recognized the man's voice. It was Jared.

"It hasn't been easy for Arnauld, these last few days. The people are growing restless. Dangerous, even. And the rumors have already begun circulating." She paused. "They say she is the Harbinger." Another pause. "And you think they're right."

"What does Childir say?" Jared asked, deflecting her.

"He says very little. But she is safe enough here...for now." The woman's hand moved away from Sahara's face, and she felt a soft cover laid over her. "Keep her comfortable, and call me if there is any change."

"Yes, my lady," Jared said.

As soon as the woman's light, quick footsteps died away, Sahara ventured to open her eyes. Jared sat beside her, head bowed, eyes closed. He looked worn and ragged, as if he hadn't slept for days.

He stirred and she shut her eyes again. Now that the delirium of fever had passed, she was so tired. And the woman had said she was safe.

"Safety," came Marsyas's voice from the shadows of her mind, "is an illusion that makes us weak."

She pushed Marsyas's memory out of her mind and drifted down into sleep.

EIGHT

When Sahara finally regained consciousness, she was lying on a cushioned platform in a cool and spacious room. A gentle breeze fluttered the garnet-hued silken curtains that dressed the colonnade of arched windows along the western wall of the room. The warm red light of the setting sun spilled on the floor. An enormous fireplace with rich wooden columns and a heavy mantle occupied the wall on the far side of the room. Strange white flowers in a crystal vase beside the bed seemed to be the source of the faint sweetness in the air.

Sahara breathed deeply and laid a hand over her forehead. It was covered with a soft bandage, as were her left arm and her ankle. Her tattered prisoner's clothes had been replaced by a clean white sleeveless shirt and wide-legged black pants that were soft but remarkably cool.

What is this place?

She remembered lying in the hot sands and that strange feeling of heaviness, like she was melting into the earth. Jared must have brought her here, and the vague memory of a shimmering city with the green trees flitted through her mind.

The sound of the door opening startled her and she sat up, her heart pounding. A man entered. He was dressed in flowing clothes in hues of black and white, with a broad red sash around his waist that hung almost to his knees. His bare feet padded noiselessly across the room as he carried a tray to the table beside her. As he set it down, he bowed low to her, hand across his chest.

"Is there anything else you require?" he asked, his voice deep but soft.

She shook her head. He bowed again and left, but before the door closed behind him, Jared poked his head inside.

"Can I come in?" he asked.

Sahara managed a smile. "Thanks," she said. "Seems I owe you."

He took a seat on the end of her bed. "This? Most of this is Aliya's doing."

"Who's Aliya?"

"Our chief Healer and the Lady of Albadir."

Vaguely, Sahara remembered a woman's face and voice and the touch of her small, cool hand. "How long have I been out?" she asked.

"Four days."

Four days. It felt like a lifetime. Sahara probed the bandage on her forehead, and he seemed to guess what she was thinking, because he added, "Your wounds are healing nicely. A day or two more and you should be able to remove the bandages."

"What is this place?" she asked.

"The Great House of Albadir. In days past, it was the High Seat: the home of the Lord Marshal and his family, and the symbol of power and justice in this district. But ever since the Drakkin invasion, it's become the home of all the noble families of the outlying regions who survived the initial purge. It's a city within the city."

Sahara's gaze snapped to his face. "The Drakkin invasion? When did that happen?"

"Years ago now. Long enough for them to suck the lifeblood out of the planet, build their labor camps, and all but annihilate our people."

Sahara could tell that he was watching for a reaction, and she kept her face carefully neutral. "They invaded my homeworld too," she said. "But my people weren't so lucky as yours."

As soon as the words were out of her mouth, she regretted them. He leaned forward, searching her face as if he were trying to read her soul. She looked away.

"What happened to them?" he asked.

She deflected the question. "Fifty noble families in one house. I'm surprised they're all still alive."

She could feel his disappointment, but he didn't press her. Instead, he picked some dates off the plate on the table and ate them.

"You're not wrong about that. For a while, everything was peaceful, but lately there are factions forming and reforming by the day. And Arnauld's chambers are under constant guard."

"You trust the guards?" she asked.

"I chose them—so yes, I trust them."

Sahara's eyes widened, and she realized that, aside from his name, she knew nothing about the man who sat across from her.

"Are you head of palace security or something?"

That made him laugh. "No. But I am a commander in Albadir's military force, such as it is."

"You're a recon specialist."

Now it was Jared's turn to be surprised. "How did you know that?"

"You have a secret forward base in the desert and you have the gear to navigate the sandstorms. It doesn't take much to put all that together."

"I guess not." He looked at her keenly, as if he were trying to decide whether there was more to her deductions than just a skill with logical thinking. "You should come to breakfast in the morning," he said. "Meals are still a great occasion around here, even with the factions and the constant threat of Drakkin annihilation."

"I don't think that's a good idea. The fewer people know about me, the better." Sahara snatched the last few dates from the tray before he could take them. "Put me on the first transport out of here and forget you ever saw me. The sooner, the better."

Jared's jaw tightened almost imperceptibly. "For us, or for you?"

"For everybody."

"When Lady Aliya says your wounds are healed, then we'll talk about what happens next," Jared said. "In the meantime, enjoy your freedom."

She met his gaze. "I'm not free."

Jared studied her so long and so intently that Sahara felt the heat beginning to rise in her face, but she refused to look away before he did.

"You escaped a Drakkin prisoner transport," he said. "I'd call that freedom."

Sahara steeled herself as the memories of the ship tumbled through her mind—the smell of burning bodies, her friends lost in the wreckage.

Jared stood and smiled. "I'm glad you're feeling better. I'll make sure they send you some more dates."

"Thanks."

Then he was gone, and Sahara blew out all her breath as a dizzying warmth swept through her. She didn't understand the intensity of the connection she felt to him, and she wondered if he could feel it too.

But he wasn't wrong about her freedom, and she knew exactly what she would do with this second chance. Her father and Marsyas had forbade her from going after her brother, and she wasn't going to make the same mistake again.

"The Taken will fill the void."

Her hands went cold as Marsyas's words drifted back into her mind.

"The Order of the Drakkin will be reborn."

She'd seen it. The figure of the dragon hulking over the ruins of the transport ship. She'd thought it had signaled another invasion—but they were already here. Jared said they'd been here for years.

It meant something else. There was more to their plan than just bleeding worlds dry—something she didn't understand.

But she felt that deep certainty that Deor was in more danger now than when they'd dragged him out of the house all those years ago.

She stared at the tray of food. Nothing looked appetizing now. She forced herself to eat the bread and drink the wine, reasoning that she would need her strength for the journey ahead, but her mouth was so dry that she could hardly swallow.

As soon as she'd finished the wine, she threw back the covers and got up. She found with relief that she could put weight on her ankle again, and she crossed the room to the window. As she pulled the curtains aside, she realized that the windows weren't windows at all, but rather an arched colonnade that opened onto a balcony.

Below her, a wide courtyard glimmered in the light of dozens of flaming torches. A network of stone pathways crisscrossed the grassy center of the space, all ending in a large fountain that gurgled sweetly in the night air. She caught the sound of voices and glanced to her right. Two men and a lady lingered in the twilight, standing beneath one of the torches.

Sahara recognized Jared immediately. The lady was beautiful in a quiet but extraordinary way, and Sahara vaguely recognized her as well. Her sleeveless dress of pale green made it seem like she belonged more to the trees and the water than this desert fortress. She was slender and almost as tall as the other man who stood close beside her, and the twisted masses of golden hair on top of her head made her seem even taller.

Sahara reached up slowly to touch her own hair. For the first time, she realized that it had been cut quite short. It felt rugged and coarse in her fingers.

The lady smiled up at Jared, her whole face glowing with joy and peace. Sahara gripped the wall. Jagged flashes of memory almost made her double over in pain.

A dark-haired woman smiling up at a bearded man. The light of love in the woman's eyes.

Sahara stumbled backward into the oasis of light and let the curtain fall into place, blocking out the growing dark. She climbed back onto her bed, curling up so that she faced away from the windows. Memories tumbled in her mind, and she clenched her hands into fists, battling to control her emotions.

Sahara dropped her bag and closed the door behind her.

Something had happened to her father. He seemed physically unharmed, but there was something horrible and hollow in his eyes... like an animal that had been cornered and beaten almost to death.

"What happened to him?" she asked Marsyas. He shifted his gaze to her father, and she took another step towards him.

"What happened to you?" she asked her father.

He managed a thin smile. "They refused."

Sahara looked again at Marsyas, then turned back to her father. "Refused what? We heard the reports this morning...they've gone."

Anguish pinched her father's face. "No. They haven't." He passed a hand over his face. "Sahara...I made a terrible mistake. I betrayed...betrayed..."

A sharp rap on the door shattered the memory. Even as she turned to tell the visitor to leave her alone, the servant entered. Without so much as a glance in her direction, he padded to the fireplace and set about lighting a fire. As soon he had the wood blazing, he took a burning twig and lit the two candelabra on the mantle. A set of pillar candles nestled together beside the flowers on her table, and he lit these as well. Then he blew out the twig.

Only then did he bow to her. "You aren't hungry?" he asked, gesturing with the smoking end of the stick at her tray.

"No."

He looked at her keenly. "Don't be troubled, lady," he said. "All things will be well."

Sahara said nothing and he bowed and left her, closing the door softly behind him.

I can't stay here. They have to let me go.

Jared had said that Aliya needed to give her permission. A quick glance out the window revealed that she was still in the courtyard, lingering by the fountain. Without another moment's hesitation, Sahara slipped out onto the balcony and climbed over the balustrade.

It was easy work to climb down—the walls were ornately decorated and gave her plenty of foot and hand holds. She dropped softly to the ground in the deep shadows of the building and crouched there for a moment, watching Aliya.

She was sitting on the edge of the fountain now, trailing her fingers in the water. Sahara glanced around. No guards were in sight, and Jared and the other man were gone. She stood and approached the fountain.

Aliya didn't notice her until Sahara was standing right in front of her. When she looked up, she started to her feet—and then her look of terror faded as she recognized Sahara.

"You!" she cried. "You should be resting! How did you get out here?"

"If you want to keep me prisoner, you shouldn't put me in a room with windows," Sahara said stiffly.

Aliya's gaze tracked up the side of the building to the balcony some three stories above their heads. "You climbed out the—"

"Yes. So clearly, I'm well enough to be on my way," Sahara said. "When does the next transport leave?"

Aliya measured her for a moment, then reached up and gently removed the bandage from Sahara's forehead. "This is almost healed," she said. "You can sleep without the bandage tonight."

"You're not hearing me," Sahara said. "I'm not staying. Point me in the direction of the space dock."

Aliya took Sahara's arm and unwound the bandage. "This too is almost healed," she said. "And your ankle is clearly not giving you trouble, if you could climb down three stories without killing yourself."

"I appreciate everything you've done for me," Sahara said. "I really do. But you don't understand. I have to go."

Aliya finally met Sahara's gaze and gripped her shoulders. "I'm sorry, Sahara. There is no space dock. Not any longer. The Drakkin destroyed it—and all our ships with it—in the First Wave. The only way off Silesia now is in the belly of a Drakkin ship."

NINE

From his balcony across the courtyard, Jared watched the light fade from Sahara's room. He was sharpening his boot-knife, the rhythmic sanding motion bringing him thoughtful calm.

"Jared?" someone called from inside his chamber. "Are you here?"

Jared turned and brushed his way through the curtains. His quarters were similar to Sahara's, but a sword rack hung above the mantle on the north wall, stocked with an impressive selection of blades both traditional and exotic. Between the bed platform and the fireplace stood two chairs and a long table littered with parchments and a stack of leather-bound books.

A young man stood in the doorway, arms crossed over his chest. As soon as Jared stepped through the curtains, he entered the room and closed the door.

"What do you want, Kirin?" asked Jared, slipping the knife into its holder with a sigh.

Kirin was probably his least favorite person in Albadir, but ever since Arnauld had assigned him to Jared's squadron, Jared couldn't seem to get away from him.

"What—I can't stop by and visit a friend?"

To hide his irritation, Jared went to a small, polished stone table holding a crystal decanter and several stubby glasses. He raised the decanter.

"Drink?" he asked.

Kirin shook his head no. Jared shrugged and poured himself a glass.

"Sit down," he said, indicating the long table. "You're making me nervous standing there. Just push that stuff out of your way."

Kirin sat down and shuffled the manuscripts aside. "Maps, maps, and more maps. How many maps of this corpse of a planet does a man need, Jared? I mean, really." He picked one up, glanced at it, then tossed it onto the heap with the others.

"As many as it takes to find what I'm looking for," Jared answered, taking the seat across from him.

"And what are you looking for?" Kirin asked.

"You didn't come here to ask me about my recon missions, so why don't you get to the point?" Jared swirled his drink and took a slow sip.

Kirin shrugged. "Fine. Tell me about the girl."

"What girl?"

Kirin leaned forward, as if this were some great secret between the two of them. "The girl you carried out of the desert."

"What about her?"

"Where did she come from?" Kirin asked. "There are rumors in the streets that she's the Harbinger."

"You should know better than to listen to rumors, Kirin." Even as he said the words, he heard the thinness of his own confidence. "They're usually lies."

"Not this time. I have it on good authority that Childir has confirmed this to be true."

Jared took another sip of his drink to hide his alarm. "Has he now?"

"Are they coming for us, Jared? That's what we need to know."

"We? Who's we?"

"Those of us who are concerned that you just carried our annihilation straight through the city gates."

Jared hesitated. What could he say about her that wouldn't reinforce the rumors? He and Aliya both knew that her coming very well might be the ragged edge of a building storm.

"If you believe she's the Harbinger," Jared said slowly, "then you must also believe the rest of the myth. There's nothing you can do to stop whatever happens next. It's already been written."

"Maybe," Kirin said. "But it's worth a try. And I am sure that Arnauld will hear me, even if you won't."

It was all Jared could do to keep from rolling his eyes. Kirin was always a busybody, eager to fetch and carry news with no regard for its actual value. More often than not, his tale-bearing did nothing but get innocent people in trouble, and Jared had already had to discipline him once for upsetting the order in his squadron.

"Arnauld will hear you...say what, exactly?"

Kirin met his gaze steadily. "That she should be sacrificed to prevent the coming onslaught."

Jared set his glass on the table. "Those rituals were expunged from Albadir years ago."

"And perhaps it's time they were brought back." Kirin rapped the table with his knuckles and left without answering.

Damn Kirin and his idiotic fear-mongering.

Jared couldn't imagine that Arnauld would hand Sahara over to an angry mob intent on human sacrifice, but Albadir had been smoldering on the edge of an uprising for months. The world was shrinking around them, and everyone knew that their days were numbered.

Some of the people still clung to the hope that they might have a chance to survive if Albadir could make itself insignificant enough to be forgotten by the Drakkin. But Sahara destroyed that plan.

If the people saw Sahara as the Harbinger, she could be the spark that would light the flame of full-out rebellion. And if it came down to saving the life of a fugitive convict or preserving the remnant of their civilization, Jared knew what Arnauld would choose.

That's what I should choose too.

He just hoped it would never come to that, because he wasn't sure he could trust himself to do the right thing.

TEN

He dreamed all night that the city was being overrun by Drakkin forces, and when he woke the next morning he felt like he hadn't slept at all.

The curtains sighed in the morning breeze, and Jared rolled out of bed. He poured water into the silver basin against the far wall and splashed it over his face and neck, shaking the droplets out of his hair. He'd hoped the cold water would drive the dark thoughts out of his mind, but it was no use. The visions of carnage and destruction now felt less like nightmares and more like prophecy.

He stepped out onto his balcony, hoping that the fresh air would lift the oppression from his spirit. The courtyard below him was still deserted, and the plashing of the fountain was loud in the quiet dawn. His eyes flickered over the windows of the east wing, lingering on the garnet curtains of Sahara's room on the third floor.

A momentary pang of guilt stabbed through him. He'd been dishonest, letting her think that she could leave this place.

I should have told her the truth.

He turned to go back inside, but Sahara suddenly thrust aside the curtains and stepped out onto her balcony. She paced back and forth, rubbing her arms as if she were comforting herself, but even from this distance Jared could feel her seething anger.

She stopped and leaned on the railing as Jared had done, staring down into the courtyard. He felt like his heart had lodged itself somewhere in his throat. And when she straightened and squared her shoulders, Jared wondered what she had decided to do.

It can't be good, whatever it is…

He wasn't sure why he felt so certain that trouble was coming, but he knew he had to try to stop her before she made things worse for herself—and for the city.

Turning on his heel, he grabbed a shirt and his boots on the way out his door. He navigated the empty corridors to her chamber in a blur and rapped on the door before he could second-guess himself.

"Sahara? It's Jared," he called.

She yanked open the door and he braced himself. "What do you want?" she snapped.

He hadn't noticed before now that her green eyes were as dark as uncut gems. Her short red hair ill-concealed the long, dark scab that ran almost the whole width of her forehead. She reminded him of the images he'd seen of Aerfen, the warrior goddess of the ancient faiths.

"I thought—maybe I should stop by and see how you were feeling." She stared at him in icy silence. "Can I come in?"

She still said nothing, but she opened the door wider and let him enter.

"I'm glad to see the bandages are off," he added, because it felt awkward to say nothing.

"Why didn't you tell me there's no way off this damn planet?"

"I didn't think you needed to hear that kind of news when you were half-dead from heat exhaustion."

"Don't you dare speak to me like I'm a child." Her voice was dangerous. "You lied to me."

Jared sighed. "I'm sorry." And then, "How did you find out?"

"Aliya told me. Last night in the courtyard." She circled him slowly.

"How did you get down to the courtyard without the guards seeing you?"

She favored him with a look that made him feel like a schoolboy. "What guards?" she said, her voice dark and dangerous. "She was out there all alone. Anything might have happened to her."

Jared caught her arm. Now it was his turn to be angry. "Are you threatening Lady Aliya?"

Again that icy look. "I don't threaten. If I wanted her dead, she'd be dead."

He released her arm. For whatever reason, he believed she was telling the truth. She left his side and sat down on the bed, feet tucked underneath her like she was meditating, and the iron grip on his lungs relaxed.

"Why were you on that transport?" he asked. When she stonewalled him, he added, "I saved your life. You said you owe me."

"I got crosswise with the Drakkin on my homeworld," she said simply.

"Anyone who breathes gets crosswise with the Drakkin. Arnauld will expect you to give an account of yourself. And for your own good I suggest you come up with a better line than that."

"Who's Arnauld?"

"Aliya's husband. The Lord Marshal of Albadir and the head of the Council of the Elect."

Sahara's eyes flickered. "And will he be at breakfast this morning?"

"He's always at breakfast."

"Then I'd better get ready, don't you think?"

He remembered that he'd come here to make sure that she didn't do anything reckless.

"You're not going to do something reckless, are you?" he asked bluntly. "Because you're already being proclaimed the Harbinger and Destroyer of Worlds in the streets."

"That's ironic."

It was a strange thing to say, but he was tired of laying siege to her life story. He opened the drawer in the base of the bed platform and she leaned over to see what he was doing. He shuffled through the assortment of clothes in earthy hues and pulled out a few selections. Everything was made of a light and flowing fabric that reminded her of the dress Aliya had been wearing in the courtyard.

"Breakfast and the noon meal are pretty informal," he said. "But the ladies usually dress for dinner."

"You're fighting for survival on this horrible desert rock of a planet and people still give a damn about dressing for dinner?"

He looked up at her scowling face. "I'm sure our customs must seem strange to an outworlder."

"Whatever. Give me those and let me get dressed."

ELEVEN

As soon as Jared was safely out of the room, Sahara scrambled off the bed and filled the basin in the corner with water. She splashed her face, more grateful than she'd ever been in her life before for the gift of water.

She shed the clothes she had been wearing and sorted through the pieces Jared had left out for her. None of them suited her, but she chose a pair of flowing black pants and a cropped sleeveless top. She dug around in the drawer and found a long, sheer duster to wear with it.

She was about to close the drawer when something caught her eye. Slowly, she pulled it out. It was a curved knife in a plain leather sheath. Sahara drew the knife and fingered the edge, and couldn't help but smile.

Finally something that's my style.

She slid the knife back into its sheath and tucked it into her pants at the small of her back. Then she opened the door and stepped out into the corridor.

Jared was waiting for her, and as she joined him, he held up a silver anklet crusted with amethysts.

"You were being so disagreeable that I forgot to give you this. Aliya wanted you to have it. All the noble ladies of our city wear one."

Sahara stared at it, a horrible burning lump rise in her throat.

I can't wear that.

She was sure she'd said it aloud, but he was already down on one knee beside her, fastening the chain around her left ankle.

"There," he said, straightening up with a smile. "It suits you."

She stared down at it and shivered suddenly, uncontrollably, as the wave of a memory crashed over her.

"Do you like it?" her father asked, smiling as she toyed with the jeweled silver chain around her ankle.

"It's beautiful," she said, bouncing up to kiss his cheek. "I'll wear it forever."

The silver anklet tinkled to the floor, shattered by cruel pliers, replaced by a prisoner's shackle. Then they marched her down that long corridor stinking of blood and death....

"Hey. Are you all right?" Jared asked, lightly touching her arm.

Sahara came back to herself with a start. She jerked away from Jared and knelt, clawing at the clasp.

"I can't wear this."

Jared crouched beside her and unhooked the chain. As soon as it was off, she sat back against the door and struggled to get control of her breathing.

"I'm sorry," was all she could manage to say.

The expression in his silver eyes was unreadable. "Not long after the Drakkin invaded Silesia, they arrested my father. I was forced to watch his execution," Jared said. "And after they hanged him, they beheaded my two older brothers at his feet. My mother died of grief two weeks later. I watched that too." His jaw suddenly tightened. "And then it was just my sister and I, until the war came. One minute we were fighting side by side. And the next..."

His eyes locked with hers. The intense smoldering of grief and anger in his eyes almost took her breath away. Suddenly, she realized that the fighter he'd spoken of back in the desert cave had been himself.

"Why are you telling me all this?" she asked softly.

"Because I have a feeling we're not really so very different," he said. "And whatever you're planning to do this morning, I've probably tried it."

"I doubt that."

Jared took her hand and dropped the anklet into her palm. "Keep it," he said. "Maybe someday you'll want to wear it."

The metal was warm from his hands, and she slowly closed her fingers around it.

TWELVE

When Sahara and Jared entered the dining hall, the buzz of conversation died like it had been severed with a machete. All of the men got to their feet, and Sahara felt the weight of their suspicion and judgment settle on her.

"A place for the stranger!" called someone at the far end of the table, breaking the terrible silence. "Jared! There are places for you here."

A young man with tawny curls and a ready smile pulled out a chair and stood waiting for her to take it. He seemed friendly enough. Maybe too friendly.

Jared mumbled something under his breath that she couldn't catch, but he led her around the table to the empty seats. She dropped into the chair the young man offered, and Jared took the seat on her other side. Gradually, the conversation in the hall resumed.

Sahara was trying to listen to the conversations around her, but the young man next to her wouldn't stop staring at her. Finally, she turned to him with an exasperated look.

"I'm Kirin," he said as he heaped her trencher with food. "What's your story?"

Sahara studied him for a moment. He was as transparent as a pane of glass. All his warmth and hospitality were nothing but show —he was here to entrap her into making a mistake.

Annoyed, she picked at her food. She would much rather have endured the acid looks of the ancient prune of an aristocrat sitting beside him than deal with this nonsense.

She glanced sidelong at Jared, but he seemed to be ignoring Kirin entirely—he was pulling pieces of bread apart with his fingers and popping them one by one into his mouth with an infuriating aloofness.

"Would you like some water?" Kirin asked Sahara. "Or some of this juice? It's delicious—made from the *edulia* fruit. E-du-li-a. It's found only on this planet, and I've heard it said that it's a delicacy on other worlds. Did you ever come by some on your world? No? Some bread, then. Do you have enough to suit you?"

"I'm fine." She tried to smile, but it came out more like a grimace. *Why doesn't he let me finish what he's already shoveled on my plate?*

As if on cue, Jared leaned across her and said, "Kirin. Why don't you let her eat what you've already shoveled onto her plate?"

Sahara's skin crawled and she glanced at Jared swiftly. "That's exactly what I was thinking," she said. "Exactly."

Jared's eyes locked with hers, and he seemed to realize the strangeness of what had just happened.

"I'm just trying to be helpful," Kirin grouched.

Sahara tasted some of the bread. It was delicate and slightly sweet, filled with dried fruits and nuts. There was cold water in her mug, and she drank it down gratefully. A small pot of something squatted beside her plate, its tiny spoon next to it. She tilted it and peered inside.

"What's this?" she asked, turning to Jared.

"It's honey," Kirin answered before Jared had a chance to reply.

Kirin leaned across her and plunged his spoon in the pot, twirling some of the golden liquid around the bowl and then lifting it out again. The honey slid back into the pot in a thick, slow stream.

"Honey?" Sahara asked. "What's that?"

"You don't know what honey is?" When she looked at him blankly, he added, "I can't imagine a world without honey. Try it."

Sahara started to tell him to leave her alone and he shoved the spoon into her mouth.

Something snapped inside her. Faster than thought, Sahara dragged Kirin out of his chair and slammed him against the wall. The dagger was out and in her hand, its curved blade pressed against the pulse in his throat.

"I knew it," he murmured, even as he lifted his hands. His lips curved up in a satisfied smile. Then he leaned his head ever so slightly toward her and whispered in a voice so low that only she could hear, "Assassin."

Behind her, chairs clattered to the floor and one of the women gave a little scream.

She heard the sound of dozens of weapons being drawn and she felt that tugging of the Sight—and the image of what was going on behind her unfolded in her mind's eye, like figures emerging through gray mist.

She pressed her left hand into Kirin's chest, the dagger steady at his throat. For all his swagger, he was trembling, his breath shallow and thready. In the next moment, Jared was beside her. He gripped the wrist of her knife-hand, forcing the blade away from Kirin's throat.

"You don't want to do this," he murmured.

A drop of sweat trembled on the end of Kirin's nose. "She does," he said to Jared. "This is what she does. This is who she is."

"Shut up," Sahara snapped.

"Sahara." Jared's grip on her wrist tightened.

Sahara dropped Kirin like a piece of dung. He collapsed onto his hands and knees, head bowed and his whole body shaking. She stepped back and sheathed the dagger. When she turned to face the crowd, no one moved.

Kirin picked himself up off the floor. "You see," he said to the room. "You have all seen what she is with her own eyes." He leveled a finger at her. "Assassin."

The word fell like a dead weight on the crowd.

"Perhaps the stranger would like to explain herself," said a clear voice from the head of the table.

Sahara looked past Jared and saw a man standing like an iron post beside his chair, a naked sword in his hand. Aliya sat beside him, her clear eyes fixed on Sahara.

That must be Arnauld.

"Explain what, my lord?" she asked.

Everyone turned to see what Arnauld would do. His face was a blank mask.

"We're not accustomed to such behavior at table here," he said. "And Kirin has accused you of practicing the shadow arts. Have you no answer?"

"Even if I had an answer, would you believe my word over his?" Sahara asked.

Jared made a warning noise in his throat, but Sahara ignored him.

"Need I remind you that you are a guest here?" Arnauld said, the heat rising in his voice. "And without our hospitality, you would be dead."

Sahara measured him. He reminded her of her father in the days before the Drakkin came; he'd been strong and unyielding too, once. And then the world had ended, and it had destroyed him.

"Who you are and where did you come from?" Arnauld demanded. "And, for the last time, I ask you to explain your actions here."

She jerked her head in Kirin's direction. "Ask him. He's the one with no manners."

Arnauld raised his eyebrows. "A knife's edge is how you deal with bad manners where you come from?"

"She was on a Drakkin prisoner transport," Kirin said. "Ask her, my lord. Ask her why."

The ladies gaped at her, and the men looked at each other uneasily. One of the older nobles across the table.

"Arnauld, if she has something to do with the Drakkin—" he began, his voice unsteady.

Arnauld lifted a hand. "Is that true?"

"Yes, it's true. The transport crashed. I escaped." Her throat closed around the words, and she felt suddenly like she couldn't breathe.

Bodies all around her...the smell of blood and burned flesh...the flames...

Impact...the cage was coming down...it would crush her....

"A Drakkin prisoner transport?"

She barely heard him. Her breathing was ragged, her mouth parched. She could feel the intensity of Jared's eyes on her, but she didn't look at him.

"Yes. The Drakkin prisoner transport. I was headed for the labor camps."

Arnauld glanced at Jared as a low murmur ran like wildfire around the table.

"Did you know about this?" he asked, his voice like a rumble of thunder. When Jared said nothing, Arnauld sucked his breath sharply through his teeth. "And still you brought her here?"

Vaguely, she heard the old prune of a woman tell Arnauld that she would walk Sahara back to the Drakkin herself if no one else would.

"Should I have let her die of exposure?" Jared asked. "Last I checked, that is not our people's way."

"It is when the Drakkin are involved!" The older nobleman planted his finger on the table. "You should have consulted the Council before bringing this into the city."

"Enough." Arnauld cut the argument short with a stern look at both parties.

"My lord Arnauld," Sahara said. "I came here this morning for no other purpose than to ask you to send me back."

"What?" Jared turned to her in surprise.

She glanced at him, then turned back to Arnauld. "Your wife Aliya said it. The only way off this planet is in the belly of a Drakkin ship. And if that's true—then that's where I need to go."

Her words caused an uproar. For a moment, all she heard were shouts of "Send her back!" and "Throw her out!"

But then Kirin's voice cut across the mayhem. "She is the Harbinger. If we wish to forestall the prophecy, there is only one path for us to take."

The silence was as deafening as the shouts had been a moment before. Jared, his face taut with rage, lunged at Kirin, but Sahara stopped him.

"What path?" she asked.

"Sacrifice."

Arnauld slammed the hilt of his sword down on the table like a gavel. "Out. All of you!" he ordered.

THIRTEEN

In a moment, the room was cleared. Noblemen and women rushed out as if the Drakkin themselves were in pursuit. Only Sahara, Jared, and Kirin remained behind.

As soon as the heavy wooden door closed, Arnauld leveled his sword at Kirin.

"We do not speak that word here," he said. "Who has been feeding you these lies?"

Kirin lifted his chin. "Ask your lady wife. She knows the truth."

Arnauld turned to Aliya in surprise. "What does he mean by that?"

"Childir believes Sahara is the Harbinger. And according to the ancient texts, her arrival promises our annihilation." Aliya raised her eyes to meet Sahara's. "I'm sorry," she said.

"I don't believe it," Jared said, stepping between Sahara and Arnauld. "The Harbinger is a myth. My father put an end to those ghost stories and dark rituals years ago! They have no place in Albadir now."

"Even you cannot deny what is happening to our world," Kirin said. "All the signs point to our destruction!"

Sahara turned to Kirin. "All the signs pointed to your destruction before I showed up. Once the Drakkin sink their claws into a world, they don't let it go until it's bled dry. You don't need a Harbinger for that. All it takes is time."

Kirin ignored her and spoke to Arnauld. "The safety of Albadir is your chief responsibility."

Arnauld nodded slowly. He looked down at Aliya, and something passed between them. "It is. But I must weigh the matter carefully." He nodded to them. "You are dismissed."

Jared bowed his head in acceptance, and then gripped Sahara's elbow.

"Let's go," he said.

She jerked her elbow out of his grasp. "I'm free, remember?" And she stalked out of the hall.

FOURTEEN

Sahara didn't realize how much Kirin's accusation had shaken her up until she reached the courtyard. She didn't want to return to her room, which now felt more like a prison cell than before, so she turned away from the Great House and followed a cobbled street into the city proper.

As she passed through the gates, the buildings seemed to close in around her. White stone, shimmering in the midmorning heat, dazzled her with its brightness. She passed a small knot of women dressed in flowing pants with loose hooded tops. They carried large baskets heaped with fruits and dried meat and flat bread, and they stared at her warily. Sahara crossed the street to avoid them.

Up ahead, a group of boys tumbled out of a row house, laughing and shouting. They raced off as a stout woman in a dust-hued gown burst out of the door.

"Come back here!" she shouted. "You forgot–"

But the boys were gone. As Sahara passed the doorway, the woman caught sight of her and her round face folded into a kind smile.

"He's always doing that, running off without his lunch," she said.

Sahara didn't really want to talk to her, but the woman descended the steps like a summer storm and stepped into Sahara's path, her generous arms folded over her even more generous bosom.

"Are you the One, then?" she asked.

"What?"

"The One. The outworlder." The woman lifted her brows expectantly. "Is that you, then?"

"If you say so."

The woman grunted and looked Sahara up and down, but her smile only widened. Then she winked. "You'll do him good, you will."

Sahara caught herself. "What? Who?"

The woman just laughed and retreated to her doorway. "Well, it's as they say, I guess. Look for something long enough, and you'll find it."

"Who's looking for—wait!" Sahara called, but the woman stepped inside her house.

Sahara vaulted up the steps after her and the woman shut the door in her face. Sahara stared at the smooth timbers and brightly-painted tilework and clenched her jaw.

Crazy old woman. What did she mean by that?

She jogged down the steps again and headed down the street. The encounter had rattled her out of her desperation, but as she walked, it came back full force.

Being trapped here was like losing her brother all over again—like watching through that window as the Drakkin hauled him away, hearing him screaming for her and being powerless to help him.

All through her training at the Shell, she'd clung to the fierce hope that somehow she would find her brother. Even when they'd sentenced her to the labor camps, she'd promised herself that she would find a way to escape.

She had escaped—but now she was trapped with people who thought she was some kind of herald of an impending apocalypse.

"If you feel like there's nothing left to live for, you could find something you'd die for...and try that."

Jared's words flooded back into her mind, and she remembered the dragon sign she'd seen above the ship.

If there was going to be a Drakkin apocalypse, then she wasn't here to announce it.

She was here to stop it.

She passed the last building on the street—a sandstone tavern that seemed strangely busy for so early in the morning. An oasis opened out below her as grassy slopes ran down to meet the slow course of the river. Trees marched down to the water's edge in orderly rows, offering pools of shade that looked almost more refreshing than the water itself. She couldn't remember the last time she had seen so much vibrant life.

She ran down the slope toward the river and stopped beneath one of the trees. The sparkling water, blinding in the fierce sunlight, murmured to her of freedom. She slipped down to the ground and leaned her back against the tree trunk. With a roar of grief and anger, she slammed the knife up to the hilt in the turf beside her.

She felt Jared's presence behind her before she saw him, but she didn't turn. He stood there behind her for a long moment, as if trying to decide what to say.

"What do you want, Jared?" she asked finally, glancing at him over her shoulder.

He came forward as if he'd been summoned. "I've been looking for you," he said, sitting down beside her. He jerked the knife free and studied it. "We should talk. About this morning."

"There's nothing to say."

Jared's mouth quirked. "I don't think Kirin will ever try shove honey in anyone's mouth again."

"Out in the desert, you told me to find something I'd die for if I felt like I'd lost what was worth living for," she said slowly. "And I'd very much like to know if you have any ideas."

"I guess that depends," he said.

"On what?"

"Well...like on what did you do to end up on that ship, for instance."

Sahara's eyes snapped to his, and for a moment she considered telling him what she'd done on Amaryl. But it still seemed to her that the less he knew, the better. "My mission failed."

He settled himself more comfortably on the grass beside her. "It might help you if you talked about it."

She was furious with herself when her eyes suddenly swam with tears. "You really don't understand," she said, barely above a whisper. "I made a promise to someone."

"To Marsyas?"

She startled, feeling the shock as if he'd slapped her across the face. "How do you know that name?"

"You said it a lot when you were sick," he answered. With the barest tightness in his voice, he added, "You seemed to have strong feelings for him, whoever he is."

"Was." She met his gaze and after a moment, she saw his expression change.

Jared picked up a stick and began to shave the bark from the smooth yellow wood inside with her knife.

"If it's a promise you're meant to keep, something will guide you to it. A way will open. But for now, you're here with us. And maybe that's how it's meant to be."

Sahara watched him work on the wood with the knife. She had to admire the deftness and delicacy with which he handled the blade. "The only thing I know how to do with a knife is fight," she said.

Jared planted the knife in the ground beside her and handed her the carefully whittled stick, now carved into the shape of a curious bird.

"Then perhaps it's time to learn a new skill."

Sahara rubbed her fingers over the intricate carvings. "Or maybe it's time for me to finish what I started."

FIFTEEN

Several days later, Jared showed up at her chamber with the news that the Council had agreed to offer her temporary asylum, so long as she stayed under Jared's supervision. Sahara bristled at this at first.

"I'm not going to watch you all the time," he said. "But this arrangement does give you greater access to the city."

And as if to prove his point, Jared took her with him to the sparring room to watch their training drills. As she watched the men practice, she realized that there was so much she could teach them.

"You have a tell," she said to Jared as they left the sparring room.

"What do you mean, a tell?"

"You signal your moves before you make them. That's why that big guy got the jump on you in that last drill."

Jared stopped. "Nobody's ever told me that."

"Why would they tell you?" she laughed, jostling him. "They need to be able to read your moves, or you'd be unbeatable." Then, sobering, she added, "You should let me help. With the drills."

Jared laid his towel across his shoulders and shook his head. "We have trainers for that. And I'm pretty sure we'd have a revolt on our hands if you got involved."

"Why? Because I'm an outworlder?" He moved off down the corridor and she followed him. "The Drakkin control most of your planet. You've lost the ability to call for aid, and I'd wager that most of your neighbors in this quadrant have already fallen to the Drakkin, even if you could get word out."

"What's your point, Sahara?"

"My point?" She stepped in front of him and stopped, forcing him to pull up short. "My point is that you don't have the luxury of standing on some kind of ceremony or custom—or whatever this is. There's no such thing as coexistence with the Drakkin. If you want what's left of your planet to survive, it can't happen with them still on it."

"Even if you're right—and I'm not saying you are—you'll never convince the Council that you should have a hand in training our military forces." He edged around her and continued down the corridor.

Sahara sighed in frustration and watched him go.

Her father had been an appeaser, trying to bargain for Amaryl's survival with the only currency they had: information. And the Drakkin had taken it from him by force, just like they took everything else. The only way to bargain with the Drakkin was at the point of a knife.

Even though Jared was supposed to keep an eye on her, he was true to his word and left her largely to her own devices. There were some days when she didn't see him at all, and she wondered where he went.

On those days, she would wander along the banks of the river, listening to the sound of the water. On one of those rambles, she'd discovered the apiary, which was tended by a kind old man named Wes. He was as industrious as the bees he tended and as languid in soul as the honey they produced, and she loved him immediately. He was kind and patient and let her help him with his work, and she appreciated the chance to keep busy during Jared's absences.

When he returned from one such absence, she confronted him.

"You're supposed to be watching me," she said. "So why don't you take me with you?"

"I thought you didn't want me watching you all the time."

"I don't—but I also don't like being left here with nothing to do."

"If I could take you, I would," was the only answer she got.

Two days later, he disappeared again, and this time he was gone so long she began to be afraid he would never come back at all. But then, one morning, as she ate her breakfast alone in a corner of the hall, she overheard two men talking about his return.

"He looked like hell," said one. "I don't know what Arnauld's got him doing out there, but whatever it is, it's going to kill him one of these days."

Sahara finished eating quickly and left the Great House. She crossed the weathered stone bridge over the river and headed for the library. It was an old domed building draped with vines, and on breezy days the smell of the fruit from the orchard wrapped it in languid sweetness. Today the heat seemed particularly oppressive, and there was no breeze at all to give any relief.

She pushed open the door and it creaked on its ancient hinges. She stepped into its musty coolness and waited a moment for her eyes to adjust to the gloom. Then she saw Jared hunched over a large tome, with a stack of parchment beside his elbow.

"You were gone again," she said, her voice loud in the stillness. "Four days this time."

"Mmm," he mumbled.

Sahara perched on the table next to the tome. He didn't look up at her and she scowled. "Why won't you tell me what you're doing, Jared? I can help, whatever it is."

"Doing with what?" he asked, blinking up at her.

"With anything! With these stupid books. With wherever you

disappear to." She planted her hand in the middle of the page and leaned into his field of vision. "Why won't you tell me?"

Jared sat back and rubbed a hand through his hair in annoyance. "This is just what I do. There's nothing to explain."

"Some men were talking this morning. They said you were going to get yourself killed."

"They don't know what they're talking about."

"Jared."

He finally looked up at her. She saw a long cut that ran down his left cheek. It had only just missed his eye. Sahara caught his chin in her hand and tilted his head.

"What happened to you?" she asked.

Before he could answer her, a shadow fell across the table from the open doorway. Sahara and Jared both turned to see a servant standing there.

"My lord Alareth?" he said with a bow. "My lord Arnauld would speak with you."

Jared pushed the manuscript into the center of the table and stood. The shadow vanished and Sahara was once more sitting in a slice of sunlight. Jared hesitated, watching her for a moment.

"I'm sorry," he said. "I have to go."

She waved a hand at him. "I know. Go."

Sahara sat there alone in the library and watched the sunlight track along the floor. At least in prison she knew who she was and what she needed to do.

I don't care what he says. I'm done following his rules.

SIXTEEN

WHEN SHE ARRIVED AT THE TRAINING RANGE, A FEW MEN WERE setting up for target practice. She watched as they each took a handgun and a single magazine from their squad leader and lined up. They fired fifteen shots into the targets downrange, and then they returned to the table and handed in their weapons.

Sahara waited to see if they would be reloaded and returned. They weren't. The soldiers began to file out, and their silence was almost more frightening than the atrocity of their aim.

Sahara stepped forward as one of the soldiers walked past her. "Wait, is that it?" she said. "That's all you're going to do?"

"Who invited you?" he snapped.

"What's your name?" she asked, choosing to ignore his tone.

"Garrett."

Sahara pointed at the targets. The edges were shredded, but very few bullets had actually found their mark. "Looks like you need more practice to me, Garrett," she said.

"Where's Jared?" he growled. "Isn't he supposed to have you on a leash?"

"I'm not talking about Jared right now," Sahara snapped. "I'm talking about your pathetic accuracy. What are you actually going to do with a gun you actually have to use it?"

Garrett glared at her and several of his squad mates gathered around them, all of them angry and murmuring. Sahara folded her arms across her chest and waited for one of them to explain or make a move. She was just in the mood for a fight.

"We get one magazine," the soldier said. "That's it."

"Since when? Last week you got at least three chances to reload."

"That was last week. Orders are orders."

Sahara glanced downrange again. "Only one of those is even close to a kill shot," she said. "You can't be done. You've got to do better than that."

"Orders are orders," Garrett repeated. "We get fifteen rounds each."

"You're wasting ammunition," she said. "Who's in charge of these drills?"

"Armon Heger," said one of the other soldiers before Garrett could shut him up.

"Get lost," Garrett said to Sahara. "Last time I'm asking nicely."

They closed their semi-circle a bit more tightly around her. Sahara planted her hand in the chest of the nearest soldier to stop him from coming any closer.

"Don't," she said. "I don't want to hurt anyone." She patted his chest and smiled up at him, then turned and headed for the stairs.

As she reached the turn at the landing, she heard voices below her and stopped to listen.

"We're critically low on ammo," said a man. "You're sure there's nowhere else we can look?"

"Why do you keep asking me that?" Sahara recognized Arnauld's voice. He sounded tired and distressed.

Sahara crept down a few more stairs and edged toward the stone bannister. Arnauld stood a flight below her, talking with a tall, heavyset man she didn't recognize.

"I've capped them at fifteen rounds for practice," the man said.

"We can't afford more than that...and even that's probably too much. We need supplies, Arnauld. We can't fight off the Drakkin with swords. Not when they have long-range tactical weapons."

Sahara's breath caught in her throat. *Are they training to fight the Drakkin? Is that what all these drills are for?*

"They have a dragon, Armon," Arnauld snapped. "What the hell kind of weapon do you think we can use against that? We have no more supplies, and we have no suppliers. So quit coming to me every month asking me the same damn questions. No help is coming. We're alone, and whatever we've got right now is all we're going to get."

Arnauld turned and his boots echoed as he jogged down the stone steps. Armon swore under his breath and headed up the stairs. Sahara flattened herself against the bannister as he swept past her. He didn't even seem to see her.

Sahara watched him go, weighing whether she should run after him and tell him that his soldiers were wasting what ammo he did have left. She decided he wasn't in the mood to hear it.

As she sat in the orchard watching the water, she thought about what she'd overheard. A strange excitement was pulsing through her veins. If they were training to fight the Drakkin, she might not have to get off-world at all to finish what she'd started.

All she had to do was bring the enemy to her, or find a way to get to them.

A momentary twinge of guilt stabbed through her. It felt a bit like she was using these people as bait.

I'm not, she told herself. *This battle is coming to them whether they want it or not.*

And, she told herself, maybe she could help them.

She wished she could talk to Jared about it all. Maybe that was where he'd been all this time, looking for supplies somewhere out in the desert. She knew that planets died when the Drakkin appeared—they drained every resource in their relentless hunt for whatever it was they were after. Infinite power, or something as close as they could get.

After two days with no sign of Jared, Sahara gave up on asking his opinion and returned to the training range.

The same squad was there again for their ridiculous little drill. They had just loaded the magazines into their guns and were preparing to take aim. Sahara strode up to Garrett and held out her hand, palm up.

"Oh, hell no," he said. "What do you want?"

"Your gun," she said.

The other soldiers laughed at her. "Go home," one said. "Doesn't Jared want you waiting in his chambers when he gets back?"

Sahara's cheeks flamed. "You think that's what I am?" she said, her voice low.

The soldiers glanced at each other, almost uneasy at the tone in her voice, and Garrett shrugged. "If not that, then what?"

"Give me that gun and I'll show you."

Garrett stepped toward her and the other soldiers closed the circle behind her. The gun was in Garrett's right hand. Sahara shifted her weight onto the balls of her feet and waited.

Garrett seized her wrist in his left hand and pulled her close to him. He raised the gun and leaned it against her temple. "See how much trouble you get into when you don't do what you're told? Such a pity. You're not bad to look at."

Sahara slammed her elbow up into his nose, then spun and kicked him in the ribs. He grunted in pain and reeled. She grabbed the gun out of his hand and aimed it at his head, so that when he heaved himself upright again, he was staring down the muzzle. She turned slowly in the center of the circle, aiming at each of the soldiers in turn. They backed slowly away.

"What else am I here for?" she asked. "Apparently I'm here to teach you how to shoot a gun."

She swung around and aimed at one of the targets. She emptied the magazine, then lowered the gun. A huge gaping hole in the center of the target marked where her shots had all gone home. Sahara smirked in satisfaction and turned to face the soldiers.

"That's what your targets should look like," she said. She flipped the gun around and held it out, handle first, to Garrett. "Care to have a go?"

Suddenly, over the heads of the soldiers, she saw Jared appear in the doorway. As Garrett stared down at the gun in his hands, she pushed through the circle and headed toward him.

"Where have you been?" she demanded. Jared opened his mouth in surprise, but Sahara heard muffled snorts of laughter behind her. She turned on the soldiers. "See to your targets," she snapped. "And they better all look like mine when you're done."

The soldiers trailed off toward the range and the noise of gunfire filled the room. Sahara grabbed Jared's arm and propelled him out onto the landing.

"What are you doing in there?" he asked.

"You've been gone," she said, "and I'm done waiting for you. They think I'm your...entertainment. I was showing them otherwise."

Jared's gaze shifted over her shoulder and his eyes hardened. "They said that?"

"They won't be saying it anymore, at least not to my face. Or yours." She folded her arms and waited.

"Maybe I can find you something to do," he said. "So you aren't bored while I'm gone."

"That's a great idea. You can officially put me in charge of these drills."

"I told you before. That's never going to happen."

"These men can't shoot worth a damn, Jared. They're just wasting what precious little ammo you have left."

Jared's gaze snapped to her face. "How do you know about the ammo shortage?"

"Because I'm not deaf and I'm not blind," she said. "Are you training to fight the Drakkin? Tell me yes or no."

"Why train for a fight we can't win?"

Sahara caught his arm. "Exactly. So how about you start training for one you can?"

"We would never win against the Drakkin, Sahara. We've run all the scenarios."

"Have you? All of them?" She searched his face. "Including the ones with me in them?"

Jared barely stifled a snort. "You're good with a knife and could probably handle yourself in the tavern. But this is the Drakkin—"

Sahara laughed quietly and shook her head. "Say something to Armon. Please. I'd do it myself, but no one trusts me, and they won't listen to me. But they'll listen to you. You have to say something."

"Fine. I'll bring it up at the next council meeting." Jared regarded her for a moment. "In the meantime, I've got another idea. What would you say to helping Lady Aliya in the Halls of Healing?"

"I'm not a healer, Jared," she said. "I'm an assassin."

Jared gently brushed her cheek with his thumb. "Remember the bird," he said. "Since when is having more than one skill a bad thing?"

He was so close that she could smell the warm sand and sunshine in the fibers of his clothes. With a smile, he turned and jogged down the stairs. Sahara's breath came in a rush, and she realized she was trembling.

SEVENTEEN

Jared took Sahara to the Halls of Healing the next morning. She was utterly skeptical and wished he would just hurry up and talk to Armon about putting her in charge of the military drills. This felt like nothing more than a useless delay.

They entered through the large double doors, and Sahara breathed deeply, appreciating the place in spite of herself. The space was shadowy with the kind of delightful half-light that comes from south-facing windows in morning. The high arched clerestory windows seemed to gather all the gentle breezes so that it never felt too warm or too cold, and a gently splashing fountain in the center of the hall was as refreshing as a drink of water on a hot day.

"Is this where you brought me?" Sahara whispered to Jared. "When you carried me out of the desert?"

"No," Jared said. He glanced at her. "This is a sacred place, not meant for strangers."

Sahara frowned at him. "So why did you bring me here?"

As Aliya came forward to meet them, Jared murmured, "You're here because you're not a stranger now."

Aliya always seemed to Sahara like she was walking on air, and

Sahara felt suddenly small and somehow unworthy in her presence. Aliya reached out her hands to Jared; he kissed them with a reverential respect. She laid one hand on top of his head in a kind of blessing. Watching the exchange, Sahara knew that Aliya was more to Albadir than just Arnauld's wife, and even more than its Healer.

She turned to Sahara with a bright smile. "I'm glad to see you again," she said. "Are you ready?"

"For what?" Sahara answered. "Jared hasn't told me why I'm here."

Jared raised an eyebrow at her, but Aliya only laughed, the rich sound echoing in the quiet space.

"You're here to help me, of course," she said. "Come."

Aliya moved away, clearly expecting Sahara to follow.

"I don't belong here," Sahara said to Jared. "I belong in the sparring room."

He smiled at her and walked away, leaving her standing alone in the vast space. "Give it a try," he called over his shoulder.

To her great surprise, Sahara found she was enjoying her work by the end of the morning. Aliya was a kind and patient teacher, and she treated Sahara with quiet respect. She never once asked Sahara about her past, or brought up that painful incident of the breakfast disaster. She seemed simply content to have an extra pair of hands, even if they weren't the most willing at the start.

They spent most of their time in silence, tending to the sick and any who were injured. There were two children who had bandages over their eyes. Once they had changed the bandages, Aliya explained quietly that they had been ill with some sort of fever, and that their eyes could not yet bear the intensity of the sunlight.

"Will they get well?" Sahara asked.

"It's hard to say," Aliya said. "We have been without access to medicines since the Drakkin locked down our world. I do the best I can with the herbs I know, and Childir helps when he can."

"Childir? I thought he was some kind of seer, not a healer."

Aliya looked at her swiftly. "He is both. He trained Jared in the art of healing and herbs—the skills that saved your life in the desert. He's our holy man."

Sahara's memory flashed back to that fateful morning when Amaryl's holy man had died during the divining—the morning that had revealed that she possessed the Sight.

"Jared is a lot like his father," Aliya continued. "Always wanting to learn—always asking questions." She sighed and rubbed her hands together slowly. "But some questions have only terrible answers...ones you would rather not know, but once you do, you can't forget."

She seemed suddenly distant, and Sahara wondered what she was thinking about. Then one of their other patients cried out for water, and Sahara hurried away to tend to her, leaving Aliya staring into the waters of the fountain.

When the bells rang for the midday meal and it was time for her to go, Aliya led Sahara back to the door and opened it for her.

"I didn't want to come here, you know," Sahara said.

Aliya reached out and pulled Sahara close, wrapping her in a fierce embrace.

"I know," she said with a smile. "But it is good for you to be here."

"Why?"

Aliya laid her cool hand against Sahara's cheek. "Because some wounds take longer to heal than others."

Sahara left the Halls of Healing feeling a strange emptiness inside. For the first time in a long time, she saw clearly the wound within her own heart—the one she thought she'd wrapped so tightly it couldn't bleed. Jared, with his healer's instincts, must have seen it, and now Aliya could see it too. It made her feel vulnerable, and that terrified her more than any battle ever could.

She turned her steps toward the orchard, which had become her favorite place in the city. As she inhaled the scent of ripe fruit and heard the gentle rush of the water, she realized that she loved it so much because it reminded her of her homeworld of Amaryl. It was all a part of that same wound: her homeworld, her brother, and the Drakkin.

She stopped under her favorite tree—the place where Jared had whittled her that curious bird that now sat on her mantle. The water was silver in the warm, bright sunshine, and Sahara clambered down to its edge. She trailed her fingers in the water and was surprised at how cool it was.

She glanced around. No one was in sight. She twirled her fingers in the water, hesitating. Then she made up her mind.

She stripped down to her underclothes and waded out into the river. As soon as she was deep enough, she took a breath and dove under the water. She felt the pull of the current and kicked her way to the surface. As soon as her head was clear, she heard a wild chorus of hoots and laughter from the shore.

She whirled around and saw a rag-tag bunch of boys crowded along the riverbank. She recognized one of them as belonging to the woman she'd met in the city all those weeks ago. He was dark-haired like Jared, with the same strange eyes, except that his were now sparkling with impish spirit.

"Hey!" he shouted at her. "This ain't the swimming hole!"

Sahara took two strokes toward them and then stopped. The boys had hold of the clothes she'd left on the shore.

"Put those down!" she called.

"Nope," said the boy. "There's a fee for swimming where there ain't a swimming hole, right, boys?"

Sahara kicked a bit closer to shore. "I know your mother!" she said. "What would she say?"

The boy's eyes widened for a moment and then he doubled over laughing. When he recovered, he said, "That ain't my mother...or leastways, she's mother to us all. Right, boys? We ain't got parents no more."

A chorus of agreement. Sahara felt a sharp pang stab through her, right through that wound she'd just re-opened in the Halls of Healing.

"I'm sorry," she mumbled. "I didn't know."

"'Course you didn't," the boy said. "You're *xenali*."

"Don't you have somewhere you're supposed to be?" Sahara asked, trying a different tack. "Like school?"

A loud chorus of guffaws. "We don't go to school," the boy said.

Sahara blew out her breath in frustration as she treaded water. This standoff wasn't going to end well if she couldn't figure out how to get her clothes back.

"Please put those down and go away," she said lamely.

The boys put their heads together and talked it over. Then the dark-haired boy took the clothes from his friends and picked his way down to the water's edge. Sahara felt a strange sense of foreboding.

"Put them down?" he repeated. "And go away? Is that right?"

"Yes," Sahara said. "That's right."

The boy grinned wickedly and held the clothes straight out in his skinny little arms. Sahara instantly saw what he was about to do.

"No! Wait!" she cried, striking out for the shore.

It was too late. The boy dropped the clothes right into the shallow water. Then he did a jig and all the boys laughed until they were crying.

As Sahara watched her clothes slowly fill with water and sink, she realized she was laughing too.

"Hey!" came a strong voice from the edge of the orchard. "Del! What are you doing?"

The boys all yelped and scattered like a flock of wild birds, Del leading them like a scrawny lightning bolt. A moment later, Jared came down the grassy sward and stopped at the edge of the water. His gaze tracked from the partially submerged clothes to Sahara, bobbing in the water with her head just above the surface, to the pack of boys fleeing the scene like a bunch of criminals.

"Nice day for a swim," he remarked casually, and she could see that he was trying not to laugh.

"Don't you dare laugh at me," she warned. "Jared—don't you dare!" But she could hardly speak for laughing herself.

Jared stooped and lifted her sopping clothes out of the water. He tossed them onto the grass beyond the muddy bank, then grinned at her.

"That doesn't help me," she said. "At all."

"You're right." Jared nodded his head thoughtfully. Then he retrieved the clothes and came to the water's edge. "Should I bring them out to you?"

"No!" Sahara cried, paddling away from him. "Just leave them and go away!"

"Sure," Jared said. He turned and headed up the bank, still carrying her clothes.

"Jared!"

He stopped in mid-stride and she could see his shoulders shaking with laughter. She swam closer to shore until her toes touched the soft sand at the bottom of the river.

"Jared!" she called again. "Haven't you put me through enough today already?"

He turned and spread the clothes out on the grass in a nice sunny spot. Then he stripped off his own shirt and came down to the water's edge. He held it out to her. "Here. It's dry."

Sahara regarded him warily. "Put it down—somewhere dry—and turn around."

Jared dropped the shirt on the grass. Then he retreated a few paces away and faced the orchard. Sahara splashed her way out onto the bank and hastily pulled the shirt over her head. It came down almost to her knees.

"Thanks," she said.

He turned around with a smile, but when he saw her, his face changed somehow. Sahara felt a sudden warmth flood through her. He didn't seem able to say anything, and Sahara felt that silence was the absolute worst thing that could happen right then.

"I'll bring it back. Later. When I'm...when it's...when everything's dry," she stammered.

She didn't dare look at him. Her hair was dripping water down her back, and she shivered, even though the sun was warm.

Jared moved a step closer to her, but she backed away. He stopped and she risked a glance into his face. Those silver eyes were unreadable, but a muscle in his jaw tightened.

"Well...I have to go," he said. He turned on his heel without another word and she lost sight of him among the trees.

Sahara blew out her breath. "Crazy," she mumbled. "I'm going crazy...or he is...or..."

She pushed the thought away and sat down under the tree to wait for her clothes to dry.

A few hours later, she rapped softly at the door to Jared's chambers. She had his shirt rolled beneath her arm, and she tried to ignore the hammering in her chest. When there was no answer, she knocked a bit louder. She was about to knock a third time when Jared opened the door.

Sahara thrust the shirt into his hands. "Thanks again," she said. "I'll see you later."

"Wait," he said. Sahara paused and he pushed the door open a bit wider. "Would you like to come in? Maybe have a drink?"

"I can't. I promised Wes I'd help him with the bees." She managed a smile and their eyes locked. Warmth surged through her, but she tore herself away and hurried down the hallway.

EIGHTEEN

THE APIARY WAS NESTLED AGAINST THE BORDERS OF THE *EDULIA* orchard. The warm air hung heavy with the scent of ripening fruit, and the lazy buzzing of the bees guided her through the long grasses.

Wes, the beekeeper, lived in a ramshackle hut at the edge of the orchard. It was hardly anything to look at—a thatched roof, rough-hewn plank walls, and wide windows that were open to the air. She loved the place, and she loved Wes's company even more. He let her help him with the tasks around the apiary—sometimes she gathered the honey, but more often she was sent to strain and jar the honey for the market and for the Great House.

She could see Wes as she rounded the bend. He was dressed head to foot in his beekeeper's suit, and he had just lifted a bar of golden honey out of a hive. She stood well back and watched as he took a knife and cut it into a wide wooden bowl that waited in the grass next to his foot.

He carefully replaced the bar and collected his bowl, and then, as he straightened, he caught sight of her.

She smiled in spite of herself as he tramped toward her, his strong steps marred by a slight limp. When he was safely out of range of his bees, he pulled off his hood.

"Sahara!" he called. "You're just in time!"

She hurried forward to meet him and he handed her the bowl. It was heavier than she'd expected, and she saw several combs floating in the thick, dark honey.

"Come up to the house," he said, jerking his head in the direction of the cottage. "I'll put on some tea."

Sahara followed in his footsteps. The warm sun held her like an embrace, and the light seemed to seep through her, soothing the hurt that had been silently weeping in her heart since that morning.

Jared had told her to find something she'd be willing to die for— and she felt, suddenly, like maybe today she'd found it.

The Halls of Healing, Aliya's warm embrace, Jared's laughter, the mischevious boys and the bees and the sound of cool water—this place that was becoming the home she'd thought she'd never find again.

I never want this to end. I'll do anything to keep this from ending.

Wes held the door for her and she set the bowl on the wooden counter in the kitchen. He stepped out of his suit and hung it on a hook near the door, and then bustled about to make a pot of tea. It was almost her favorite thing about this place—his *edulia* flower tea, sweetened with just a tinge of fresh honey. She sat down on a chair with a battered green cushion and tucked her legs beneath her.

The house was sparsely furnished with just the necessities—a rustic table and chairs, a wooden bed in one corner, and a shelf above it with a few books that looked like they hadn't been opened in years.

"What brings you down this way?" he asked as he set the kettle to boil. "I didn't expect to see you today."

"Nothing really," she said. He placed a steaming mug in front of her and then took the seat across from her. "Maybe I just came for some tea."

"And you are always welcome for that," Wes said, crinkling his eyes at her.

She felt that glow of happiness again, but when she looked at the shadow of her chair on the floor, she saw the shape of the dragon. The Sight tugged at her insides, and she felt sick.

He watched her steadily as she sipped her tea. "Something's troubling you."

"Nothing's bothering me."

Wes leaned back in his chair and stuck his legs straight out in front of him. He sniffed and leaned his head back, as if sorting through options. Then he snapped his fingers.

"Something you haven't let go," he said.

"More like something that won't let me go."

He raised his wild eyebrows at her, and she sighed. It seemed there was no putting him off, so she added, "Nothing lasts, no matter how much we wish it would."

Wes nodded. "Bees, now," he said. "Bees understand. Things have seasons. The trick of it is to stay with the season you're in. Gather honey when it's honey time." He winked at her. "And from the soundings of it, seems you have honey to gather. Am I right?" There was such an impish look in his face that she smiled in spite of herself.

"What's that supposed to mean?" she said.

"And why not?" He regarded her for a moment and then added, "Jared's father was a fine man. His son will be a better."

"Who's been feeding you rumors down here?" she asked, trying to laugh but feeling her cheeks on fire. "He and I aren't like that. And anyway." She fidgeted with her mug and then set it on the table abruptly. She didn't know how to tell him. The wound was still as fresh as the day it had happened. Love meant betrayal; it meant loss and and endless wound. "It's not easy for me."

"Love is easy," Wes said.

"Losing isn't," she fired back.

The beekeeper sighed and leaned his hands on the table. "That I know too well," he said softly.

Sahara regarded him in surprise. It had never occurred to her that he'd had any other life than this—the life he spent alone with his bees.

"They took her years ago," he said.

There was something in his voice, such a deep sadness, that Sahara's eyes filled with tears and she looked away, out at the orchard and the bees. Wes covered her hand with his and jiggled it until she faced him again.

"If you let loss kill the love in your heart, Sahara, then they've already won."

Sahara dragged in a breath and stood. "I have to go," she said, her voice tight with tears. "Thanks for the tea."

Wes leaned back and released her hand, and she left the house. Somewhere in her heart, she heard the whisper of that voice that had once meant so much to her.

"Don't let it consume you."

She shoved it away, and her angry tears broke loose like a summer storm.

Too late for that, Marsyas. Too late.

NINETEEN

The next morning, Sahara arrived at the Halls of
Healing at the appointed time, half hoping that maybe Aliya would
send her away. Her talk with Wes had left her feeling like her heart
was filled with the smoke of anger.

All night she had dreamed of the ones she'd lost—Marsyas, Killa,
Ivy, the twins, her mother, her father. Deor.

And everywhere she looked now, she saw the dragon in the shadows. They were coming. She didn't know how, or when, but the
threat was imminent.

She pushed open the door and stepped inside. The hall was clean
and smelled of fresh pressed herbs, and the fountain splashed in the
silence. Miraculously, none of the beds were occupied, and she didn't
see Aliya anywhere.

She checked the supply room, thinking that perhaps Aliya might
be using the time to prepare fresh tinctures and organize their waning
supplies. But the room was empty, and Sahara wandered back to the
fountain and sat down on its stone lip.

But when she looked in the water, there it was again.

The shadow of the dragon.

She fled the Halls and went in search of Jared.

But when she reached the Great House, the guards told her that he had been pulled into an emergency council meeting.

"Did something happen?" Sahara asked.

The guards glanced at each other but said nothing. And no matter how many times she asked, they remained silent.

Sahara turned on her heel and left the Great House. She hesitated as she reached the turning that led down to the apiary, but she didn't want to face Wes again, not after what had happened yesterday. So she took the other way instead and wandered toward the pastures that rolled away east of the city.

The pastures butted up against the edge of the desert sands, and the grasses here were tough and hearty enough to survive without much water. Albadir boasted a small herd of strange, shaggy animals that provided both milk and meat for the city. They smelled pungent but had sweet, if stupid, dispositions. They were exactly the company Sahara needed.

As she approached the fence, she saw a group of boys out in the field. Their hair was as tousled and tangled as the hides of their four-legged charges, but she recognized them as the same bunch from the riverbank. When they saw her approaching, they let out a collective whoop and ran to meet her.

"She got out!" they chortled. "You got out of the river! Tell us how you got out!"

"No," Sahara said.

The boys clambered up onto the fence and took seats. Their eager, sunburned faces were all shining with enthusiasm, and Sahara felt a little of the anger seep out of her.

"Come on," said the chief boy, whose name, Sahara remembered, was Del. He patted the fence beside him. "Up you get."

Sahara climbed up beside him and he offered her a piece of long, sweet pasture grass. All the boys were chewing one, she realized. She put it in her mouth and Del's grin widened.

"That's it," he said. "You're one of the gang now."

"I heard you about knifed Kirin, right in the dining hall," one of the other boys said.

Sahara glanced at him and carefully removed the tender stalk from between her teeth. "You always believe everything you hear?"

"When it's about Kirin almost getting knifed by a girl, absolutely," Del said.

Sahara stared out over the undulating grasses and stuck the grass between her teeth again. "Well, he shouldn't have shoved honey in my face."

The boys all guffawed, and Del could hardly contain himself. "It's true, then? You really did it? Really really?"

Sahara rolled her eyes. "Yes. And they won't forgive me for it."

"Show us the knife!" Del said, jostling her.

She drew her knife from its sheath at the small of her back and hefted its weight. Then she flipped it and caught the tip, then flipped it again. When she slipped it back into the sheath, they all groaned in disappointment.

"That was nothing!" Del said. "Come on, show us something!"

"No way," she said. "Everyone already thinks I'm a bad influence."

"Nah. You're not so bad," one of the other boys said. "You can chew grass all right."

"And flip a knife," added another.

"And swim," said Del with a wicked smile.

Sahara regarded the row of boys and had to smile. They reminded her so much of her brother Deor, and she felt that same fierce resolve to do anything to keep them from sharing his same fate.

"Thanks. I think," she said. She slipped off the fence and tossed her piece of grass into the pasture. "Time for me to go."

The boys all jostled each other and Del's grin lit up his silvered eyes. "Tell Jared he better be nice to you," he said. "Or he'll have us to reckon with!"

Sahara laughed and gave him a push. He toppled into the long grass of the pasture, and the boys all roared with laughter.

Sahara waved and left them to tend the animals. She smiled all the way to the tavern.

It was a sober place for a drinking hole. Giant vats of ales slumbered in dark casks along the western wall. Only twenty or so other people were gathered in the long room, most of them young men with quiet voices and fiercely intense faces. They clustered around tall tables in knots of four and five, carrying on hushed conversations.

Three young women lingered at the bar, which was by far the most cheerful part of the place. Its towering shelves of exotic liquors were lit by strangely incandescent stones of red and blue and green, and it spanned almost the entire expanse of the north wall. The women watched her with unfriendly eyes, and Sahara was glad when she spotted Jared sitting alone in a corner booth.

"You look happy," Jared remarked as she slid into the seat across from him.

Sahara realized, with a bit of a shock, that she actually was. "I guess I am."

"That's good," Jared said. There was a strange expression in his eyes.

"What happened today?" Sahara asked. "Aliya wasn't in the Halls of Healing, and the guards told me—"

"Nothing. Nothing happened."

His answer was so sharp that it caught Sahara by surprise. He clearly seemed in no mood to talk, so she

In the corner of the tavern opposite their table, two rough and burly men were engaged in a serious-looking dagger throwing game. Sahara recognized one of the men as Armon, the captain responsible for training the men at the firing range.

He's hardly better with a knife, she thought, watching him throw a dagger at the target. When the other man's throw went even wider off the mark, she shook her head.

"Do you at least have any news for me about the training?" she asked.

"Armon doesn't think you can handle it," Jared said, his tone still clipped and sharp. "And Arnauld agrees with him."

"He doesn't think I can handle it," she repeated.

She stood up and started for their table, but Jared caught her arm. "What are you doing?"

"You're being a beast, so I thought I'd play daggers with them."

"You don't know how to play."

"I think I can figure it out." She pulled her arm out of his grasp.

"There's betting involved, you understand."

"Of course there is. That's what makes it interesting."

She snaked her way between the tables and heard Jared slide out of the booth to follow her. Even better. Let him sit there and watch.

Armon and his companion were in the middle of an argument when she walked up.

"I want in," she said.

Armon and his companion turned and looked her up and down.

"You again," Armon said. "Why don't you get lost?"

"These knives are sharp, little miss," the other man said. He drew a calloused thumb along the edge. "You might cut your pretty self, and we don't want that."

"What are you afraid of? If you win, I'll buy a round for the whole tavern. And you're sure to win, right?"

The promise of a free drink made the man grin. He glanced at Armon and jerked his head at Sahara. "What d'you think, Armon? Let her play?"

Sahara kicked off her sandals and rose onto the balls of her feet, testing her balance. Armon watched her, rubbing the jagged scar on his jaw thoughtfully.

"And who knows?" Sahara added. "I might be able to teach you something about hitting a target while we're at it. And then you can pass it on the tips to your troops at the firing range."

Out of the corner of her eye, she saw Jared plant his forehead on his fist.

Armon stiffened. "What the hell's that supposed to mean?"

"Your men can't hit a target worth a damn, and you're wasting precious ammo. You might as well shoot blanks."

She thought she heard Jared groan, but she ignored him. He should have talked to Armon himself if he didn't want her to handle it.

Armon's expression was dangerous. "If you're gonna play, where's your weapon?"

Sahara drew her knife, balanced it, and threw it. The tip buried itself in the center of the target.

"Your turn."

She perched on the edge of Jared's table to watch as the men tried to dislodge her dagger.

"You didn't have to say that," Jared said in a low voice. "About the firing range."

Sahara glanced at him. "You promised me you would talk to him," she said. "You lied to me, Jared."

"Only to keep you from getting yourself into trouble."

"I don't know why you think I need saving, Jared." She jumped down from the table. "I can handle myself."

Armon threw his final dagger. It went wide. He turned around, face red and his left hand clenched in a fist.

"Too bad," Sahara said. "Want to play again?"

"No." Armon took a step toward her.

"You really should consider my offer to take over the training drills," she said.

"You think this proves anything?" Armon said, his voice a throaty growl.

"You have some other test in mind?"

"You should have been sacrificed," Armon said. "But no—now our own people have to pay the price!"

Jared jumped to his feet and his chair toppled over. "Shut your mouth before I have you arrested," he said.

"What's he talking about?" Sahara asked, turning to him. "What price?"

"Keep your girl under control, Jared," Armon said. "Isn't that what Arnauld told you this morning?"

"Let's go," Jared said to Sahara.

Armon grinned wolfishly at her. "Seems you need a man who can handle you. Maybe I'll tell Arnauld he should give me that job instead."

Sahara snorted. "You can't handle your dagger well enough."

Jared gripped Sahara's elbow. "Time to leave."

Sahara yanked her arm out of his grasp and planted her finger in Armon's chest.

"You sit around here in your little bar and play your little games, or you go to the training range and shoot at little targets, and you pretend there are no stakes if you lose," she said. Her vision swam, as the Sight tugged at her. Everywhere she looked, she saw the shadowy form of the dragon. "There is a reckoning coming! They are coming for you—for all of you! Where will you go when they come for you? There's nowhere left for you to run."

Sahara came back to herself with a gasp, and Jared made another attempt at her arm. She shook him off.

An angry murmur swelled in the tavern behind her, and she realized that there was now a crowd standing around them, watching. If the breakfast incident was any indication, rumors would spread like wildfire after this, so she decided to give them something to talk about.

Armon folded his arms across his chest, a triumphant sort of smile on his face. "Kirin told you she was the Harbinger," he said to Jared. "And you wouldn't believe him."

"I can show you how to fight the Drakkin," Sahara said, raising her voice. "And what's more—I can show you how to win."

A hush fell over the room. Even Jared was staring at her with something between respect and disbelief in his eyes.

"You better get something straight," Armon said. "We don't need you. We don't want you. So why don't you go back to wherever the hell you came from and leave us in peace."

"If I could get off this damn planet, I promise you I'd already be gone," Sahara said.

She pulled out her dagger out of the target and slipped it back into its sheath. Then she stepped so close to Armon that his breath ruffled her hair.

"If you're afraid to risk it all to win," she told him, "then you'll lose. Every time. Against me...and against the Drakkin."

Armon shoved her so hard that she hurtled backward into the table, breaking the chair on her way down. She felt a searing pain in her ribs and for a moment, she was too stunned to move.

"Didn't see that coming, did you?" Armon jeered.

Sahara scrambled to her feet just in time to see Jared lay Armon out flat with a stunning right hook.

"Guess you didn't see that coming either," Jared said to Armon mildly. Then he turned and grabbed Sahara's sandals and took her by the hand. "Come on," he said.

He propelled her out of the tavern. As soon as they were outside, Sahara took a deep breath and winced.

"I think I bruised my ribs."

"What the hell was that?" Jared said, turning on her. He tossed her sandals at her feet. "Do you want to get yourself killed? Or thrown into prison? Or what?"

She arched her back and rubbed her side. "I can help you, Jared. And I'm tired of trying to tell you that."

"You think getting in a bar fight is supposed to prove something? Dammit, Sahara, if you wanted people to trust you, that isn't the way to do it."

She tipped her chin up to meet his gaze. "So I should try lying to him instead? That's how you get people to trust you, right?"

Jared blew out his breath and dropped his gaze. "The politics of these things are complicated. You have to let me handle this."

"You seem to think I don't get how this works. But I do. And I understand how dangerous it is to let popular opinion and petty rivalries push you down a road you shouldn't take. Believe me—I have seen where that gets you. Sometimes you have to do what's right, even if it seems like its burning everything to the ground."

"If someone's going to set a fire, it shouldn't be you."

Sahara wrapped her arm around her throbbing ribs. "Who else is going to do it? You?"

Jared swung away from her. "Come with me," he said. "I've got something you need to see."

TWENTY

Sahara picked up her sandals and trailed after him. With each step, the cool stones of the path seemed to draw the heat of her passion out of her. She looked up into the hazy sky, and realized with a sudden shock that she was absurdly homesick.

I wish she would listen to me.

It was Jared's voice, and she scowled, all her anger coming back in a rush. She jogged a few steps and caught up with him.

"I do listen to you," she said. "Just not when you're wrong."

Jared startled. "What?"

"I said—"

"I know what you said, but—" He stared at her with the strangest expression on his face. "Forget it."

He moved ahead of her again and she fell in behind him. The path swerved to bring them into the courtyard by a little arched gateway dripping with white and purple flowers. Sahara paused and cupped her hand around the tender blossoms. At her touch, they yielded their softly sweet fragrance, and Sahara closed her eyes, drinking in the scent. It made her think of home again, and her heart ached.

When she opened her eyes again, she found Jared watching her with that steady, unreadable gaze that made her spine prickle. After a wordless moment, he turned and they continued along the way.

Jared led her straight to his chambers. He opened the door and held it open for her to enter. She stepped inside and immediately caught sight of the rack of swords over the fireplace.

"Very nice," she murmured, moving closer to examine them. She reached up and touched one, a viciously curved scimitar with a widening point and a jeweled handle.

She turned to Jared in surprise. "This is a Drakkin blade. Where did you get this?"

Jared poured himself a drink. "I took it."

"You took it. How?"

"You can't hang on to a weapon when you're dead, can you?"

Sahara considered him for a moment. If he was telling the truth about that, then he was more skilled as a warrior than she'd guessed. She removed the scimitar from its place and tested its weight and balance. It was curiously light, and she tried several passes with it.

Jared's eyes flickered as he watched her, and he sat down and crossed his boots on the table. "I had that off the Drakkin chieftain who killed my sister." He paused and took a long drink from his glass.

"Is there a Drakkin fortress here? Or is their presence limited to the labor camps?

"They have a fortress up in the mountains."

"How many are based here?"

"Of the leadership? Hard to say." He swirled his drink. "We never see them unless..." His voice trailed off and he shook his head. "It's hard to say."

Sahara replaced the scimitar and joined him at the table. She gestured at the pile of parchments and books next to Jared's boots.

"What's all this?" she asked. "Are you some kind of wise man?"

"Depends on who you ask, I guess," Jared said with a grin.

"That's not what I meant."

"I know what you meant. Take a look if you want."

Sahara lifted the topmost sheet off the stack and studied it for a moment. "These are maps, Jared," she said. "What do you need maps for?"

"That's what I wanted to show you," he said.

Sahara studied the map for a moment, then raised her eyes to his. "This map stops at that ridge of dunes where you found me all those weeks ago." She flipped through the rest of the stack. "And not one of these goes much further west than that." She tossed the parchment onto the desk and leaned back in her chair. "What does this mean? I don't understand."

"There used to be settlements to the south. Prosperous little villages and cities. And the Great City sprawled over the banks of the River Alba, just where it flows out into the southern sea. Its king ruled all these lands, all the way up to the mountains, and his city had amassed such riches as have never been seen in this world before or since."

"Those places aren't there any longer?"

After a long silence, Jared answered slowly, "It's been three years since we heard anything from the Great City. The council thinks it was destroyed by the Drakkin, but no one has been able to find out for sure."

"So what does that make Albadir?" Sahara asked. "The last remaining human stronghold on this horrible desert world?"

"I've been searching all the records I can find. It's like our world has shrunk. Everything beyond Albadir is a dead zone. We don't venture outside the circle."

"You do," she said. "You've been out beyond this line."

"Yes. But I'm the only one. And the last time I went out, I was nearly caught by a Drakkin scout here." He pointed to a spot on the map well within the circle. "They're closing in on us, Sahara."

Sahara hesitated, wondering how much she should tell him about the Sight. "I know."

He frowned at her. "What do you mean, you know? How could you know?"

"It's hard to explain," she said. "But I have a gift—on my home-world, they called it the Sight. I can sense the enemy. Think of it like a spiderweb. When they move, they disturb the web. And I can feel it. I've felt it, ever since my ship crashed. They're coming for you."

"*The Order of the Drakkin will be reborn. The Taken will fill the void.*"

"Funny you should mention that," Jared said. "Arnauld has had me watching the crash site ever since you got here."

"And?"

Jared traced the wood grain of the table with his fingertip. "And it seems pretty clear that they know someone is missing." He raised his eyes to her face. "They've been scouring the desert, searching for you."

Sahara stood abruptly. "You have to let me go," she said. "You have to let me finish what I started. It's the only way to stop what's coming, Jared."

"They're dredging the sands looking for a corpse," he said. "It doesn't seem to have occurred to them yet that you could have survived. But it won't take them long to figure it out—and when they do, you heard Armon tonight. There are those in Albadir who want to offer you in sacrifice in exchange for the city's survival."

"That's what we all thought, back on my homeworld," she said. "Sacrifice the one and save the many. But the truth is, the Drakkin don't work like that, Jared. They will take the one, and then they'll take the rest. You have to let me go. Let me do what I was trained to do—what I was born to do."

"You said tonight that you could teach us how to fight them and win, and I don't know why, but I believe you." He leaned forward. She could feel his intensity when she met his gaze. "We don't have the numbers for an all-out assault on the fortress, and every time we've tried a rebellion, it has cost us dearly."

"I never said anything about an assault," Sahara said. "I'm no general, and I'd be lying if I said I was. I'm talking about a plan that would risk fewer lives. Probably just mine, actually. But I would need a team."

"A team for what?"

"Mission support. Backup in case things go sideways and I need to get out fast." She tried to shrug away the memory of what had happened to her team last time she'd tried a mission like this.

"You said you're no general. What are you, then?"

"Kirin's right, Jared. I'm an assassin."

For a long moment, he held her gaze. His expression was unreadable, and Sahara wasn't sure if he was impressed, surprised, or completely nonplussed.

"That explains a lot," he said at last.

"What's that supposed to mean?" Sahara felt the heat rising in her cheeks.

"You fight your battles alone."

"Because I'm all that's left." She hesitated, then reached out and gripped his hand. "You told me to find something I'd die for. Well, I have. And it's you."

Jared's eyebrows lifted in surprise, and the air between them suddenly felt charged.

"It's this place," Sahara said, stumbling over the words. "Your people. This city. I couldn't save my own homeworld. Let me try to save yours."

He pulled his hand out of her grip and rose. He crossed to the fireplace and gripped the mantle, staring up at the scimitar.

"I won't let you do this thing alone," he said. "It wasn't an accident that you walked out of that wreckage, and it wasn't an accident that I'm the one who found you. We both have unfinished business with the Drakkin."

Sahara closed her eyes, fighting with every fiber of her being not to scream out that she had to do this alone because she couldn't bear to lose him like she lost Marsyas.

"And I think I know someone else who'll join us," Jared added.

"Someone else who'd take a shot at revenge in a heartbeat. But if Arnauld finds out about this, we're finished."

Sahara opened her eyes and smiled up at him. "The shadow arts are my specialty, remember?"

TWENTY-ONE

The next evening, they sat in the darkest corner booth the tavern had to offer, and Jared scanned the room like his head was on a swivel. She wondered, as she so often did, what he was thinking.

"So who is this person we are supposed to meet?" Sahara asked.

"A friend," he said.

Sahara sipped her ale and idly spun the mug on the table. Every time she glanced around, she felt like unfriendly eyes were watching them. She wished Jared had chosen a different place to meet this person. This was all too public, too exposed.

She was just about to ask if they could leave when a man slid into the booth beside Jared. He seemed to be a man of contradictions: rugged but carefree, fierce but with a disarming smile that seemed to reveal his whole heart. Sahara wasn't usually one for snap judgments, but she liked this man instantly.

"It's good to see you, Rafe," Jared said.

"So," he said, clasping Jared's hand, "you really think we have a chance?"

Jared turned to Sahara. "Rafe Margolis," he said. "I've had him out patrolling the south."

"A recon specialist?" Sahara asked Rafe.

"Me? Nah. I'm a street fighter who happens to be unlucky enough to be this guy's friend. So when he has a shit assignment, yours truly gets called up." Rafe grinned at Jared, then turned back to Sahara. "And you're the outworlder. Jared's told me about you."

"I hope that's a good thing," Sahara said.

Rafe winked at Jared. "Mostly good." He folded his hands on the table and leaned forward. "So. Who else is in on this?"

"No one," Jared said.

Rafe gave a low whistle and looked at Sahara. "Terrible odds," Rafe said. "I like this plan already."

Before Jared could say another word, a commotion rose from the other side of the tavern.

"There she is!" cried a loud voice.

They turned and saw Armon, staggering through the middle of the tavern. Five men, all as drunk as he was, crowded close behind him. He leveled a finger at Sahara.

"There she is!" he shouted again.

"Oh, this isn't good," Sahara murmured.

Two of the men lurched forward and grabbed her roughly, hauling her out of the booth.

She struggled against their hot, sweaty hands, but they dragged her into the middle of the tavern. A crowd gathered around Armon's men, and she saw Jared and Rafe shoving their way forward. Her gaze connected with Jared's and she shook her head.

My fight.

He stopped, gripping Rafe's arm, that strange expression on his face. She nodded at them in thanks and then turned her attention to Armon.

"You," Armon said to Sahara, slurring his words. "They're looking for you. You will bring all hell down on us."

A frightened and angry murmur rippled through the crowd.

"All hell is coming for you anyway," she said. "Let me teach you to fight. Freedom is better than fear."

"Yeah. We get rid of you–that's our freedom." he said. "No need for fear when you're gone."

Sahara saw Jared start forward again and she stopped him with a glance. "You think handing me over will save you?" She turned to include the crowd standing around them. "Is that what you think?"

"That's what I think," Armon said. A few half-hearted cheers bolstered his courage, and he seized Sahara's wrist and raised it high. "Who votes to sacrifice her to the Drakkin?" he shouted.

No one moved or even seemed to breathe. It was as if he had uttered the unspeakable. Some of the crowd peeled away, and Sahara saw them hurrying out the door. Armon seemed to lose some of his nerve, and she felt his grasp on her wrist slacken just a fraction. She faced him and used his grip on her to pull him close.

"You can turn me over," Sahara said, "but they are coming for you. Not me. You. It's only a matter of time before they wipe you out."

"One life for all," Armon said. "That's how it works. That's how it's always been. That's how we keep them away. And this time I say it should be you!"

There was something in Armon's voice, some heavy sadness, that filled her with a sudden doubt. When the Drakkin had come to her own homeworld, they had systematically eliminated her people. There were no demands, no options for barter or exchange. It was a steady and inexorable annihilation.

But maybe it was different here, and she had the sudden feeling that Jared had kept something from her.

"She's an outworlder," said Rafe, lifting his voice above the murmuring crowd. "The Drakkin won't take her as payment for our debt."

Sahara glanced at Jared. *What debt?*

"Oh, no. They'll take her," Armon countered. He twisted Sahara's arm behind her back and caught her other arm. "Bring rope!" he shouted to one of his followers.

The man obeyed and handed Armon a length of cord. But as he

struggled to secure her arms, Sahara slammed her head back into Armon's face. He let out a howl and lost his grip on one of her arms. She twisted free and kicked him full in the stomach. He reeled back and collapsed on the floor, his face a mess of blood.

Two of his henchmen stepped forward and Sahara drew her knife and flipped the grip. Then she waited, breathless, for one of them to make the mistake of challenging her.

"Don't," she cautioned. "I will kill you."

The two men looked at each other and then one shook his head. He backed away and almost tripped over Armon's legs. Sahara took one step towards them and they turned and fled. As soon as they were gone, she swung around to face the crowd.

"I am an outworlder," she said. "And I don't belong here. But believe me when I say that Albadir is all I have left." Her voice was raw, and for one awful second she hesitated. It was too late to hold back now. "If you doubt me, here's my proof."

She dropped the knife and it clattered on the ground. Then she turned and slowly lifted the back of her shirt, revealing the scars that crisscrossed her skin. She could almost feel the eyes of the crowd boring into her, and she forced herself to breathe slowly and evenly. Another low murmur rippled through the room, and she lowered her shirt again and faced them.

"The mark of K'ilenfir," someone whispered.

Armon scrambled to his feet, his face twisted with anger and drink. He stumbled to the door and out into the night, his followers on his heels. As soon as he was gone, the tension in the room was broken. The crowd broke up and returned to their tables, but as the swirl of talk once more filled the tavern, Sahara could feel their eyes returning to her again and again.

She collected her knife and sheathed it. When Jared and Rafe joined her, she jerked her head toward the door.

They didn't speak again until they were safely in Jared's room with the door bolted. As Jared poured drinks, Sahara and Rafe sat down at the table.

"Why didn't you tell me she'd survived K'ilenfir?" Rafe asked Jared. "I would've come to pay my respects sooner."

"Did you know about the scars?" Sahara asked as Jared served the drinks and joined them.

"Aliya told me," he said. "When you were ill. You were such puzzle to us."

"So you think you understand who I am?"

"I think I'm beginning to have some idea," Jared said. He smiled suddenly, and a strange warmth tingled through her. "Though I can't pretend to read your mind." As soon as the words were out of his mouth, he got quiet and a frown settled between his eyebrows.

"Well, I sure as hell had no idea who you were," Rafe said. "But that was damn brave, what you did just now."

"Is it true, what he said?" Sahara asked. "Do the Drakkin take someone in sacrificial payment in exchange for keeping the rest of the city alive?"

Jared and Rafe exchanged a glance. "It's true," Jared said.

"Why didn't you tell me that?" she demanded.

Rafe raised his hand. "He didn't want you charging out there to be a martyr."

"That's not his call," Sahara said, glaring at Jared.

"Nobody has to be a martyr," Jared said. "They aren't looking for you. They're looking for a body. So let's give them a body."

"That's your plan?" Sahara asked.

"It will stall them and buy us enough time to figure out our next move."

"Maybe, unless Armon or somebody else has ratted me out and told the Drakkin where I am."

"Armon wouldn't dare venture outside the city walls," Jared said. "No one's been out there but me. I promise you."

Sahara measured him for a long time, and then a smile crept over her face. "In that case—this could work."

"This could work?" Rafe said. "This is crazy! And where are we going to get a body?"

TWENTY-TWO

JARED STOOD AT THE FOOT OF A LONG, WINDING FLIGHT OF steps. He hadn't come here in months, and he was suddenly unsure that Childir would even agree to see him. When Jared had left his service to become a soldier, Childir had been angry with him, and Jared had never understood why. Since then, Aliya was the only one who had dealings with the holy man.

Jared blew out his breath and started up the steps. There was nothing for it but to try.

Unearthing his sister's bones was a sin he needed forgiveness for.

And there was something else he needed to know too. He'd seen the strange tattoo on Sahara's back, almost obliterated by the scars she bore: a circle enclosing a small, three-petaled flower. He'd seen that symbol in the manuscripts, and he thought he knew now why the Drakkin wanted her back. But he needed Childir to confirm that he was right.

The stairs ended abruptly at an oaken doorway, and before he second guessed himself, Jace rapped his knuckles against it.

"Come!" called a voice from within.

Jared opened the door and entered quietly. Light flooded the room from the open north windows, and the faintest breath of a breeze whispered through bunches of dried herbs hanging along the ceiling, releasing their sweet and savory fragrances. Childir sat at a table facing the door, surrounded by piles of books. A plate with cheese and bread and a cup of water sat untouched at his elbow.

"My lord Childir," Jared said with a bow. "I hope you are well."

If the sage was surprised to see him, he didn't show it. "As well as ever, I suppose," he replied.

Childir gestured to a chair against the far wall of the room, and Jared sat down obediently. He resisted the urge to squirm under Childir's steady gaze.

"It's...hot today, my lord," Jared said lamely.

"I hardly think you came here after all this time to discuss the weather." Childir tilted his head and regarded Jared with the ghost of a smile.

"No, my lord, I didn't."

"Speak what's on your mind, then."

"It's about Sahara. And...something else."

Childir's eyes flickered. "Yes. The outworlder. Well? What about her?"

"I don't know how much Aliya has told you, but she was bound for the Drakkin labor camp. The transport ship crashed in the desert and she escaped."

"Everyone knows this much," Childir said. There was a hint of impatience in his voice, and when Jared glanced at him in surprise, he said smoothly, "Aliya has kept me informed. She is not so remiss in her attention to me as you are. I have more or less kept up with her comings and goings. I know she finds disfavor with many of our people. And I have even heard rumor of a growing faction that wishes to sacrifice her to the Drakkin."

"That faction, I think, is much smaller than it was," Jared said flatly.

"Oh? And why is that?"

Jared brushed the question aside. "She bears the mark, my lord.

The three-petaled flower. And I hoped you might know what it all means."

Childir's face changed ever so subtly. A line appeared between his brows, and there was something sharp in his eyes. It made Jared's insides curl, and he suddenly wished he hadn't come. What started as a simple wish to understand now felt like a betrayal.

"Did she show you this herself?" Childir asked.

"Yes." He hesitated, then added, "Me and everyone else in the tavern last night. But I don't know if anyone else recognized the mark."

Childir watched him with an intensity that made him thoroughly uncomfortable. "And how much do you know about what you saw?"

"The scars are from the flagellation, but anyone who is taken prisoner by the Drakkin and sent to K'ilenfir receives that much. I've seen the three-petaled flower symbol in the manuscripts, but I'm not sure I know what it means."

Childir rubbed his jaw, his eyes fixed on the line of mountains visible outside the windows. "What it means? Time will tell."

"Is it some kind of prophecy?" Jared asked.

"You could say that, I suppose."

Jared waited expectantly for the seer to continue, but he seemed lost in thought. "That's all you have to say?"

"For the moment, yes."

Jared stood abruptly. "I'm sorry I bothered you with all this."

"Wait. You said there was something else." Childir regarded him with interest. "What more did you want to say?"

Jared hesitated. He didn't know why he shouldn't tell Childir of their plan to put the Drakkin off Sahara's trail, but something made him pause. Some change hovered just outside his conscious perception. The room was the same. Childir's face was lined with the same wrinkles, and his wizened hands still showed the bluish veins and the knotted knuckles. But there was something about his eyes...some strange darkness in their depths that Jared didn't understand.

"Oh, it was nothing," Jared said. "Nothing important."

"Bring her with you, next time. I should like to meet her."

Jared bowed his head to Childir and slipped out the door. He faltered his way down the steps, feeling the heaviness of betrayal in his heart.

He had told the others to meet him at the gate of the burial grounds, and the heaviness within him grew with every step he took in that direction. It didn't help when he saw Rafe and Sahara waiting for him, their faces lit up from laughing. Rafe had always been funny, and he couldn't blame Sahara for appreciating his friend's sense of humor. But faced with what they were about to do, laughter seemed like a profanation.

"There you are!" Rafe called as he approached. "Where have you been?"

"I went to see Childir."

"The holy man?" Sahara asked when all Rafe's smiles dissolved in an enormous scowl.

"Why the hell would you do that?" Rafe asked, ignoring Sahara. "He's gotten strange, that old man. And you haven't been to see him in ages."

"Aliya trusts him, Rafe."

"Yeah, well, I don't."

Jared bit back the words *I don't either* and moved past them to the gate. "Let's do what we came to do," he said.

Rafe caught his arm. "Before we step foot in there," he said, "whose body are you planning to dig up?"

Jared glanced from his friend's intense face to Sahara. She was staring at him as if she could read his thoughts, and he quickly turned back to Rafe.

"Someone who would volunteer for this mission without a moment's hesitation if I asked her," he said quietly.

Rafe squeezed his arm until Jared almost cried out in pain. "No. No you're not. No way in hell."

"She would want—" Jared began, but Rafe cut him off.

"I said no!" He shoved Jared away from him and pushed his

hands through his hair. "I cannot believe—how could you even think—"

"Who are you talking about?" Sahara asked, stepping between them. "What's going on?"

"His sister!" Rafe cried. "He means his sister—the love of my life." He turned on Jared with a ferocious anger. "I have just as much say over what happens to her as you do! And if you want to dig her up, you're gonna have to kill me first!"

Sahara stepped between them and planted her hand on Rafe's chest. Then she turned to Jared. "Don't do this for me," she said. "Please."

"It's the only way we put them off! And this isn't just for you—you said yourself that they're coming for us no matter what!" Jared looked over her shoulder at Rafe. "That mark on her back—"

Sahara sucked her breath through her teeth. "Do you know that mark? I didn't think anyone here would recognize it."

"I would know the mark of the Shell anywhere."

Rafe's eyebrows shot up, and for a moment he forgot his anger. "The Shell? You're a member of the Shell?"

"Yes." She frowned at Jared. "How do you know the mark?"

"It's in many of the manuscripts of our history. The stories are dark and terrifying—a shadow order with the power to raise up and topple whole systems. But when the Drakkin first arrived here, Arnauld wanted to recruit them to help us, but the Shell, it seemed, had vanished. None of our contacts knew where to find them."

"That explains why you think you can teach us how to defeat the Drakkin," Rafe said.

"I was trained for one purpose: to take down the Drakkin leadership on my homeworld of Amaryl," Sahara said. She faltered for a moment, then added, "That's why they're hunting for me."

"She is our only hope of ever being free of them," Jared said to Rafe. "And Rhea died for that freedom, Rafe. She would want us to do this."

The mention of Rhea's name sent Rafe wild again and he lunged at Jared. Sahara held him back.

"I don't give a damn what you say!" he shouted. "I will not let you do this!"

"You have a better plan?" Jared asked. His gaze slid from Rafe to Sahara.

"My plan is to do what I was trained to do," Sahara said. "Get intel on their fortress and take them out."

"We don't have that kind of information," Jared said.

"I know that," she said. "So let's go out there and get it."

TWENTY-THREE

They camped that night in the same cave where Jared and Sahara had stayed all those weeks ago. Sahara sat on one of the patterned rugs and watched Jared build a small fire in the brazier as Rafe heaped their trenchers with dried meat, nuts, and withered fruits.

I guess I've come full circle.

As Rafe offered her a trencher, she shivered a little, wondering suddenly if her life was on a permanent loop. She'd started down the same road again—the road that always seemed to end in the same place.

A holding cell and a sentencing.

How many times can I escape something like that?

"If the Drakkin scout follows his usual pattern," Jared said, joining them and taking a trencher from Rafe, "he should be patrolling the dunes around midday tomorrow."

"I hope you're right," Rafe said, tearing some of the dried meat with his teeth.

After they ate, Jared prepared a syringe with a thick needle and capped it carefully.

"What is that?" Sahara asked.

"A truth serum."

"You had Aliya compound a drug?" Sahara cried. "I thought this mission was supposed to be secret!"

"She didn't compound it—I did." Jared placed the syringe on one of the chests. "I just hope it works."

As they rolled themselves in blankets to sleep, Sahara's veins were humming with adrenaline. Memories tumbled through her mind, filling her with uneasiness and doubt. Memories of the crash. Of her life before the Drakkin. Of her brother, carried off through the night by a Drakkin soldier.

But this was what Marsyas had trained her to do. And as she looked at Jared and Rafe over the rim of her mug, she smiled.

This time, I won't fail.

But her dreams that night were nightmares.

The scaled face loomed over her, its jagged teeth bared in a growl. Its hot breath, smelling of dead things, curled around her. And the awful weight of its boot pressing into her chest...in a moment, he would crush the life out of her.

"There is no escape for you," it hissed. "Not this time."

Sahara sat bolt upright, sweat drenching her hair. Her dagger was in her right hand and she clutched at her chest with the other.

"Hey," said Jared. "You okay?"

"What?" she gasped. She blinked as her surroundings came into focus. She blew out her breath and rubbed her hand over her face. "I'm fine," she mumbled. "Just a bad dream."

Jared dropped her pack beside her and laid a hand on her shoulder. "I was about to wake you anyway," he said. "It's time to go."

She nodded and he moved away to talk to Rafe. She opened the pack and took stock of what was inside. Three water skins, a bunch of pressed herbs wrapped in a clean cotton cloth, another cloth bag filled with rations, and an extra knife.

Jared and Rafe each carried crossbows and hip quivers. Sahara pointed to them. "Those aren't going to be much good against a scout," she said.

"They are if you know how to aim," said Rafe with that irrepressible grin.

"Let's suit up," Jared said. "Time to move."

They left the cave and headed out into the sands. The air swarmed with tiny particles of sand, and the desert still seemed to be trembling from the force of the night winds. There was no glow of light yet along the eastern horizon, and Sahara could see the stars.

The beauty of it made her catch her breath. The sky was as clear as if it had been scoured with an iron brush, and the brilliance of the stars seemed close enough to touch. Sahara thought she could make out patterns, but none of the constellations were familiar to her.

Not that I ever paid much attention when I had the chance.

Once she had entered the Shell, she'd had only one purpose. Knowing the constellations wouldn't have helped her combat skills, and Marsyas never really took the time to show her anything else.

She spent the rest of the morning's journey lost in melancholy. But as the sun rose higher and they drew closer to the dunes where they would wait for the scout, Sahara felt a growing knot of doubt in the pit of her stomach.

How are we supposed to conceal ourselves out here?

She stopped for a moment and adjusted her pack, studying the blazing expanses of sand.

"Don't worry," Jared called over his shoulder. "We've got camouflage."

Sahara stared at him in stunned silence for a moment. *Did I say that aloud?* Maybe the sun was getting to her again. "What are you talking about?"

"We have adaptive camouflage suits," he explained. "They're ancient pre-siege tech, but they work. Even if someone looked straight at us, he'd see only sand."

"I know what adaptive camouflage is," she snapped. She didn't care about the suits at the moment—it was the weirdness of his timing that she couldn't handle. He regarded her quizzically with his silvered eyes but before he could say anything, Rafe interrupted them.

"Let's move before we all bake!" he called from a few paces ahead of them.

"Coming," Sahara said. She shouldered past Jared and jogged to catch up with Rafe.

As they trudged through the shifting sand, Sahara wished that Rafe would say something funny to take her mind off the fact that Jared seemed like he could read her thoughts. But Rafe was oddly quiet and focused, and Sahara didn't press him.

Some time later, Jared finally called a halt. Sahara looked around at the endless dunes and saw nothing that could serve as any kind of location marker.

Jared and Rafe were already busy setting up a small tent that could provide them shelter from the fierce afternoon sun.

"Is this the place?" she asked.

Jared paused for a moment and looked around. "Yeah, this is it," he said.

"You sure?"

"I'm sure."

"Okay." Sahara shrugged and drank some from her water skin. She didn't know how he could be so certain. Everything looked dizzyingly the same to her out here.

As soon as the shelter was ready, they crawled inside. The cool of the shade made Sahara shiver a bit and she took another long drink of water.

"Better than the first time you were out this way, isn't it?" Jared asked.

She nodded. "Are we on schedule?"

"We are. Remains to see whether he'll show up on time. We can rest here for a bit and then we need to get into position."

"Sounds good to me," Rafe said. He rolled onto his back and

crossed his hands behind his head. He shut his eyes, and a moment later, he was breathing softly.

"Where did you get camoflage tech like this?" Sahara asked. "This was black market stuff back on my homeworld. Or at least, it was when I left."

"Believe it or not, Silesia used to be the main trading hub in this quadrant. And we didn't just trade—although that would have made us wealthy enough. We were also a center for manufacturing. We partnered with our sisterworld Askalon, which was rich in raw materials but had very few skilled workers. They would send raw materials to our factories and guilds in the Great City and we would produce the finished goods. But when the Drakkin came, they cut off our communication with other worlds. They withered our cities away, literally bleeding our world dry. Whatever advanced technology we had, we hid. We keep it only for emergencies now." He permitted himself a smug smile. "Don't let the ammo shortage fool you. We've still got some surprises left."

"I hope so," she said. She glanced at Rafe and then leaned over to stare into his face. "Is he actually asleep?"

"He's spent years perfecting the art," Jared said.

His gaze intensified, and the hazy warmth of the muted sunlight made her feel strangely giddy. She took another drink from her water skin and cleared her throat.

"How do you know him?" she asked finally.

"Rafe?" Jared asked with a laugh, and the electric moment was over. "We've been friends since we were boys getting into trouble together. We were both apprenticed to Childir for a time, but Rafe went rogue and decided he liked street fighting better than herb lore."

"You weren't a street fighter yourself?" she asked. "I thought you left Childir's service too."

Jared laughed aloud at that. "Do I look like I was a street fighter to you? No. I learned the arts of war the civilized way—from a master at the training range. But Rafe? Well, let's just say that if I told you the number of times he's had his nose broken, you'd think I was lying."

Sahara smiled. "No...I'm pretty sure I'd believe you."

"When my sister fell in love with him, we pretty much became like brothers." Jared looked away, and Sahara felt how much the thought of her still hurt. After a long silence, he sighed and nudged her. "What about you? You've never told me your story."

Sahara swallowed hard. Now it was her turn to re-open a wound. She drew her dagger and turned it over in her hands. "I never wanted to be this," she said slowly. "Part of the Shell. An assassin. But when the Drakkin came, it didn't matter what I wanted anymore. My father couldn't protect me...I had to learn to protect myself."

"Your father taught you to fight?"

"No." And with a rush of bitterness, "The only thing my father taught me was that trying to bargain with the Drakkin destroys you and everything you love."

"When you were ill, you kept saying a name," Jared said. "Marsyas. Was he your brother?"

Sahara closed her eyes for a moment at the mention of his name. When she opened them again, she found Jared watching her intently.

"No. Marsyas was my teacher."

There must have been something in the way she said it, because Jared's eyebrow lifted just slightly. "Teacher."

"He made me everything I am," Sahara said. She blew out her breath and stared down at the knife in her hands.

And you loved him. It was Jared's voice in her head.

"You're right. I did love him," she said before she could catch herself.

"I didn't say that," Jared said.

"Yes, you did."

"Really?"

"I heard you say it right now!" she said, but then she caught herself and frowned. Had she really heard him say it?

He looked completely puzzled for a moment, and then he shook it off. "Okay. But you did have a brother, right?"

"Yeah. Deor." She stopped and clenched her jaw. She dragged the point of the dagger through the sand.

"What happened to him, Sahara?"

Jared's voice was gentle but prodding, and Sahara took a deep breath to steel herself against tears. She might as well tell him.

"When the Drakkin invaded my homeworld," she said, "they started a program of systematic extermination. Our capital city of Actaeon was the last stronghold of our people. Kind of like Albadir, I guess. Three years after they arrived, they rounded up all the male children left and just...took them away." She stopped, fighting against her ragged breathing. "I was sent away to train when I was seventeen. And after that, my mother...she just gave up on life."

He covered her hand with his, and the warmth of his touch almost broke her. "And your father?"

"My father sent me and fifteen other girls to the Shell, to learn the black arts of the assassin from Marsyas. We were supposed to be our world's last best hope for freedom. And I let them down."

"You can't carry the fate of an entire world on your shoulders, Sahara," Jared said.

She squinted at him. "Can't I?" When he said nothing, Sahara pulled her hand out from under his and sheathed her dagger.

"If you'd told Arnauld that you were part of the Shell I think everything would have gone very differently."

"I guess we'll never know."

Jared's gaze was intense and unreadable, so she turned and stared out at the northern edge of the dunes. They stretched away to a haze of shimmering dark haze of mountains on the horizon. Everything was utterly and completely still and silent. It made her shiver.

Rafe suddenly took a relaxed deep breath and opened his eyes. He stretched and then propped himself up on an elbow. "Am I late?" he asked with a yawn.

"Right on time, as always," Jared answered.

Rafe grinned and when Sahara smiled in spite of herself, he winked at her. "You ready to do this?" he asked.

"Always."

Sahara looked out at the dunes again, then frowned and squinted against the glare. A dark speck formed against the shimmer of the sands, and it seemed to be growing larger by the moment.

She drew her knife.

"It's coming," she said.

TWENTY-FOUR

They pulled their camouflage suits out of their packs and wound the fabric around their heads and over their necks and shoulders, pulling the fabric so that only their eyes showed. They tossed aside their sand-colored battle jackets and stepped into their camouflage jumpsuits, then pulled covers over their boots.

"Remember," Jared said softly, his voice now eerily disembodied except for his eyes. "We need him alive."

Weapons at the ready, they crept cautiously out of the tent and positioned themselves in stages along the side of the dunes.

And then they waited. The sun beat down on Sahara's back, and sweat trickled down her nose. The scout came on steadily but slowly. He was on foot, and he seemed to be alone. Its mask of beaten and burnished metal gleamed every now and again beneath its dark cowl.

As he approached the place where they lay hidden, his steps slowed, and he drew a heavy blaster. His head swung from side to side, as if he were sniffing them out.

Sahara hardly dared to breathe for fear she would be heard. As the scout turned toward Jared's position, Sahara saw a small place just under the scout's left arm where one of the scales of his mail shirt was twisted out of place. It was only just big enough for a crossbow bolt.

I hope Jared's a good shot.

The scout edged forward again and then stopped suddenly, his boots right above Sahara's head. Jared was the only one with a clean shot at him now—Rafe was too far away to see the target.

A sharp *whizz* suddenly cut through the silence, and a bolt slammed into the scout just below his left shoulder. It bounced off without penetrating the armor, but the force was enough to knock him off balance. As soon as he had purchase in the sand again, the scout swung around to Jared's position and aimed his blaster at the sand.

Sahara drew her dagger and coiled herself. As the scout's finger closed on the trigger, she sprang on him and caught him around the waist. The rough metal of his armor bit into her skin and the smell of him washed over her in a sickening wave. His shot went wide, sending a spray of sand harmlessly into the air.

She heard someone shout, but everything was lost in the blinding heat of the sand and the scout's stench as they rolled together down the other side of the dunes. A dull pain seared through her as the scout's gauntleted hand smashed into the side of her face.

They slid to a stop at the foot of the dune and Sahara scrambled to a crouch. The scout was splayed in the sand beside her, one leg twisted unnaturally sideways.

The weak place was exposed.

Before the scout could shield himself, Sahara sprang on him again and straddled his chest. She slammed her dagger into the vulnerable spot and the scout roared in mad pain and rage. She dragged the blade free as he flailed beneath her.

The blood was pounding in her ears, and her vision clouded. She ripped the cowl from her head and then raised the dagger high, hilt tight in both hands.

"For Deor," she whispered.

"Sahara, no!" Jared shouted.

As she plunged the blade downwards, Jared tackled her and toppled her sideways. She shoved him off and scrambled back toward the scout. Jared caught her legs and then straddled her back, holding her down on the sand as she bucked to get free.

"Sahara! We need him alive!"

The scout, wheezing and gurgling on dark blood, scrabbled weakly in the sand. He reached for his blaster. Rafe plunged down the side of the dune in a shower of sand and kicked the scout in the head before he could reach his weapon. The scout fell backward in the sand and didn't move again.

Panting, Jared released Sahara and shoved the cowl from his head. Sahara got to her knees and glared up at him, rage still pulsing like liquid metal in her veins.

"I had him!" she shouted. "Why did you stop me?"

"Because killing him wasn't the damn mission," Rafe said, unwinding the cowl from his own head. "Remember?"

Sahara knelt there for a moment, panting. As her rage subsided, the pain in her face and body throbbed into her awareness again.

"That's a nasty bruise," Jared said. He took her chin gently and turned her face.

"He hit me on the way down." Sahara touched her cheek gingerly and winced.

"Let's get him back to the cave before he wakes up," Rafe said.

It was a long walk back to the cave carrying the scout's dead weight, and the harbingers were starting their vicious swirl when they finally reached it. They dragged the scout inside and dumped him in the middle of the of the floor. Rafe tied him hand and foot and then they crouched nearby and watched.

They didn't have to wait long. The scout came to with a violent jerk that carried him halfway to the wall. Rafe hauled him upright by the shoulders and forced him to sit up. His wound was seeping dark blood and he growled in pain and rage.

"You will burn for this." The scout dragged in a breath choked with spittle through his teeth. "You will all of you burn!"

Jared crouched just out of reach of the scout's feet. Then he looked up at Rafe and nodded.

Rafe grabbed the syringe from the top of the chest where Jared had placed it the night before. He flicked off the cap and jammed the needle into the scout's neck. The scout let out a grating howl and then sagged in Rafe's grip. Jared counted silently and then shoved the scout's head upright.

"Tell us the best approach to the fortress," he said.

"Not...telling...anything," the scout slurred.

Sahara moved to stand behind Jared, her heart pounding. She hoped Jared's serum would actually work—and if it did, maybe she could find out more than just the intel on the fortress. Maybe she could find out about Deor.

Jared punched the scout upside the head. "The approach."

The scout looked past Jared at Sahara. He hissed and growled. "That one belongs to us."

Jared raised his hand to strike the scout again but Sahara stopped him. He looked up at her in surprise as she stepped around him. She took a knee beside the scout's head and leaned in.

"You want me? Then tell me the path to the fortress. I'll turn myself in."

The scout's breathing quickened and he angled his head to look at her. "You lie."

"You have something I want," she said, keeping her voice low. "And I will trade myself for him."

"What?" Rafe said, starting forward. Jared caught him by the arm and held him back.

The drug was beginning to take effect, and the scout shook his head once, and then again. "The pass," he slurred. "North of the city...in the foothills. Take the pass."

"How many guards?"

"No guards." The scout slumped forward and Sahara jerked him upright again.

"You're sure? They want me alive, and if a guard should kill me—"

"Want you alive." The scout's speech was so slurred now that she could barely make out the words. And then he started to laugh, choking on blood and spittle. "Alive until you become one of us...just like him."

The Taken will fill the void.

In one blinding motion, Sahara drew her knife and slashed it across the guard's throat. Rafe and Jared jumped back as the dark, foul blood sprayed onto the stone floor.

"I don't believe you," she said.

She wiped the dagger on the scout's leg and sheathed it.

"Why the hell did you do that?" Jared asked. "We didn't get anything out of him!"

"We got enough," she said.

"He didn't tell us anything we didn't already know!"

"He did tell us that the pass isn't guarded," Rafe put in.

"What use is that if we don't know where to go when we get through?" Jared fired back. "This was supposed to be about saving Albadir, not your brother!"

"Look," she said, "I promised I would help save your city. But I made him a promise a long time ago—and if I have a chance to save my brother, I will take it."

"Even if taking that chance means you sacrifice the rest of us?"

For a moment, Sahara and Jared faced each other over the pool of blood spreading across the floor. She could feel his anger as if it were her own, and it made her pause.

"If you could have saved your sister, wouldn't you have taken the chance, no matter the cost?"

"No," Jared said, his voice suddenly strained. "Why do you think she's dead?"

Sahara's breath caught in her throat and she looked at Rafe. He nodded once and she turned back to Jared.

"You sacrificed your sister...for what?"

"For the city. For the greater good."

"Did it work?"

Jared said nothing, but his face was crumpled with anger and grief.

"That's why the three of us are here, isn't it?" she asked, looking at Rafe. "We're here because we want revenge. And when we take our revenge, Albadir will be free."

She turned back to the body and stripped the scimitar. She tossed it among their packs, then jerked her head toward the door of the cave.

"Get rid of the body," she said.

Rafe hitched his hands under the scout's armpits and dragged him out into the howling storm. A moment later he was back, his hair wild and blood on his hands. He went to one of the stone jars of water and rinsed off the blood, then dumped over the jar to wash the floor.

"Well, even if we didn't exactly get what we came for, there's one fewer of them now," Jared said.

Sahara watched the bloody water swirl down the drain hole in the center of the floor.

She had set them on the path, and there was no turning back now.

TWENTY-FIVE

As they made their way back into the city, they found preparations underway for a festival. Women were hanging long garlands of lights and flowers in the square, and the men rolled in vats of ales and stacked them for easy access. Everyone was smiling and laughing, and the disconnect between the seriousness of the cave and everything that had happened there and this desperate, shining life of the city hit Sahara like a punch in the stomach.

"What's happening?" Sahara asked. "What are they doing?"

"It's the Summer Festival," Jared said.

"We're celebrating another year of survival," Rafe added. "And another year without the payment being collected."

He waved a hand and disappeared into the crowd.

"Rafe, wait!" Sahara called. She moved to follow him but Jared caught her arm.

"Let him go," he said. "We'll see him later."

"What did he mean about the payment?" she said. "Whose lives do you trade for the city's survival?"

"Don't worry about that tonight. Tonight, let's celebrate."

"Celebrate? How can we celebrate? We just slaughtered a

Drakkin scout back there, and now you're telling me we should go to a party and ignore the fact that you're buying all of this with the blood of your own people!"

Jared sighed. "I'm not ignoring it. We remember the dead and honor the life they have given us. And we celebrate because there are no guarantees that any of us will be alive tomorrow."

"Have fun with that," she said and swung away from him.

"See you tonight!" he called after her.

She ignored him and headed for the Halls of Healing. She was still fuming when she reached the doors and Aliya came forward to greet her, but she had the beginnings of a new plan.

"What happened to you?" Aliya asked, looking Sahara over with deep concern in her eyes.

Even though Sahara had taken pains to scrub the blood from her hands and face, she knew she was covered with grime and the dust of the desert.

"Nothing," she said. "But I need your help with something."

Aliya's usual warm smile faded suddenly and she gripped Sahara's arm. "Where have you been?"

"Out. With Jared. But this festival—"

"Yes. It's tonight."

"I know that."

"Is that what's troubling you?" Aliya asked with a little laugh. "You don't have to do anything special, you know. It's just a chance to enjoy food and dancing, and—"

"Dancing." Sahara swallowed hard. The last time she'd danced, it had been with Marsyas. That was before the Shift. Before she had become all this. "Yeah—I can't go."

Aliya took both Sahara's hands in her own and squeezed them. "Of course you can! I put a dress in your rooms for you to wear. You deserve to enjoy a bit of happiness and fun."

"I heard something, and I need you to tell me if it's true."

"What did you hear?" Aliya said, the lines of concern reappearing between her delicate brows.

"That you buy the city's survival with the blood of your own people."

Aliya's face looked suddenly as if Sahara had driven a knife through her stomach.

"Of course not," she said, but it was feeble and the look in her eyes put the lie to it.

"What a relief," Sahara said. "I was afraid he was telling the truth."

Aliya motioned at several baskets of clean bandages and mumbled something about folding them, and then she left Sahara and disappeared into the back rooms. Sahara went to the stone basin to wash her hands.

She stared down at her skin beneath the surface of the water. She had scrubbed them before they left the cave, but they still seemed to have blood on them. She swirled them slowly, watching the ripples. The water was clear, but all she could see was the swirl of bloody water slowly sliding down the drain in the desert cave.

She splashed water over her face and leaned over the basin. It was better for her to go alone. Jared and Rafe would come if she asked, she knew, but she didn't think she could survive it if they shared the same fate as Marsyas.

As she folded the bandages, she thought about what supplies she would need. When her work was finally done, she returned to her rooms and sorted out her pack. Weapons weren't a problem, and she wasn't expecting a long journey, but it wouldn't hurt to pack some food and a canteen. If they were setting up food for the festival, no one would notice if she took some.

She tied the pack shut again and rummaged through her drawers looking for dark battle dress pants and a shirt. There was nothing remotely useful here. She would have to raid the armory.

Might as well take a gun while I'm at it.

As she shouldered her pack and turned to the door, she caught sight of the dress Aliya had left for her. It was draped over the back of the chair. She lifted it up and looked at it. It was sleeveless, and the color of shallow water over white sand.

For one moment, she hesitated. Maybe it would be better to put them all off their guard by showing up to the party, just for a little while. Then she could slip away when they were all too drunk to miss her.

She lowered her pack to the floor and then went to the mantle and felt beneath the flowers she had placed there. Her fingers found what she was looking for and she drew it out. The amethyst chain sparkled in her hand, and she bent and fastened it around her ankle.

———

The night was lovely and dark, and the lights danced on the garlands in the hushing night wind. Several long tables, heaped with all manner of meats, breads, fruits, and sweets, stood under the eastern colonnade. Children piled their plates with sweets and ran off before their mothers could catch them. Men filled their tankards from the casks that had been brought earlier that day. Everywhere she looked, people were happy.

It hurt her insides to look at their faces, and she almost turned and ran back to her room. But then she stopped.

Jared stood with a knot of young men, all of whom were on at least their third tankard of ale, and none of whom could hold their liquor. He was smiling, and Sahara's heart lurched in her chest and a strange warmth seeped through her veins.

"—and so she says, she says," guffawed one of the men, gripping Jared's arm and leaning into the circle, "she says she won't come tonight because her fool bag of omen stones told her it wasn't safe."

"If it's not safe here, it's not safe in her bed either!" one of the others said.

"Sounds like it's not safe for anyone to be in her bed," another added. This drew a hearty round of laughter, and he jostled the first speaker with his elbow. "You got lucky, I say. Let her sleep with her rocks. Cold comfort, that."

Jared drained the last of his ale and left the group, heading for the food tables. Sahara watched him, wondering if he would turn and notice her.

I hope she hasn't gone and done something stupid.

It was Jared's voice in her head and it startled her. What did he mean by that? And then she remembered her pack, ready and waiting, by her chamber door.

Nothing stupid...not yet anyway.

He turned suddenly, as if he heard her voice, and his eyes locked with hers across the square. He stared at her as if he didn't recognize her, and she made her way through the crowd until she stood in front of him. The expression on his face made her veins buzz with a strange kind of heat.

So beautiful.

Sahara smiled. "You really think so?"

"What?" he asked stupidly. His eyes lingered on her face, and she felt her cheeks grow warm.

"So I decided to come after all," she said.

"You weren't going to come?"

She shook her head. "I had something—I mean, I wasn't sure I could." She shrugged. "But I'll miss all this, I guess."

He frowned at her. *What's that supposed to mean?*

Now it was her turn to scowl. Why did she keep hearing his voice in her head? It was starting to scare her. "Don't worry about it. I guess it'll all become clear soon enough."

"What the hell are you talking about?" The strangeness of the conversation seemed to be getting to him too.

"I don't need to explain myself to you," she said. He only stared at her stupidly and she shook her head. "Forget it. Let's get a drink."

As she turned away, he caught her arm. "Wait," he said. "No knife-throwing contest tonight. Promise?"

She laughed then. "I promise."

Jared offered her his arm, and Sahara took it. She could feel the muscle beneath his shirt, and the feeling that rushed through her was almost enough to make her run back to her room. But then he smiled at her, and all her fear melted away.

He led her to a table under one of the arches. Bottles of some kind of drink were clustered here and Jared poured a glass of it for Sahara to try. She downed it in a single draught. The bubbles caught her by surprise.

"It's like drinking sunshine!" she said.

"It's *estevalia,* and you should be careful," Jared warned. "It'll knock you out faster than any ale."

Sahara smiled and held out her glass. "Then I think I'll have another."

A sudden commotion drew Jared's eye, and she followed his gaze. Armon and several other soldiers clustered together at the edge of the courtyard. One of them was speaking urgently to Armon and kept gesturing in the direction of the river.

Sahara looked up at Jared and he frowned. Something wasn't right.

"What's going on?" she asked.

"Not sure," Jared said. He led her to the edge of the fountain and she sat down with her glass. "Wait here," he said. "And don't fall in."

"Why do I have to stay here?" she asked.

"Armon doesn't like you for starters. Give me a minute to find out what's happening. If I need you, trust me—I'll call you."

"Fine."

She watched him thread through the crowd and then downed her second glass of *estevalia.* A crowd of revelers passed between her and the soldiers and she lost sight of Jared. When they finally moved out of the way again, he and one of the soldiers were gone.

Sahara jumped to her feet and scanned the crowds. There was no sign of him anywhere. Then she spotted one of the other soldiers standing nearby and she joined him.

"Where's Jared?" she asked.

"They said they saw something," the soldier answered. His expression was grim. "Down by the river."

"What was it?" Sahara asked, though she already knew the answer.

"They thought it might have been a Drakkin scout."

Sahara closed her eyes briefly. The moment she'd been dreading was actually here, and Jared had left her behind.

"No need to panic," the soldier said with a feeble attempt at a reassuring smile. "They'll take care of it."

"Right. I'm sure they will."

She turned away from the soldier and melted back into the crowd.

TWENTY-SIX

She returned to the fountain and perched on the edge.
There was nothing to do but wait for Jared to return. He'd said he
would come for her if he needed her help, and trying to track him
down would only waste time.

Besides, if he can't contain it, this is where I need to be.

As she waited, the music began—a beautiful haunting melody
with an insistent throbbing bass. The courtyard filled with people, all
dancing with rhythmic abandon, totally unaware that there was
anything for them to fear. Sahara saw Del and his friends take the
center of the space. They moved with unbelievable agility and grace
in a series of complicated steps, feet pounding, hands clapping, losing
themselves in the music and the ritual.

As Sahara watched them, she realized she would give anything to
be out there with them, dancing to honor the dead.

"I'm surprised to see you here, Sahara."

Sahara started and looked up. Kirin stood beside her, watching
her with something between suspicion and admiration. She scowled
at him.

"What do you want?"

"I was thinking," he said. "Can't we let the past be the past and be friends, just for tonight?"

Surprisingly, he seemed genuine, and Sahara narrowed her eyes. "Only if you promise not to shove a spoon down my throat."

Kirin laughed. "No fear! But I will get you another glass of *estevalia.*"

"No thanks," she said. "I've had enough."

He looked around and then asked, "Where's Jared?"

"I don't know."

"He left you sitting here all alone and didn't even tell you where he was going?"

Sahara bristled. "I don't need to track his every move, Kirin."

"Well, since he stood you up, would you care to dance?" he asked. Kirin held out a hand and she eyed it warily. "Come on," he said. "Dance with me."

Sahara glanced toward the southern end of the courtyard where the band was playing. The music was tempting her, calling her. As she swiveled back to face Kirin with a "yes" on her lips, she noticed that the rest of the soldiers were gone.

Instantly, the spell of the music snapped, replaced by the insistent tugging of the Sight. She rose up on her toes, trying to see over the crowd. In every shadow, she saw the dragon.

"What are you doing?" Kirin asked. "Is something wrong?"

"Don't talk to me right now." She edged around him to scan the tables where the ales had been set up, but no one was there either.

"You're looking for Jared, aren't you?" he asked as Sahara turned back to him with a frown. "I bet you'd dance with him if he asked."

"I don't want to dance."

"Why not?" he asked. "Are you afraid of me?"

Sahara wanted to laugh at the almost wishful tone in his voice, but she checked herself. "Nothing about you scares me, Kirin."

A scream tore through the crowd. The music jangled to a confused stop and people looked around. A low, worried murmur swelled into a chaos of questions with no answers.

And then a blast like a bolt of lightning shredded the courtyard, and three bodies crumpled to the ground, limbs severed by the blast.

The crowd erupted in screams and the people stampeded for the street. Sahara jumped onto the ledge of the fountain, kicking over her glass. It shattered on the stone.

Another blast from the shadows of the colonnade caught a dozen people from behind, ripping through their bodies and showering the stones with blood.

"What the hell is that?" Kirin shouted up at her.

Sahara skirted the edge of the fountain and tried to get a better look at who—or what—stood in the shadows of the columns. But as the crowd parted, she froze.

The scorched and mangled bodies of Del and his friends lay in the center of the courtyard.

Sahara couldn't even scream, and for a moment, she thought she would vomit. She dragged in one shattered breath after another, spacing them evenly, just like she'd been trained.

I will show neither pain nor fear. I will show—

Below her, Kirin caught a woman by the arm as she bolted past him. "What's happening?"

"They've come!" the woman screamed.

She dragged herself out of Kirin's grip and disappeared into the stampeding crowd.

All Sahara's nausea faded in a hot rush of adrenaline. Everything within her felt like it was on fire, heightening her senses and her reflexes. Sahara scanned the colonnade. At the edge of the courtyard, just beyond the reach of the torchlight, she could just make out a dim figure.

As she watched, he raised his massive blaster, glowing golden at its core, and fired again into the crowd.

The blast sent scorched bodies flying in every direction. A shower of stone and dirt rained down around Sahara and splashed in the fountain. She ducked to shield her face and then hiked up her skirt to draw her dagger.

"What are you doing?" Kirin shouted. "Are you insane?"

"Get out of here before you get yourself killed!" she said. "And if you find Jared, tell him to open the armory!"

Another blast made Kirin bolt. She didn't think he would go looking for Jared. She was alone.

Sorry, Jared. I know I promised I wouldn't get into a knife fight tonight. She glanced at Del's body and clenched her jaw. *But I can't sit this one out.*

She edged around the fountain to get a better vantage on the situation. The figure fired again, sending what was left of the crowd into a murderous frenzy. The bodies of the dead and dying were trampled under pitiless feet.

Sahara tested her grip on the dagger. Trying to cut through that seething mass would probably get her killed. Besides, she wanted the element of surprise. She circled back around the fountain and jumped off on the far side.

She thought she'd avoided the bulk of the crowd, but even so the press of bodies around her nearly suffocated her. Her feet barely touched the ground as she was swept away. For a moment, panic choked her. What if she couldn't get out? What if she fell? If she did, she knew she would never get up again.

Another blast behind them sent chips of stone and dirt showering down on the crowd like shrapnel. The stampede crashed against the refreshment tables, toppling them. Bottles and the giant barrels of ale shattered on the cobblestones, and ale and *estevalia* ran like blood through the crevices.

The pace of the crowd slowed as people bottlenecked at the entrance to the courtyard, and Sahara saw her chance. She angled her way to the left, shoving her way through the crowd until she broke free.

For a moment, she crouched against a pillar of the colonnade, fighting to calm her jangling nerves. After a few deep breaths, she got to her feet and shifted her grip on the dagger again. She slipped into the shadows and edged her way toward the hulking shape on the far side of the courtyard.

"You picked the wrong party," she said softly.

The last of the crowd drained out of the courtyard, leaving a wreckage of bodies and broken stone in its wake. Sahara crept forward in the shadows, her eyes never leaving her target. The figure finally stepped out from beneath the colonnade and Sahara got a look at him. His mask, made of some dark burnished metal, hid his features. The rest of him was concealed in the folds of a dark cowl, like he carried his own shadows with him. But as he paced slowly through the pools of torchlight, Sahara caught the glint of the armor that covered his body like scales.

His head swung from side to side as he surveyed the damage in the courtyard. Suddenly, Del groaned softly. The scout stopped and riveted on his body.

Everything inside Sahara turned to ice. She'd never imagined that the boy could be still alive.

"No," she whispered. "No, no, no..."

The scout turned his heavy steps toward Del and stood over him for a moment. Sahara held her breath.

"Where is the outworlder?" the scout asked, his voice a throaty growl. When Del shook his head, the scout grabbed the collar of his shirt and half lifted him off the ground. "Where is she?"

Del's gaze shifted past the scout and found Sahara in the shadows. She didn't know how he could see her, but she was certain that he did. The tiniest ghost of a smile touched his lips and he looked back up into the scout's masked face.

"She's not an outworlder," he croaked. "She's one of us now."

The scout dropped Del on the stones and placed his placed his booted foot on Del's chest. Sahara heard the sickening crack of his ribcage as the scout crushed his chest.

She bit down on lips until the blood came to keep herself from screaming. Everything inside her melted in the hot rush of rage and grief, and with a supreme effort, she channeled it all into a single point of focus.

The scout kicked Del's shattered body aside and returned to his scan of the carnage. Sahara edged into position behind him, moving silently as a shadow herself. Then a sharp noise on the other side of the courtyard startled her and the scout's head snapped up.

Armon and two other soldiers edged out from the relative security of the colonnade, machine guns raised.

"Not another step," Armon said. His voice was shaking with fear.

The scout made no answer except to turn its slow, heavy steps to advance on Armon's position.

Sahara's pulse pounded in her temples. The soldiers opened fire and Sahara dropped onto the blood-soaked pavement to avoid being hit. Not a single shot found its mark.

Damn their useless drills!

She drew herself up into a crouch. Then she saw Jared step out of cover to Armon's right. The scout swung toward him and raised his blaster.

Faster than thought, Sahara flipped the grip on her dagger and launched herself at the scout.

She hit his arm and the scout's blast went wide, slamming through the stone column to Jared's left. It buckled and collapsed in a shower of stone and she lost sight of Jared in the cloud of dust.

Sahara gripped her legs tight around the scout's waist and drove her dagger into the soft fleshy point where the scout's neck met his shoulder. He roared and dropped his blaster, then clawed at her with his gauntleted hand. The metal nails raked the flesh of her calf and Sahara gritted against the red wash of pain.

She dragged off the mask that shielded the scout's face and it clattered to the ground. The scout clawed her again, the claws gouging her deeper this time. She lost her grip and crashed down on the stone.

The scout turned on her and she scrambled backward. Her knife still protruded from his neck, and dark blood streamed from the wound to slick his breastplate. The scout's reptilian face, so scaled that it was almost impossible to tell where the armor ended and skin began, was set in a snarl, revealing razor-sharp teeth.

The scout dropped his blaster and drew his own jagged knife. As he advanced on her, Sahara crawled backward and her hand bumped a large stone. She flung it at him and it bounced off his shoulder. His growl intensified and sprinted at her. He stomped on her ankle with his massive boot and pinned it against the stone. Sahara cried out in pain as the scout leaned his weight on it.

"You belong with us," he growled.

And then she heard a single blaster shot. The scout pitched forward and fell beside her on the stone. Dark blood oozed out from his massive skull, and his lizard-like eyes were glassy and fixed on her face.

Sahara scrabbled away from him and got to her feet. She cried out and almost fell again when she tried to put weight on her ankle. Strong arms caught her just before she hit the ground.

"Are you all right?" Jared asked. "Sahara, are you all right?"

She swiped a hand across her face and realized she was crying.

"It's okay," Jared said. "I've got you. Come on."

Jared slipped his arm around her waist and helped her across the courtyard. Armon and his soldiers stood waiting for them under the colonnade. Sahara could barely see them through the cloud of tears, but anger burned up hot within her.

"You almost got us killed!" Sahara shouted at him. "You and your damn useless drills!"

Armon said nothing, but his gaze shifted to Jared.

"What do you want me to say?" Jared asked. "She's right."

He pushed past Armon and helped Sahara through the rubble until they reached the street.

As the adrenaline ebbed, the burning pain in her leg and ankle intensified. Sahara leaned against Jared, feeling the roughness of his linen shirt under her cheek and the strength of his arm as he supported her. The gentle breeze hushed around them, cooling her burning skin and drying the tears on her cheeks.

"You saved my life back there," Jared said.

"Well," she said, her voice gravelly, "I guess we're even."

Jared said nothing, and she was thankful. They limped along the street in silence until she couldn't go any further. She stumbled and he stopped.

"I can't," she said simply. Blood trickled down her leg to pool on the stone. "I can't."

Without a word, Jared lifted her in his arms and carried her toward the Halls of Healing, just as he had done all those weeks ago. She laid her head on his chest and the tears she couldn't hold back any longer burned down her cheeks.

"I'm going to destroy them all," she sobbed.

TWENTY-SEVEN

Sahara stood silently with Jared under the boughs of a spreading tree as Aliya's sweet, deep voice wound through the shadows of the funeral grove. The entire city had gathered for the burial rites, holding tiny candles that shivered in the night breeze.

Sahara's throat tightened with tears she couldn't shed, and she stared down at the small barrow that was just long enough to hold Del's broken body. Beside his resting place lay thirty more.

As Aliya finished her song, Childir stepped forward bearing his own small candle. Sahara had some vague notion that he had come to see her while she was ill all those weeks ago—but then, as she tried to fix the moment in her mind, she suddenly wasn't sure. He reminded her a bit of Tol, her own city's holy man. That memory made her shiver, and she shifted ever so slightly closer to Jared.

Childir raised a hand in benediction over the graves.

"May the river guide your spirits to a place of refreshment," he said. "May the sun warm your faces and the rains fall gently. May beauty surround you forever. May no evil trouble you, nor sorrow hold you here. We release you."

He blew out his candle. One by one, all the tiny lights winked out. Sahara held hers tight, unable to catch her breath enough to extinguish it.

"Sahara," Jared said softly.

I can't, she thought. She didn't even have the voice to speak.

Jared bent his head and blew gently. Sahara's light vanished, and a tiny curl of smoke stung her eyes.

In knots of twos and threes, the crowd dispersed back to the city. Out of the corner of her eye, Sahara saw Arnauld slip his arm around Aliya's shoulders and lead her away.

"Are you ready?" Jared asked, his voice low and gentle.

"Ready for what?" She felt heavy, so unbelievably heavy.

Jared touched her arm and she looked up. "We shouldn't linger among the dead."

"Go ahead and leave if you have somewhere else you need to be," she said, realizing how harsh she sounded only after the words were out of her mouth.

But Jared seemed to understand. He gave her fingers a squeeze and left her standing there alone in the gathering dark. Sahara sat down cross-legged on the grass and wrenched a stalk from its roots. She stuck it between her teeth with trembling fingers.

"You were made for peace," she said to Del's barrow, her voice taut with tears. "I guess this world just couldn't hold you."

There was nothing but silence in the glade, and Sahara chewed the grass furiously, fighting down the flood of tears that burned behind her eyes.

"Damn," she said at last.

She drew out a knife, almost identical to her own, in a delicately tooled leather sheath.

"Meant to give you this at the festival. Boys said yesterday was your birthday." She turned over the sheath in her hands. "I guess maybe you don't need it where you are now." And then, "I hope you don't, anyway. But here it is."

She leaned forward and laid it on the barrow. Then she traced a tiny symbol with her finger in the dirt beside it. A circle enclosing the three-petaled flower.

"You're one of us now," she said, her voice taut. "So watch out for me, Del, would you? I'm going to need someone to show me those pastures when I get there."

Then she buried her face in her hands and sobbed.

For a week after Del's death, Sahara stayed in the Halls of Healing. Her physical wounds healed quickly thanks to Aliya's skill, but she didn't want to leave. As long as she stayed within those walls, she could hide from the questions that she knew were coming. At the same time, her fears made her ashamed. She wasn't trained to run. No matter what the situation, Marsyas would have wanted her to stand and fight.

But somehow, this time, she just didn't have the strength.

On the eighth day, as Sahara stared out the window at the sands beyond the city walls, Aliya approached her quietly and stood for a moment beside her.

"I know I can't stay here any longer," Sahara said without turning around. "But I don't know how to leave."

"Do you know what they call you?" Aliya asked.

"Outworlder?" Sahara offered bitterly. "Outcast? Murderer? Assassin? Traitor?"

Aliya slipped an arm around Sahara's shoulder. "No," she said. "That's what they *used* to call you. But since the festival, they call you *gennai*."

"What does that mean?"

"*Brave one.*"

Sahara leaned her hands on the ledge of the window and bowed her head. Aliya stroked her hair gently, as if she were a child.

"He was alive when the scout got to him, Aliya." She closed her eyes, battling the memory that still haunted her. "And I did nothing. I let him die. How is that brave?"

"I know," she said gently. She leaned her cheek on Sahara's shoulder. "But when everyone else fled in panic, you stayed. Jared owes you his life."

"And I owe him mine. I wasn't the only brave one that night."

Aliya leaned over to look into her face. "Do you think he was wrong to save your life?"

The question made Sahara pause. How many times in the last week had she wished she could have traded places with Del? That it could have been her beneath that boot?

"Maybe."

"You are here for a reason, Sahara. Maybe now is the time."

Sahara glanced up. "Time for what?"

"It is time for you to stop hiding, *gennai*," Aliya said. "It is time for you to be who you were always meant to be."

"And who is that, exactly?" Sahara asked.

Aliya smiled and gave her shoulders a squeeze. "I think only you know the answer to that."

Her soft footsteps died away, and Sahara lingered at the window for a moment longer. Then she drew in a deep breath and headed for the door.

TWENTY-EIGHT

J ARED HEADED DOWN THE PATH TOWARD THE RIVER, HOPING TO find Sahara there. Aliya had told him that morning that she had left the Halls of Healing, and he'd loitered around the Great House to see if she might come home. She didn't, and after three aimless hours, he gave up waiting and went looking for her.

Arnauld had called a council meeting, and he had requested that Sahara be there. Jared wasn't sure what the summons might mean, and he didn't like uncertainty.

It's not like what happened was her fault.

But even as he thought it, he knew what they would all say.

It was her fault because she was here. And it was his fault too for bringing her here. The two of them had blood on their hands as certainly as if they'd murdered all those people themselves.

Maybe, after all, they were right.

He rounded the bend in the path and saw Sahara sitting beneath a tree, staring out over the water. Her hair was bound up in a silver cloth, and she wore black battle dress. A gear pack sat beside her.

"Sahara!" he called as he angled down the slope toward her.

She glanced over her shoulder and welcomed him with a faint

smile. Her eyes were rimmed with red. As he settled down beside her, she turned away to look at the water.

"Nice day for swimming," he said.

"I haven't tried." She didn't look at him, and her voice was taut.

"I understand." It was a lame thing to say, he knew, but it felt foolish to say nothing at all.

"You told me once that maybe that I could be something more than my past. And this morning Aliya told me that it's time for me to become who I am meant to be." She finally turned to him. "I was hoping I'd have the chance to say goodbye."

"You can't surrender to them, Sahara," he said. "You're one of us now. If the Drakkin come for you, they come for us all."

"I'm not talking about surrender." Her eyes burned hot and bright. "I'm going to take the path through the foothills and finish what I started. And I'm going alone."

Jared stood suddenly. "Come with me," he said. "I want to show you something."

"You're not going to convince me not to go," she said. "I don't care what you have to show me."

"Just—come with me." He held out his hand. "Please?"

She stood and hefted her pack. He led her across the bridge to the library and pushed open the heavy door. It was dark and cool inside, and he breathed in deeply. The spicy, musty air smelled of dry parchment and old leather, and it always made him smile.

"I never understood your love affair with this place," Sahara said.

"My father was the official scribe of the city, so I practically grew up here. He spent many days and nights transcribing messages, accounts, birth and death records into a vast database. Whatever might be useful in constructing a picture of daily life in Albadir, he collected." He went to a set of bookshelves in a small alcove. "When the Drakkin came, they destroyed all our communications and our technology...but they left us the books."

"Why did you bring me here?"

"Arnauld has called a council meeting, and he wants you there," he said. "But before you face them, I wanted to tell you more about our history with the Drakkin."

"Why?"

"If things go sideways at that meeting, maybe it would help you understand why."

Sahara took a deep breath and blew it out. Then she gestured at the parchment. "Tell away."

"There are two things that come up in all the stories about the Drakkin. One is that the Alba River—the main water source for Albadir and the Great City—is controlled from the Drakkin fortress. They have some kind of sluice which they can close at will and cut off all our water. I don't have to tell you that without water, we wouldn't last long. The desert would bury us within days."

"So they control the water. What else?"

"In payment for keeping the sluice open, they require blood," Jared said. "One life for many, as they say."

Sahara scowled suddenly and the ferocity in her eyes surprised Jared. "Is it actually one life, or do they claim more than that when they come to collect?"

"Depends. In the past, they've taken anywhere from fifteen to fifty men. But they always take a woman. From what I can gather, the men are shipped to the labor camps north of here."

"Where I was supposed to go," Sahara said. "And the woman?"

"She is a blood-offering to the Drakkin."

A dark foreboding gathered in Sahara's stomach. "So if they came tomorrow and demanded their payment, who would be sacrificed?"

"Aliya."

Sahara's hands convulsed into fists. "No."

"It's been years, Sahara. There's no predicting when they'll—"

"Well, we have a problem now. I've attracted their attention and we killed their scout. They will come for me again, and when they do, they'll probably take her too. And they might still cut off the water, because you've become an annoyance."

"And I think that's why you're being summoned to the council meeting," Jared said.

Sahara perched on one of the long wooden tables and leaned back on her forearms. She tilted her head to look up at the domed roof and frowned. He followed her gaze. The dome was decorated with gold stars scattered on a blue field, and at the apex was a three-petaled flower.

"What's that?" she asked.

"It's the most ancient symbol of our city," he said. "We call it the *lilia-dir*. It used to grow along the banks of the Alba River. It's said that they all died when the Drakkin came, but we still preserve its memory. I believe that it will grow along the river again someday."

Sahara sat up and leaned her elbows on her knees. "It's the same flower as the tattoo on my back, Jared."

"I know."

"What does that mean?"

"I was hoping you could tell me." He hesitated, but then thought better of telling her that he had consulted Childir about it.

"When I entered the Shell, this was the tattoo we received. I never thought it had any significance beyond the Shell itself. But maybe it does." She gestured at a stack of parchments. "Have you found any answers?"

"In the mystic texts I've read, the three-petaled flower and the Drakkin are almost always pictured together. There is a deep antagonism between the children of the *lilia-dir* and the Drakkin which goes back as far as our recorded history."

Sahara straightened. "And how does the Shell come into all of this?"

"I don't know. But I think you are more deeply connected to Silesia's fate than you realize." He smiled at her and gestured at her pack. "I guess I'm asking you to give them a chance to support you before you do something reckless."

TWENTY-NINE

The council hall was filled to capacity. As Arnauld called the men to order and they took their seats around three sides of the heavy table, Sahara felt like she'd been summoned before the bar of judgment.

The room was oddly oppressive—its dark wood walls closed in on her, and the stained glass ceiling filtered shards of reddish light down onto the council. The panels of stained glass seemed to be depictions of moments in Silesian history, and they held little meaning to her. But the final panel in the series showed a city consumed in fire and an enormous dragon crouched on the summit of the mountains.

There's always a dragon, at the end. Always.

Her breath caught in her chest as the shard of a memory erupted into her consciousness.

The voices of the Drakkin rolled over her like a suffocating wave, drowning her in the darkness. She stood in the center of the oubliette, hands pinioned behind her in iron chains. She couldn't see the Council, but she could hear them.

"We sentence you to life on the desert planet of Silesia for your crimes and your insurrection."

In a way, it was a triumph. She was dangerous enough to warrant it. And maybe someone else would be inspired to take up the work where she'd left off.

And life in a labor camp might not be so bad...or for that long. She would find a way to escape. And when she did, she would make them pay.

"Are you okay?" Jared whispered, nudging her with his elbow.

Sahara came back to herself with a little gasp. She stared at Jared for a moment before she recognized him or where she was. As his question registered, she nodded.

At that moment, Arnauld leveled a finger at her.

"There were those who warned me not to trust you," he said. "And I think perhaps I should have listened."

"She saved my life," Jared said. And then, before she could stop him, he said, "And she's a member of the Shell, Arnauld."

Slowly the stony looks melted and the council members murmured to each other. Arnauld leaned forward in his chair, a sudden intensity in his face.

"What?" he said. Then, to Sahara, "Is this true?"

"Yes," she said.

"Why didn't you tell us this before? Do you know how long I have prayed that we would find you?" Arnauld continued, his voice rising. "How many years I have hoped some word of you would reach us, even as the shadow around us grew darker?" And then, thunderously, "Why didn't you tell me who you were?"

Sahara lifted her shoulders. "I was a stranger here, and I didn't know how I might be received. But now you know." She hesitated, and then added, "And if you know the Shell, then you know what I am trained to do. You can't hide from the Drakkin any longer, and I know what that means for your city. But I also know what that means for you, my lord Arnauld."

He stiffened and Sahara stopped. She didn't dare look around at the others, but she could feel the tension in the room building.

"My lord Arnauld, my son was slaughtered that night because we are harboring a fugitive!" a young nobleman cried. "You can't seriously be considering allowing her to stay, not after what happened!"

"If it weren't for her, the creature would still be among us," another man protested.

"That's not true, Terrence!" the young nobleman protested. "Armon said it was Jared, not that woman, who brought down the beast!"

"What do you want?" Terrence demanded. "To feed her to the Drakkin?"

"And what if that is exactly what I want?" the nobleman said, starting from his seat. "We don't need her here!"

Sahara sat very straight and kept her eyes fixed on the banner that hung on the wall behind Arnauld's chair. It was emblazoned with the sign of the three-leaved flower that Sahara had seen in the library—the same mark she bore on her back.

It has to mean something. The fact that it's here, and so am I.

Arnauld pounded a small gavel on the table and the two men sat back, scowling at each other.

"It would seem that we have much to discuss," he said. He gestured at the door. "Sahara, I would ask you to withdraw."

Sahara glanced at Jared and he nodded once. She moved to the door, but before she stepped across the threshold, Jared caught her arm.

"It won't be long," Jared whispered. "Don't go far."

As soon as she was out in the corridor and the heavy wooden doors swung closed again, Sahara blew out her breath and leaned against the wall. After a moment, she slid down to rest on her heels.

The moments ticked by and she could hear raised voices through the heavy door. She wanted to leave and see Wes. He would have some tea and some wisdom for her, and she needed both so much right now.

She stood up and paced up and down in front of the door.

"Hey," said a voice behind her.

She turned and saw Rafe approaching. He grinned at her, but it faded into a scowl when he saw the closed council door.

"What's going on?" he asked.

"They're deciding whether or not to hand me over to the Drakkin." Rafe started to laugh, but she shook her head.

"What, you're serious? Is this because of the festival?"

"There's no good way out of this now. If they hand me over, it won't stop the Drakkin from exterminating them. But if they let me stay, there's a faction that will resent Arnauld and Jared...and I don't know what that could mean." She sighed and leaned against the wall again. "Have I ever told you how much I hate politics?"

"I agree with you," Rafe said. "But I disagree that there's no good way out. The way out is for us to take the fight to the Drakkin and end this once and for all."

Sahara looked at him as if seeing him for the first time. "Marsyas would have liked you," she said.

"Who's that?"

"He was my teacher. The Guardian of the Shell."

Something must have changed in her expression, because Rafe nudged her with his elbow and she looked up at him. "It'll all work out as it's meant to. You'll see."

At that moment, the door swung open and Jared stepped into the corridor. He had a strange expression on his face that set Sahara's stomach churning.

"They're ready for you," he said. He glanced at Rafe.

"I'll wait here," Rafe said. He winked at Sahara. "It'll work out."

Jared ushered Sahara back into the council hall and closed the door behind them. Several of the members smiled at her as she entered, but there were many more who looked grim or downright angry. Arnauld rose from his seat at the head of the table.

"Sahara Acwellan, you have been granted pardon and asylum in Albadir."

I didn't realize I was on trial.

Jared nudged her with his elbow as if to rebuke her, and she glanced at him with a frown.

"Through the exercise of my executive prerogative to ensure the safety of our people," Arnauld continued, "I have decided that we will prepare for an assault against the Drakkin, and that you, Sahara, will take over the training and command of our forces in the field, effective immediately."

It was as if all the air had been sucked out of the room.

Sahara wasn't sure what had just happened, but it was like something out of a nightmare.

"My lord Arnauld," she protested. "I am no military commander. I'm an assassin. Please don't—"

"I am glad you accept your post," he interrupted. "I expect your report on our readiness in three days' time."

Sahara turned helplessly to Jared, silently pleading for him to intervene—to explain to these people that this wouldn't work. But he only gave her the tiniest shake of his head and opened the door again.

Nod and smile, came his voice in her head. *And get out fast.*

Sahara obeyed. She bowed her head to Arnauld and then retreated into the hallway. She almost barrelled into Rafe, who steadied her.

"What happened?" he asked.

As soon as Jared emerged from the Council chamber and the door closed, she grabbed his jacket and gave him a shake.

"What the hell was that?" she shouted. "This can't be happening —do you realize what this means?"

"It means maybe our troops will learn how to aim," Jared said.

"What happened?" Rafe repeated, glancing from one to the other.

"She got a promotion," Jared answered.

"To what?"

"Commander," Sahara said.

She turned on her heel and stalked down the corridor, heart thundering in her chest. The tugging of the Sight was almost unbearable, and she knew in the depths of her bones that Arnauld had made a fatal mistake.

THIRTY

Sahara stepped out into the courtyard and crossed it without slowing down. She had to get somewhere where she could breathe and think. She heard Jared and Rafe following her, but she didn't stop until they reached her favorite tree beside the river bank. Then she turned on them.

"Maybe it won't be that bad," Rafe said. "You'll do a better job than Armon, that's for damn sure. He's done nothing for us but waste resources."

"You don't understand," Sahara said. She clenched her fists. It was impossible to make them understand—to make them see the looming shadows that she saw everywhere, even in the blazing sunshine. "This is a mistake. This isn't what I was trained to do. This isn't how it's supposed to end." She turned to Jared. "How could you let him do this?"

"There was nothing I could have done to change his mind," Jared said. "As soon as he found out you were a member of the Shell, his mind was made up. Nothing anyone said made a difference to him. It was as close to a unilateral action that I've ever seen in my time on the Council."

"Great," she mumbled. "That's even worse."

She sank down on the grass and flung a stone into the river. It landed with a satisfying plop and she threw another, more viciously this time.

"I should have left without saying goodbye," she said bitterly. "I would have been halfway to that fortress by now."

Jared and Rafe sat down on either side of her and Rafe skipped a few stones over the surface of the water.

"You don't mean that," he said.

She turned and smiled at him. "No, I guess I don't."

"I've got an idea," Jared said. "Arnauld asked for a report on the state of the army. If you make the case that a full-out assault on the fortress will be a massacre, then maybe he'll listen to a different plan. Your plan."

"That's very wise," Rafe said. "And then you don't have to face those bastards alone. You'll have Jared and I to back you up."

Sahara's heart twisted in her chest as he skipped another stone on the river. "Right. It's a good idea—if Arnauld will listen to reason."

"Are you ready to take stock of the armory now, General?" Jared asked.

"The sooner we get this nightmare over with, the better," she answered.

They got to their feet and Jared led the way back to the Great House. The armory was just off the training wing, behind a heavy bolted metal door that was controlled by a keypad mounted into the wall.

"I guess easy access to these weapons wasn't part of the design," Sahara observed.

Jared punched in the code and the door slid open. "Why do you think it took me so long to get back to the festival?" he said.

In spite of the dire warnings she'd heard about the availability of weapons, the armory seemed well stocked.

"It's not enough to wage a war against the Drakkin," Sahara said.

She lifted a machine gun off the rack and checked it over. "Not even close."

She selected a pistol and let it lie in the palm of her hand for a moment before she closed her fingers around the grip and aimed at the wall.

"Marsyas didn't think much of weapons like these," she said.

"You seem expert enough," Jared observed.

"Oh, he made sure we could use them...but there's a fundamental problem with them in combat situations, so Marsyas always encouraged us in another direction."

"What problem?"

She looked at him and gestured at the shelves around them. "The ammo runs out." She pulled the trigger and the gun made a soft snapping sound. "And when it does, you're finished."

"You're right about that," Rafe agreed. "But are you really suggesting we should train a bunch of soldiers how to use a combat knife?"

"Don't be ridiculous," she said. "A combat knife is for close quarters fighting, not an assault. But the Drakkin have advanced weapons with significant range. There's nothing here that even comes close."

"What are you going to tell Arnauld?" Jared asked.

"I haven't seen the men yet," she answered. "So maybe it's time for a review."

"Done. Rafe, come with me. Let's get everyone assembled in the courtyard."

———

That afternoon, Sahara stood on a balcony of the Great House and studied the array of soldiers gathered in the courtyard. There were only a few hundred of them, and most stood with shoulders slumped, in spite of Armon's orders to present themselves. She could see at a glance that their hearts weren't in this fight.

When Jared and Rafe joined her on the balcony, she shook her head.

"Exactly what I was afraid of," she said. "They're not ready for a fight."

"It's been seven years since the last rebellion," Jared said. "We lost so many. No one has the stomach for a fight—not when we can keep the Drakkin at bay with a few sacrificial victims every year."

"Tell them to go home," she said.

Jared signaled to Armon and he barked the dismissal order. The men shuffled out of the square, and many turned worried faces up toward the balcony where she stood. Some glared at her with a murderous rage.

"They're afraid I'm going to send them to be massacred," she said softly. Then she turned to Jared and Rafe. "Let's go. It's time to try another way."

She left the balcony in search of Arnauld, trying to swallow her doubts. The last time she put a plan like this in motion, she lost everything she loved best in the world.

Marsyas had taught her never to say the word "fail"...but it loomed there in her mind all the same.

Right along with the word "betrayal."

THIRTY-ONE

Sahara and Jared met Arnauld in the Council Hall, surrounded by all the proofs of Albadir's desperate circumstances. Sahara looked cool and confident, and he could feel the iron strength of her resolve.

But Jared dreaded the outcome of this conversation. There were only two ways this could go, and neither option made him happy. Either Arnauld would ignore Sahara's report and push his men into the field against an enemy they could never hope to defeat, or he would listen to her—and send her to what would almost certainly be her death.

He wished Sahara had come to Albadir under different circumstances, or that he'd met her somewhere bright and beautiful, like at one of the gala events they used to hold in the Great City, where the best musicians from Askalon would entertain the highest social circles on Silesia.

He wished they'd had more time.

"So? What do you have to report?" Arnauld asked after they'd taken their seats.

"You aren't ready for an assault on the Drakkin," she said. "Your weapons stores are dangerously low, and too primitive to be effective against the Drakkin's more advanced technology. If you think you will save Albadir and your wife by marching against the fortress, you will destroy us all."

Jared held his breath. No one spoke to Arnauld that way, and for a moment, the air was charged with tension.

But then Arnauld sat back in his chair, folding his arms across his chest. "*Us?*"

Sahara pointed to the banner with the three-petaled flower. "I don't understand it," she said, "but somehow, for some reason, I am meant to be here. Like it or not, my path is intertwined with yours, and I can't escape it any more than you can. No matter what happens next, you are going to ask me to risk my life for this city and these people. So yes, *us.*"

Jared wanted to smile, but kept his face carefully neutral.

"You say we aren't ready," Arnauld said. "Do we have any chance at all?"

Sahara shook her head. "It would be a massacre."

"Unless you have some other idea, I don't know what else to do," Arnauld said. "We cannot continue on as we have."

"I don't like raising problems without also offering a possible solution," Sahara said. "I'm an infiltrator and an assassin. And we have reason to believe there is a way into the fortress."

Arnauld glanced swiftly at Jared. "How did you come by this information?"

"That's not important right now," Sahara said. "What is important is that they have a weakness, and I can exploit it."

"Why don't you lead our army to attack this weakness?"

Sahara shook her head. "Too risky. But if I go alone, I can slip into the fortress and eliminate the leadership. Once I cut off the head, then you can lead the army in to sweep away any remaining resistance."

"What do you think?" Arnauld asked, turning suddenly to Jared.

Jared hesitated. This was the question he'd dreaded. "I think it's the best chance we have to rid ourselves of the Drakkin."

"Please don't make me lead your men into a battle we can't possibly hope to win," Sahara said. "This is the better way. I promise you."

Arnauld measured her for a moment in silence. Then he said to Jared, "You're no assassin. But am I to understand that you want to go with her?"

Jared shook his head. "I will do whatever she tells me to do. Maybe that's going with her." He glanced at Sahara. "But maybe it isn't. And you should know, my lord, that Rafe Margolis has also agreed to help."

"So you think the three of you can bring down an empire? And what if you fail?"

"We won't fail," Sahara said quickly. *Not this time.* "I give you my word."

Arnauld thrummed his fingers on the table. Jared watched his jaw tighten, and his heart sank. Finally, Arnauld shifted his gaze to Sahara.

"No," he said.

"How can you say no?" Sahara countered. "Haven't you heard anything I've said?"

"There is strength in numbers," he said. "You will get the men ready, and you will lead them through this secret way to make an assault on the fortress. You were right—we have been cowards, trying to pretend that the inevitable would never come. I will not have my people go into this dark night without a fight."

Sahara sat very quietly for a long time, and Jared could feel the intensity of ner struggle.

"Why won't you listen to me when I tell you that I haven't been trained for this?" she said finally. "Why don't you lead your own men on this suicide crusade instead of asking me to do it for you?"

Arnauld's eyes glittered at her. "Freedom must be paid for with blood. Isn't that the teaching of the Shell?"

Jared saw Sahara's hands tighten into fists. As he looked into her face, his vision swam and something else appeared before his eyes.

A young man with strong and chiseled features paced before ranks of young women, clad all in black, silent, at attention. Sahara stood in the front row, staring straight ahead, chin up, eyes fixed on the hewn stone wall behind the young man.

"Freedom must be paid for with blood," he said. "While there is life, there is hope. Where there is hope, there is opportunity. Where there is opportunity, strike first and strike hard."

The image drowned in darkness and Jared came back to himself with a low gasp. His head felt like it would split with the intense pounding. He could barely see straight, but through his blurred vision, he saw Sahara's face. She looked as hardened and pale as she had in that vision, or memory, or whatever it was he had just seen.

"It is the teaching of the Shell that you don't send people to slaughter when there's a better way," Sahara said.

Arnauld slammed his hand down on the table. "Enough."

Sahara shoved back her chair and stalked out of the room. Arnauld watched her go, then turned to Jared.

"My lord—" Jared began, but Arnauld raised a hand and cut him off.

"Consult Childir. Ask him to choose the most favorable day for the attack."

He inclined his head and took his leave. As soon as he stepped into the corridor, he took a deep breath and leaned against the wall. His head still hurt so badly that his vision swam.

"Hey," Sahara said, and he straightened. "Are you okay?"

"While there is life, there is hope. Where there is hope, there is opportunity."

Sahara reeled back, face pale with shock. "How do you know those words?"

"I saw...I heard...you were all in black. In some kind of bunker."

Sahara retreated until her back touched the wall. "How could you know—"

"Did you see it too?"

"Of course I saw it!" she snapped. "That was my life. How can you see into my mind?"

"Is that why I'm hearing your voice even when you don't say anything?" Jared asked instead. "Sometimes I hear you like you're talking to me."

"I can hear you too. Sometimes, I mean...not always..." She held up her hands. "Make it stop."

"I don't know how."

"Ask Aliya! Aliya would know."

Jared shook his head and the pain made him dizzy. "No. I don't think she would."

"Who then? Childir?"

"Maybe."

Sahara crossed the corridor in a single stride and seized Jared by the shoulders. "You have to ask him! Find out how to make it stop. You can't—you can't be in my head."

Jared took her arms gently and looked her in the eyes. "You aren't nearly as dark inside as you fear," he said. "All I feel is light."

Her expression was unreadable. "We're going to see Aliya," she said stiffly. "You're delirious."

THIRTY-TWO

As Jared lay on a bed in the Halls of Healing, he stared up at the high vaulted ceiling. Why could he read Sahara's thoughts? It didn't make sense. As his headache subsided, he grew more puzzled.

Aliya approached with a damp cloth in her hand. Jared managed a smile for her as she sat on the edge of the bed beside him.

"Feeling better?" Aliya asked.

She laid the cloth over Jared's forehead. It was cool and smelled fresh and clean, with a scent that seemed to weave into his brain and release the tension.

"Yes," he said. "Just confused."

"It must come as a shock that you aren't superhuman," she said, nudging him with a smile.

"Why would you say that?" he asked, an edge in his voice. "I'm no different from anyone else."

"I'm teasing you, Jared."

He sat up and handed the cloth back to her. "I need to speak with Childir," he said. "Thanks for letting me rest here for a bit."

"I hope he lets you in," Aliya said. "The last time I tried to speak to him, he wouldn't allow me into his chambers."

Jared frowned. "That's strange."

"I think the deaths of so many at the festival must have taken a toll on him," she said with a lift of her shoulders. "He has isolated himself since then. I have tried not to disturb him, but—"

"But what?"

She sighed and managed a smile for him. "I have much on my mind. And it would be nice to have someone to talk to."

"You can't talk to Arnauld about what's troubling you?"

"I don't want to burden him with my worries," she said with a laugh, but it was hollow. Jared sat up and took her hands in his.

"You can talk to me."

"Not about this, I'm afraid." She regarded him for a moment. "Something is troubling you too. Do you want to talk about it?"

"Nothing's bothering me." He swung his legs over the side of the bed and stood. "Thanks again."

He hurried out of the Halls of Healing and made his way back toward the Great House. As he reached the staircase that led to Childir's chambers, he met Armon coming down.

"What are you doing here?" Jared asked in surprise.

"I can consult the holy man same as you," Armon said. "Just because you apprenticed to him don't make you any more special than the rest of us."

Jared scowled at him in annoyance. "Did he agree to see you?"

"Of course he did."

Armon brushed past him and Jared watched him disappear around the corner. Why would Childir see Armon and not Aliya? It didn't make sense.

He went slowly up the stairs, feeling the heaviness and confusion in his heart grow with every step. It made him feel bitter inside, like he'd swallowed some kind of acid. He reached the top of the stairs and stood there in front of Childir's door, suddenly unsure.

"I know you're out there, Jared," came Childir's voice from within the chamber, "so you might as well come inside."

Jared opened the door and peered inside. Childir sat in a chair by the open window. A crow, black as nightmares, perched on the arm of the chair and Childir stroked its sleek feathers with one bony hand.

"Aliya told me you didn't like to be disturbed these days," he said.

"Are you here on her behalf?"

"No...on Arnauld's."

"Then come quickly and tell me what business you have with me. I don't have much time, you see."

Jared looked around the room, but saw nothing out of the ordinary save the crow. "He wishes to consult with you about a possible move against the Drakkin," he said. "He wants to know what day is most favorable."

Childir angled around at this, and so did the crow. A shiver of a chill ran down Jared's spine as that bird cocked its bright eye at him, as if it were listening to—and understanding—everything he said.

"That's a new pet," Jared said, gesturing at the bird. "Where did he come from?"

"Tell me more about this plan of Arnauld's."

"That's all I can say. Just tell me the day."

Childir's eyes, unblinking as the crow's, remained fixed on his face. "Who leads this force? You?"

Jared felt the heaviness inside him grow as the bird stared at him, head tilted. Childir leaned forward.

"If not you, then who?"

"What does it matter?"

Suddenly, Jared remembered that Armon had been here before him, and he wondered if the seer already knew more than he was letting on.

"It matters very much." Childir stroked the crow's feathers again. "How am I to pick a favorable day when I don't know whose star is on the ascendant?"

Jared hesitated. The heaviness was so unbearable now that he almost couldn't breathe. But through the fog of his thoughts, he felt the cold certainty that keeping Sahara's role in all of this a secret from Childir was somehow important.

"I am," he lied.

Childir's eyes narrowed just the tiniest fraction. "You said it wasn't you."

"I never said that. I said nothing. But this is all I've ever wanted, you remember."

"Yes. I do remember." Childir's gaze hardened and he turned away to look out the window again. "Come back tomorrow and I will tell you what I read in the stars."

Jared bowed and backed out of the room. As soon as the door closed on the old man and the crow, he hurried downstairs and into the bright sunshine. It wasn't until he got outside that he realized he hadn't asked Childir how to sever the connection to Sahara's mind.

But instead of frustration, he felt only relief. Somehow, he knew that revealing that information to Childir—and to that horrible crow —would have been a terrible mistake.

THIRTY-THREE

A few days later, Sahara stood in the observatory room on the top floor of the Great House and tried to make her peace with death.

She'd almost left the city when she'd put Jared under Aliya's care in the Halls of Healing. But something Aliya had said to her made her stay.

"Do you know why the *lilia-dir* has three petals?" she'd asked Sahara as she laid a cool cloth on Jared's forehead.

"Because that's what it looks like?"

Aliya had laughed that lovely, silver laugh and led Sahara to a nearby window. "No," she said. "Though that is true. The *lilia-dir* was chosen as the symbol for our people because it reveals our strength. We are best when we are united, when we support each other. Prince, people, planet." Her eyes searched Sahara's. "Do you understand?"

At the time, Sahara had refused to see what she meant. But in the days that followed, she thought she understood.

Maybe her mission on Amaryl had failed because she hadn't

trusted her team enough. She had relied too much on her own strength—and not enough on theirs.

Maybe, just maybe, Arnauld was right. Maybe this would be the better way after all.

And so, she had chosen to stay.

Today was the day Childir had picked for the attack. Jared had come to her and told her the news in the Halls of Healing, and Aliya had overheard it all. When Jared had said some nonsense about the day being marked with favorable omens, Aliya's eyes had shone so brightly that Sahara hadn't dared tell them that she didn't trust such things.

The meaning of omens all depended on where you were standing, and somehow they always seemed to go hand-in-hand with death.

She thought back to that fateful day, when Tol had died and she'd seen the dragon in the sands.

You could use the Sight.

She ignored the tugging sensation and buried the thought.

She had made a vow to herself that she would never use that power again, not after what had happened to Marsyas. If it couldn't show her the vanishing of her brother or the death of the man she'd loved, then it was worthless.

With a heavy sigh, she bent to tie her sand-colored boots. She belted on her handgun and strapped the holster to her thigh, then slipped the spare magazine into the pocket of her battle pants. Then she fastened on her shoulder scabbard and pulled on her gloves. She checked that her knife was ready, and slapped it back into its sheath.

Swords and handguns against the Drakkin. It was more than ridiculous.

All we need to do is draw them away from the fortress, she reminded herself.

They'd given strict instructions to their commanders that they were not to engage beyond a certain point. A pitched battle would be a slaughter, and she couldn't live with that on her conscience. All she needed was a diversion—enough to let her slip in and take out the commanders.

A noise behind her startled her and she turned. Jared stood in the doorway.

"Ready?" he asked.

"No. But the only way out is through." She gave him a wry smile. "Anyway, you said this day is blessed."

He shrugged. "In my experience, seers speak one truth and twenty lies." He scowled out the window. "Something about this doesn't feel right."

She heard his thought. *Maybe because I gave Childir the wrong name.*

"Whose name did you give him?" Sahara asked. "Yours?" He gave her a look, and she laughed. "I don't give a damn about seers and stars. One day's as good as any other to die. Follow the plan and this will all work out."

"I wish I had your confidence," he said.

"Promise me that you will let me go, no matter what happens."

He gripped her shoulders and searched her eyes. "I promise," he said. "You are *gennai*. Never forget that."

THIRTY-FOUR

The Drakkin artillery bombarded them without mercy, rippling the sands around them and shattering her lines even as Sahara tried to form them for the charge. Shells whistled overhead as Albadir's few cannons returned fire, trying to give her the chance to get the men safely underneath the range of the enemy's guns.

She led them at a run through the rain of fire to the foot of the cliffs that surrounded the Drakkin fortress. As they reached the rocks, the men hunched under the meager protection they offered and Sahara tried to collect her scattered wits.

Two of her squadrons had been trapped in a pitched battle just to the south along the ridge, and almost none of them had made it back alive. In spite of all their efforts to draw the Drakkin out of the hills, they had failed.

As the chaos around her intensified, panic threatened to crush her. For a moment, she felt like she couldn't breathe. Then she saw Jared emerge from the clouds of smoke that swirled around them, and the iron bands around her chest suddenly loosed. She gulped air, sand, and smoke all at once and leaned back against the rocks to catch her breath.

Jared placed a hand just over her shoulder and leaned in to speak so that only she could hear him.

"My men have scouted the approach to the fortress. They're waiting for us there too, Sahara. That scout lied to us. If we go that way, we'll die."

Sahara closed her eyes. The scout hadn't lied. She was certain of that. They'd been betrayed.

"They knew we were coming," she said. "But how?"

"It doesn't matter. Sound the retreat and let's hope they don't pursue us back to the city."

"We'll never get another chance at this, Jared," she said, gripping his arm and searching his face. She feel his concern for her run like electricity through body. "I told you—you had to let me go, no matter what."

For a long moment she watched him wrestle with his own demons. Finally, his mouth hardened and he raised his eyes to hers. They glinted silver like a knife's edge.

"If we make one last charge, maybe it will buy you enough time."

She pointed in the direction of the battlefield. "Tell the commanders to make one last charge and then sound the retreat to the city."

He pushed away from her without a word and disappeared into the swirling clouds of sand and dust. Sahara blew out her breath and then knelt in the sand, planting her sword in the ground in front of her. She drew her knife, checked the edges, then slapped it back into its sheath. She felt a vague uneasiness but pushed it away.

Can't be worse than the Shift. Not the hardest thing you've ever done.

As the memories of the fight in the tower room of the fortress of Ilan flooded through her, she buried them.

It won't go that way. He won't follow me.

Boots crunched in the sand next to her and she looked up. Rafe crouched beside her. His face was marred with blood and dirt, and he had a monstrous black eye. But he grinned and winked at her with his one good eye.

"Got any water?" he rasped. "I'm out." She handed him her canteen and he drank greedily. Then he said, "What's next?"

Sahara jerked her sword out of the sands and sheathed it. "Time for me to go."

He didn't protest like she thought he would. Instead, he handed her the canteen and peered through his binoculars, studying the ridge.

"Not looking good along the ridge," he said.

"I'm leaving you in command of my squadron," Sahara said, taking a drink from the canteen. "Jared is going to lead one more charge against their position and then fall back to the city. Just make sure you don't let the bastards through."

She took another drink and swiped her lips with the back of her hand. Rafe watched her with unusual intensity.

"It's risky," he said. "Maybe too risky."

She met his gaze. "Whatever happens," she commanded, "do not follow me. Tell Jared. Don't follow me."

Rafe nodded brusquely and Sahara got to her feet. They clasped hands and the wrists and she swung away from him.

"Sahara!" he called. "Good luck."

Glancing back over her shoulder, she managed a smile. "You too."

Without another word, she left him. She cut quickly around the lines, staying low and out of sight so that her soldiers wouldn't see her. Just as she reached a tumble of boulders near the entrance to the path the scout had told them about, she heard a general roaring of shouts and saw Jared and Rafe leading the men in one last desperate charge.

This was it. Her last chance to finish what she started all those months ago. A thrill almost of excitement rippled through her.

I promised I'd never forget...and never forgive. Today, I'm keeping that promise.

Without another moment's pause, she pushed forward up the trail. It was a steep path, full of scree and pocked by deep holes that made the climb grueling and treacherous. At least the path was empty, and she wondered if Jared might have been wrong about the guards.

Wouldn't be the first time he's lied to try to protect me.

At last, after three massive steps that required her to leap like some kind of mountain-dwelling predator, the ground leveled out and she stopped, breathing hard. She pulled off her helmet. Her hair was matted with sweat, and even the hot breeze felt good.

Sahara!

The voice came from somewhere within her, but it wasn't hers. It was Jared's. Faint and far away at first, it swelled until it crashed against her consciousness so sharply that it brought her to her knees in the dirt. She shook her head to clear it, but it pounded painfully. She pushed a shaking hand through her damp hair.

What the hell was that?

She tried not to be angry with him—neither of them knew how to control this power—but she needed to be sharp, and now she felt like she'd been run through some kind of shredder.

She pushed herself back to her feet. The path was still empty, save for the first swirling hints of the harbingers. But then, suddenly, she sensed that someone was behind her. She reached for her dagger.

A sibilant, dark voice came close to her ear, "Touch it and I'll have your arm for a trophy."

Almost before the voice finished speaking, something hard slammed into the back of her head and she felt a stabbing pain in her lower back. She crumpled in a heap in the swirling sands.

THIRTY-FIVE

THE NOISOME SMELL OF DAMP ROCK MADE HER RETCH, AND THE heaving of her stomach brought her roughly into consciousness. Sensation returned to her body in a rush, and she winced at the rough stone digging into her hands. As her eyes adjusted to the gloom, she realized that she was in the corner of a dank cell.

She scrabbled to the middle of the floor and sat up, rubbing the back of her head. A large bump weltered there where she had been struck, and pain radiated through her head when she touched it. She left it alone and gazed around at her surroundings. The walls arched up above her into sheer darkness, and to her left, a twisted metal gate caged her in.

And then she heard singing.

Even as her mind framed the question—*Who would sing in this horrible place?*—she knew who it was.

Her breath caught in her throat and the ecstasy of recognition made her forget pain, damp, and loss. It was the voice she thought she'd never hear again.

She dragged herself to the door.

"Jared!" she croaked, and the singing stopped abruptly. "Jared, is that you?"

One breathless moment later, he was there on the other side of the door. Sahara bowed her head against the metal, overwhelmed by relief.

"You're alive," she whispered. "You made it out alive."

Jared gripped her hands in his. "Barely. But yes."

He chaffed her hands to warm them and tried to smile. Sahara stared at him through the bars.

"What happened?" she asked finally. "Where are we?"

"The prison moon. K'ilenfir."

She couldn't help a short laugh. "That figures."

"Rest now," Jared told her. "I can tell you the rest later. We've got all the time in the world now."

She shook her head, and then she frowned at him. "Why aren't you locked up?"

Jared shrugged and grinned. "The guards decided they liked my singing enough to let me out to entertain them during their meals." He winked at her. "My father always told me, 'Train all your talents, boy, for you never know which one will save your skin.' I always thought he was full of it, but I'm glad I listened to him."

"So am I." She managed a smile for him and he brushed her cheek with his thumb.

"Don't run off and do something reckless, okay?" he said.

He got up to leave but she snatched his hand. "You were right. I never should have attempted the pass."

"Well," he said, his voice matter-of-fact, "I shouldn't have tried it first."

Rough voices shouted for him, and he pulled his hand gently out of hers. He slipped into the shadows of the corridor and a moment later, she heard him singing again.

Sahara crawled back to the middle of her cell and curled up on the stone, her head on her arm. All her bones and muscles ached, but she let Jared's melody flow around and through her. Her eyes drifted closed and she slept.

———

Something hard and metallic clanged against the door of her cell and jarred her awake. Her eyes flew open, and the struggled to recognize the sound.

The rusted door squealed on its hinges and she realized the sound had been keys. She stayed still and tried to pretend she was still asleep, but the tramp of heavy boots approached her. The guard slammed his foot into her side and she grunted in pain.

"Get up," he barked.

Sahara pushed herself to her feet, every muscle screaming in protest. The guard secured her hands behind her back with iron manacles attached to a long chain. The metal cut into her wrists and she gritted her teeth.

You will show neither pain nor fear. Neither pain nor fear.

The guard shoved her forward and she stumbled out of the cell into the rank corridor. The guard took his position in front of her and jerked on the chain to get her moving. As he led her down the row, she strained her eyes to see if Jared was being kept in any of the cells. They all seemed to be empty.

"Where are the prisoners?" she croaked.

"Shut up." The guard yanked hard on the chain, almost bringing Sahara to her knees. He laughed at her as she stumbled to stay upright. "Keep moving."

"Where are you taking me?" She shook her hair out of her eyes and forced her feet to keep pace with his long strides.

"Time for you to learn your fate." He jerked her forward again, speeding up their pace.

As they turned the corner and stepped into a broader stone corridor, Sahara glanced back at the row of cells. With every step she took, she was more and more certain that she would never see Jared again. All she could do was hope that he would be treated with mercy.

But even as the hope formed in her heart, she banished it.

You know better than that. There's no such thing as mercy in hell.

THIRTY-SIX

The guard led Sahara through a maze of passageways, and gradually, the light seemed to increase. She'd never been in this part of the facility, and she wondered if there were windows somewhere. Then she realized that there were luminescent stones set in the walls high above her head. She angled to look at them as they passed, and the guard pulled viciously on the chain to keep her from falling behind.

Finally, the corridor ended in a heavy door that seemed set into the slab of stone in front of them. The guard unlocked the door and it swung open silently. Then he removed the manacles from her wrists and shoved her through the door, slamming it behind her.

Sahara collapsed on the floor, her legs shaking and her mouth completely dry. She dragged herself back to the door and pounded on it.

"Hey!" she shouted. "Get me water!"

Her voice sounded feeble in the tiny space, which seemed to devour sound. If Sahara had stretched out on the floor, she would barely have had room. Everything about the space seemed designed to make her feel like it was closing in on her. The only light came from one of those luminescent stones set in the ceiling. One wall seemed to be dark glass, and Sahara edged toward it. She saw nothing but her own reflection.

What would Marsyas say if he saw me now?

She fingered the metal collar that the guard had left around her neck. Her hair was matted with blood and dirt. Her face was almost unrecognizable, and her clothes were in tatters. She took a deep breath.

He would say, you're alive. Where there is life, there's hope. Where there's hope –

"There is no opportunity for you here." The voice was harsh and reminded her more of the sharp hiss of a lizard than anything else.

She stumbled back as the other side of the glass slowly became visible. Two Drakkin lords stood there, hooded and cloaked completely in black, their features hidden in the shadow of their dark cowls. Their hands were inside their sleeves.

Sahara had the strange sensation that perhaps there were no hands there at all, and no faces either. She pushed the thought away. She knew better.

They could bleed. She had made them bleed.

"Why do you lead rebellions on Silesia?" said the Drakkin on her right.

She curled her hands into fists, willing herself to be calm when the sight of those robed figures filled her with a rush of rage and hate so fierce it took her breath away. "Why?" she said. "Because I can."

Some hideous sound that could only have been laughter fell dully on her ears. Even the pulsing stone above her head seemed to be laughing at her.

"Apparently you can't," the Drakkin on the left said. "You have failed...and rest assured, we will not make the same mistake with you again."

For just an instant, the figure's veil of concealment was disturbed. A stabbing pain seared through Sahara's head—and just as she had once read the sands all those many years ago, she now read the shadows.

Like two wisps of smoke, one after the other, Sahara saw the emaciated, almost skeletal face of a man and then the fierce blood-red eyes of a dragon. Her eyes burned and she blinked. The vision faded, but the throbbing pain in her head only intensified.

"We have been searching for you," the other Drakkin said. "Assassin."

"Chrysalis."

The word was out of her mouth before she could stop herself. It was as if everything froze. The two Drakkin lords seemed to shrink—almost imperceptibly, but she felt a surge of power within her as she realized the truth.

"You fear me."

The glass faded again, leaving just a dark screen that threw the reflection of Sahara's filthy, ragged self back into her face. But now she smiled.

In spite of the chains, in spite of everything, they feared her.

No matter how weak she felt, no matter how desperate, she had a power inside her. A power that she had only begun to tap into.

And now she realized that the purpose of the Shift had been to reveal that power to her. But she hadn't fully embraced it. Some part of her had resisted.

The Shift had opened the door. It was time for her to step through it.

The guard entered the room and clipped the metal chain back onto the collar around her neck. She watched his movements in the mirrored glass.

"Time to go," he said.

He dragged her out the door, and for now, she let him take her.

He led her back down the corridor through the thick, heavy gloom, but when she thought he would take the turning to the cell bay, he dragged her up a different passage. This one curved around gently as it ascended.

Without warning, the wall on her left ended and the edge of the passage dropped away into nothingness. A massive metal cage sat on the edge of the chasm. The guard opened the door and shoved her inside. He unclipped the chain from her collar, shut and locked the door, and then whistled.

Sahara scrambled up and backed against the edge of the cage that sat on solid ground. She gripped the bars as she felt the cage tilt slowly toward the darkness. The guard whistled again, and the cage was lifted off the floor and swung out over the chasm.

And then it plummeted.

Sahara screamed. She clung to the bars as the wind rushed up past her. She was sure she would be pulverized at the bottom of the chasm...if it even had a bottom.

Then, almost as suddenly as the cage had dropped, it stopped. Sahara's body slammed against the bottom of the cage, and for a moment she was too dizzy to move.

A strange dancing light seemed to flare along the metal bars, and she blinked her eyes, trying to get them to focus. She finally realized it was torchlight, and she pushed herself to her knees.

She gripped the bars and peered below her. Some twenty feet beneath her lay a massive triangular hall illuminated by three huge braziers, one in each corner of the room.

She lifted her eyes and saw another cage just like the one that held her, not more than a stone's throw away. Jared was inside, gripping the bars and watching her.

Sahara's heart constricted and she felt suddenly that she couldn't breathe. This was worse than any nightmare.

Images of Marsyas's execution tumbled through her mind.

No. Not this time. Not this time.

She flung herself against the door of the cage, but it was secured. The shock jarred her bones, but she shook it off. No way out that way.

She crushed herself against the bars and angled to see above her. In the darkness, all she could make out was the heavy chain that suspended her cage. Even if she could manage to get on top of the cage and climb up the chain, she had no idea how far she had fallen. And if she did reach the ledge, she had no idea whether she could get to Jared's cage from there.

She tried to squeeze herself through the bars, but the gaps were too small. She slammed her hands against the bars. It rocked violently.

What are you doing? came Jared's voice in her head.

Getting you out of here.

She backed up and flung herself against the bars. The cage swayed and Sahara felt giddy with success. She did it again, and the cage started to swing.

Just as she was getting some momentum behind her, the massive doors below her opened and the Drakkin Council filed into the hall. They were all hooded and cloaked like the figures who had questioned her.

As they filled the benches that curved in stiff semi-circles around a raised dais, Sahara realized that the colors of their cowls were subtly different, so that soon the hall was filled not with figures in black, but figures in every possible shade of grey. The Drakkin lord in the black cowl—the one who had questioned her—took his seat on the dais with a Drakkin clad all in white.

The dark Drakkin spoke first. "This Council is called to order."

The assembly took their seats with a whispering of robes on stone benches. They waited. Sahara didn't dare move, and her cage swung in a silent and sickening arc above the assembly.

"We have summoned you from your domains to decide the fate of the prisoners. Jared Alareth, rogue agent and revolutionary, from the planet Silesia."

The cowled heads rotated slowly to look at Jared. She thought she heard a low murmur of disapproval.

"The other is known to us. Sahara Acwellan, the one they call the Chrysalis."

A hiss, like breath escaping through hundreds of jagged teeth, filled the assembly hall.

"Six days ago, she helped Alareth to lead a rebellion on Silesia. But thankfully, her efforts were prevented by timely information."

So there __was__ a traitor. Who was it?

Jared didn't answer her, and she clenched her hands into fists.

A delegate in a variegated silver robe rose and addressed the dais. "Why has she not been dealt with in the customary way? Why must we all be present for this again?"

Right. The customary way. Like a life sentence in the labor camp on some barren planet. Because that worked out so well last time.

"The Chrysalis is a threat to our order," answered the Drakkin in white. "It is time for us to extinguish her with the full exercise of our power."

Chrysalis...why didn't you tell me? Jared's voice inside her head drew her attention away from the drama below them. She looked across the gulf of darkness at Jared.

I didn't know how.

The silver-robed Drakkin was not prepared to let the matter drop. "She assassinated the High Drakkin Lord Zhezhna-ban on Amaryl. Why did this Council not take her then? If you will remember further, it was I who suggested that she pay the full penalty—"

"We all remember it, Gar-Nublai," said the dark Drakkin. "But surely you will recall why this Council voted against you. She has the Sight. She was to accelerate our search in the desert."

Search? Jared asked inside Sahara's mind. *Search for what?*

In a rush, she remembered the words of the Drakkin guard as he refused to kill her. He'd dragged her face so close to his that she could smell his foul breath.

"You have the Sight," he'd said. "Guess it's time for you to use it."

They never told me what they were looking for. They never had the chance.

"Of course that's what you thought," Gar-Nublai retorted. "But she escaped, as we might expect a member of the Shell to do."

"The others were not so lucky, were they?"

Sahara closed her eyes and offered a silent prayer for her friends. So many lost. She opened her eyes and caught Jared's gaze across the gulf of shadows. Her desperate fear that they would take him too welled up inside her again.

"But," added the dark Drakkin, "she found our defenses much more effective on Silesia than they were on Amaryl. We have learned from her."

Sahara leaned her head against the bars. She'd made too many rash assumptions about their protocols and her own skill. The timely information they'd been provided...maybe it hadn't come from a traitor. Maybe it had come from her own prior actions.

"What about the other?" a Drakkin in a charcoal cowl asked, rising to address the dais. "Let us not pretend he is innocent. He has Drakkin blood on his hands too. Or have you forgotten the day we lost Klei Kali on the battlefields of Albadir?"

Sahara's gaze locked with Jared's. *We are more alike than we thought.*

Maybe, but I'm not the Chrysalis.

"Send them both to Al'alsunne," a Drakkin in a dark gray robe offered. "Let them rot in an oubliette of ice and darkness."

A murmur of approval rippled through the hall. Sahara caught the bars as a vision rushed through her.

A mountain in the dark, the rush of wings, and a world on fire.

"No!" she cried.

Her voice echoed in the vast chamber, and every head turned up toward her. The Drakkin lords on the dais rose to their feet. She came back to herself with a rush and realized that she had spoken aloud. She sucked in her breath and looked desperately at Jared.

His face was almost wild, his eyes dark discs. *Don't you dare. Please don't.*

She tore her gaze away and addressed the dais.

"One life for many," she continued. "Isn't that the way of the Drakkin Lords of Silesia?"

A low murmur ran through the hall.

"Take my life and set him free," she said. "You said it yourself. It is time for me to be extinguished."

"No!" Jared shouted. He shook the bars of his cage. "Sahara! I won't let you do this!"

"I'm the one you want," she said to the Drakkin, ignoring him. "I am the Chrysalis. Take my life and pay the blood that is owed!"

There was a long silence that dragged from moments into minutes. Sahara wondered what they were doing. Would there be no debate? She hazarded a glance in Jared's direction.

"Don't do this," he begged aloud, shaking the cage again. "Don't do this for me."

The white-robed figure on the dais rose and held up a scroll etched with a red script. "The Drakkin lords of Silesia have laid claim to her as their blood-offering," he said, with a subtle nod in the direction of a contingent of silver-robed figures in the corner. "One life for many. Return the man to his people."

Without warning, Jared's cage was dragged up into the darkness.

"Jared!" Sahara screamed, seizing the bars of her cage and staring after him. "Jared!"

There was no answer from the shadows. And then her own cage lurched into motion.

Where there is life, there is hope. Where there is hope, there is opportunity.

The cage grated to a halt and the door opened. The guard reached in and dragged her out by her legs, scraping her entire back against the metal of the doorframe. She clenched her teeth against the burning pain as he hauled her to her feet and snapped the chain to her collar once more. The manacles were next, the metal biting into her wrists.

Where there is opportunity, there is freedom.

THIRTY-SEVEN

Four days later, Jared staggered into the crowded council hall in Albadir, hardly aware of where he was or why. He pulled up short as he registered the wall of surprised and stunned faces around him. Rafe toppled his chair as he charged at Jared and threw his arms around him. Jared blinked slowly, shaking his head to clear it.

"I thought you were dead!" Rafe said. "You crazy bastard! She told you not to follow her!"

Jared stepped back and gripped Rafe's shoulders. "Well, to be perfectly accurate, she followed me," he said with a wobbly grin.

Arnauld rose from his seat. All the color had gone out of his face, but he was smiling. Chair legs scraped on the stone floor as everyone stood, waiting to see what would happen next.

"Jared," Arnauld said. He edged around the table and seized Jared in a rough hug. "You look like hell!"

"Guess it rubbed off on me," he said, rubbing a hand over the dark stubble on his jaw.

"A goblet of hot spiced wine for my lord Alareth!" Arnauld called to a steward.

As the man bowed and disappeared down a hallway, Arnauld gestured for Jared to sit, and he and Rafe returned to their places. The rest of the council resumed their seats.

"What happened to you?" Arnauld asked. "We never thought we'd see you again."

Jared stretched out his legs with a soft groan. A servant set a goblet of spiced wine in front of him and he drank deeply.

"First, I want to know what's happened here since I was captured," Jared said, replacing the goblet on the table.

"There's not much to tell," Rafe answered. "After Sahara left, we retreated as she had commanded. We waited as long as we could for you to get back, but when the harbingers kicked up, we had to bar the gates. We sent search parties out for days...but they found nothing. We thought you were gone."

"We've done nothing but wait," Arnauld said. "Wait for the storm to break on our heads."

"There's been no movement from the fortress," Rafe added. "We brought everyone inside the city walls for protection. All our outposts are abandoned and the outlying villages are empty. There's nothing more we can do."

Jared nodded, swirling the wine in his goblet. For a long moment, there was silence.

"Tell us what happened to you," Arnauld said at last.

"Drakkin soldiers ambushed me in the pass. They bound me, stuffed a gag in my mouth, and then dragged me onto a hovership. It felt like hours that I waited there in the dark. And then...."

"And then?"

The voice that pressed him was new, and Jared looked up. A young man with fair hair sat across from him, and one look at his eyes told Jared that he was an outworlder like Sahara.

He turned to Arnauld, who lifted a hand to forestall his question.

Jared turned back to the stranger. "It's difficult to explain." He stopped again, and then took a deep breath. "It was like I could see what was happening to her. Like—a vision. Sort of. She didn't know the Drakkin was behind her. She didn't see. But I saw. So—" his voice faltered, but he continued— "I called to her with my mind, and she heard me."

The council members whispered among each other until Arnauld flattened his hand on the table. Instantly, there was silence in the room.

"That's a myth," Arnauld said. "Speech between minds—that's nothing but a story for children. A fable."

"That's what I thought too, until it started happening to me," Jared said dryly.

"You mean you could talk to her right now if you wanted?" Rafe asked.

The fair haired man leaned forward across the table, quivering with excitement. "Can you call her for us? Can we speak to her?"

"It doesn't work like that," Jared said. "I don't know how to explain it to you, and I'm certainly not going to be your interplanetary comm system."

"But she heard you. You're sure she heard you?" the strange young man asked.

"I'm sorry. Who are you?" Jared asked, and then turned to Arnauld. "What is he doing here?"

"This is Brytnoth," Arnauld answered. "He wandered into the city out of the desert three days ago and has been recovering in the Halls of Healing ever since. He is here today to tell his story...but then you barged in and interrupted everything."

"Wandered out of the desert...from where, exactly?" And when Brytnoth shook his head, his eyes suddenly vacant, Jared said, "You don't know?"

"Let him be," Arnauld said, laying a hand on Jared's arm. "He'll tell us in good time."

"Well, to answer your question even though you can't answer mine—yes, she heard me," Jared said. "I called her name, but that was all I could do. I must have lost consciousness after that. When I came to, she was there beside me on the hovership, unconscious, gagged, and bound."

"Why did they let you go?" Arnauld asked, his voice quiet.

Jared drained his goblet and set it carefully on the table. "I finally discovered why Sahara was on that prison ship bound for the labor camp all those weeks ago. We know she was a member of the Shell. But she was on that transport because she assassinated the Drakkin Chieftain on her own homeworld."

There was utter silence in the room.

"She *assassinated* him?" Rafe repeated, incredulous.

Arnauld leaned back in his chair. "That explains a great deal."

"Where is she, then?" Brytnoth asked. "They didn't release her too?"

"No. She has paid my debt. She has paid it for us all." Jared glanced around the table. "The Drakkin lords of Silesia took her as the ritual blood offering."

Arnauld bowed his head. "She did this willingly?" he asked softly.

"Yes."

"Then I have been unjust towards her," Arnauld said.

Jared pushed back from the table and stood. "Probably," he agreed. "But they haven't sacrificed her yet, and there is no way I'm going to let her die."

THIRTY-EIGHT

The sun was sinking in the western sky as Jared left the council hall, and he could feel the gentle brushings of the night winds beginning. He paced beside the cool fountain in the courtyard. He had sworn not to let Sahara die, but he had no idea how to save her.

He didn't know where the ritual sacrifices were held or how to get there. They'd already tried to infiltrate the fortress, and that had been a catastrophic failure. He couldn't take a risk like that again if he hoped to do Sahara any good at all.

And he had no time to rummage around in moldy old books and parchments in the library, researching ancient records and deciphering old runes. He leaned on the rim of the fountain and glanced back at the Great House.

The only one he knew who could help him was Childir. He choked down his doubts and headed for the Great House.

He jogged through the winding corridor to the kitchen. The cooks were still busy at their work, and there was a noise of pots and an aroma of stewed meat and fruits. His stomach growled loudly, but he ignored it. He took the steps that led to Childir's chambers three at a time and then stopped to listen outside the door.

He heard no sound from within the sage's chamber, but a spicy, sweet smell seeped under the door. It was from the *edulia* fruit that grew in the oasis gardens, and as Jared inhaled, a memory sliced through his consciousness.

Sahara was laughing. She stood below the branch of the edulia tree, where he sat drinking in the smell of the ripening fruit.

"What are you laughing at?" he asked.

Something seemed to make her suddenly awkward. "Why do you care about the smell so much? It's just fruit."

"You say that because you've never tried one." He plucked a fruit, heavy with juice and warm from the sunshine. He jumped down next to her and offered it to her. "Here. Taste it."

She took the fruit and bit into it. As the juice exploded in her mouth, her eyes met his in surprise and delight. And then, suddenly, she flung it away.

"Why did you throw that away?" he asked. "I would have eaten it."

"I don't like it."

Her voice was fierce but hollow, and he saw tears on her cheeks.

"I don't believe you."

Jared dragged in a breath and came back to himself with a start. "What the hell is wrong with me?" he muttered.

Shaking off the force of the memory, he turned the handle and pushed open the door. Childir sat at his table, surrounded by old manuscripts and bunches of dried herbs. A plate heaped with slices of *edulia* fruit and a thick wedge of cheese sat on the table next to his elbow. He glanced up and crinkled a smile at Jared.

"Back from the dead, I see," Childir said. "You look troubled. It isn't enough for you to be alive?"

"The price for my life was too high."

"Sit."

Childir beckoned toward a seat with the end of his quill pen. Jared obeyed and the old man returned to scratching some notes on a parchment. Jared clasped his hands, letting his head hang down almost to his knees, and waited.

"Now," said Childir after a moment, "speak the heaviness in your heart."

Jared hesitated. So many questions tumbled through his mind, and he still felt that he wasn't in complete possession of his senses.

"The *edulia*?" Childir asked, seeing Jared's eyes fixed on the plate. "Do you want some?"

Jared shook his head, not trusting his voice. Childir studied him intently and Jared cleared his throat.

"What do you know about the stories of speech between minds?" Jared asked.

Childir's eyes flickered. He set down his quill carefully, then folded his hands. "It is not something you can seek, this power."

"I don't want to seek it," he said. "But if someone had it...what should they know about it?"

There was a long silence. Childir never moved, but his eyes remained fixed on Jared. "With whom do you share this power?"

Jared clenched his jaw for a moment, suddenly unsure how much he wanted to reveal, but feeling like he'd gone too far to take back the question.

"With Sahara."

Childir studied Jared so intensely that he felt like he was being read like one of the old man's manuscripts. He shifted in his seat and cleared his throat again. He'd felt this way once before, when Childir had caught him eating a fruit that he was saving for a scholarly experiment. Jared had been subjected to exactly this sort of silent interrogation then, and it unnerved him as much now that he was a grown man as it had then, as a boy.

"Do you love her?" Childir asked.

Jared sat back, trying to keep the stunned expression off his face and sure he was failing miserably. Childir seemed amused, but that strange flicker was in his eyes again. Jared's stomach clenched in sudden panic, though he didn't understand why.

"It's a simple enough question," Childir prodded. "Do you love her?"

"I fail to see how that's relevant." Jared's voice was flat and he felt as transparent as a bee's wing.

The old man rubbed his hands together slowly. "I am trying to make sure that what you think is mind-speech isn't just the height-ened awareness of love." His eyes bored into Jared's. "You know what I mean by that?"

Jared wrestled again with how much he wanted to tell the sage. There were moments when he could hear her voice in his head, and when she seemed able to hear his. But there were so many countless other times, when he felt her feelings, sensed her emotions. And there were the nights, filled with the gentle hushing of the sandstorms outside the city walls, when he thought he could hear her breathing as she slept, even though her chambers lay on the other side of the garden courtyard from his.

"You do know what I mean," Childir said.

Jared came back to himself with a start and rolled his shoulders in a careful shrug.

"I never said that," Jared said. "I'm not sure I do."

Childir bit off a piece of his cheese. "I think you are mistaken about this power you think you have. I suspect it is nothing more than this hyperawareness. And yet—" his eyes bored into Jared again— "perhaps not. We must wait for clarity."

"Will you tell me what it is?" he asked. "Just in case it...happens again?"

"Why don't you tell me exactly what happened to you?"

Jared hesitated, then decided there was no other way to find out what he wanted to know. He explained what had happened on the hovership, feeling more and more foolish. Finally, his voice trailed off and he glanced up at Childir, who was still watching him steadily.

"That's all?" Childir asked.

"Yes."

Childir grunted and pressed his fingertips together. Jared

dropped his head into his hands, overcome suddenly by weariness. He closed his eyes.

"Regardless of your answer to my question, it seems that you have a very strong connection to her," Childir said, but his voice seemed to come from far away. Jared looked up, but Childir's face was fuzzy and Jared had to squint to see him. "Even now, I feel something in the air. Like a presence, but thin...faint..."

Jared shook his head to clear his vision. But it blurred until he couldn't see the room around him. He gripped the chair as if it were the only solid thing left in his world.

And then he saw her.

She was huddled in the deep shadows, surrounded by walls of dark stone. Her knees were hugged to her chest, and she looked like she had been beaten. Then she lifted her face and looked straight at him.

The shock of the connection sent a spear of pain through Jace's mind. Just before he lost the vision, he heard her speak.

Jared. Don't be angry.

Jared came back to himself with a shattered gasp. He pressed his palms into his eyes for a moment, and then he looked up. Childir was watching him with a ferocious intensity.

"You saw her," he said.

Jared lifted his heavy lids and felt a little knot of dread coil itself in his stomach. Childir leaned forward, his hands gripping the chair until his knuckles showed white. His expression was full of a raw hunger that Jared had never seen before, not even when the sage was on the brink of some discovery.

"Did she speak to you?"

Jared couldn't make his voice work, but Childir seemed to get some satisfaction from his expression. He studied Jared for a long time in silence.

"There are wheels now in motion," Childir said, his voice suddenly sharp and brilliant, like a diamond. "Nothing can stop it now."

"I will," Jared said. "I will stop it."

"It is better to let the wheel turn," Childir said, his voice still altered. The strange tone reminded Jared of something—something that made him afraid—but he couldn't place it. His mind was too fogged by pain for anything to make sense. "Sahara Acwellan has been marked. This is her destiny. There is nothing you can do to prevent her death."

A chill shivered down Jared's spine and he pushed himself to his feet. The room tilted and he caught the back of the chair to steady himself.

"I don't believe you," he said.

THIRTY-NINE

The guard struck Sahara across the face so hard that the blow split her lip. The metallic tang of blood filled her mouth, and she spat on the stones in front of his feet.

This was a human guard, not some half-monstrous creature the Drakkin had dragged out of the tunnels of some backwater mining world. She wondered, as she looked at his face, where he had come from. She wondered if her brother might have shared the same fate. Was he doing the Drakkin's dirty work now in some prison on another planet?

"You must've messed up bad," she said, "to be sent down here to rough me up."

"There is much that you know—and the Council has left it to me to find out exactly how much."

"Then they should have sent somebody else."

The guard moved to a table on the other side of the cell and opened a leather pouch. Sahara saw the glint of metal—small metal spikes, thin as a woman's hairpin. She swallowed hard and twisted her hands in their chains.

"I can tell you are surprised," he said. "You've only seen the brute guards. You wonder, I imagine, why I am here. Where I came from."

"I don't give a damn where you came from," Sahara said.

"But of course you do. It is the nature of humans always to seek connection with each other. We do it through our stories. Shall I tell you mine?"

"No," Sahara said.

The guard shook his head and chuckled, and somehow that was even more horrible than the blow across her face.

"You have no idea what they are capable of," he said. "What they put us through. The training we must endure, to be worthy of our new lives of service."

Sahara pushed the thought of her little brother out of her mind. Fear for him—for his fate—made her vulnerable.

"They obviously didn't train you in interrogation," Sahara said. "If you want information, you actually have to ask me questions."

His eyes flickered at her, and she felt suddenly sure that it was she, not him, who was lacking in training.

"I was just a boy when they took me away from my family," he continued.

He arranged the tiny spikes on the leather cloth, perfectly spaced, perfectly ordered.

Sahara swallowed hard. *Don't think of him. This isn't his story.*

"What world?" she asked, before she could stop herself.

"I'm surprised you can't guess that," he said, eyeing her.

A damp chill of horror washed over Sahara. She stared at the guard, trying to see if there was any resemblance...

"That was the hardest part, you know," he said. "When it became clear that my family had abandoned me to my fate. I hated them after that. I will never forgive them."

"Why are you telling me this?" Sahara said, her voice shaking. "I don't give a damn about you or where you came from."

"Because you, too, will feel this pain," he said. "To leave and to be abandoned are two very different things."

Sahara's mind spun. There was no way. This disgusting human

being who was preparing to torture her couldn't possibly be Deor. They wouldn't know. They couldn't possibly know.

But nothing she said to herself eased the horrible ache in her heart. She had made a promise to find her brother. She had gone through the Shift to save him. But instead of keeping her promise and tracking him down, she had abandoned him. She'd let herself get caught up in someone else's fight, and now Deor was lost forever. He was either already dead, or he'd been warped into a monster like the man in front of her.

The guard regarded her steadily, as if he were taking some kind of measurement. "So. Let us begin," he said. "You led the rebellion on Silesia."

"That's not a question," Sahara snapped.

The guard selected a metal spike and returned to Sahara's side. "There are those who think that heavy blows and severe trauma deliver more pain than little things. But I have found that little things —" and he slowly slid the spike into Sahara's thigh until she writhed in silent agony— "are so much better. Like a needle in your brain, driving you mad...."

Sahara's breath came in ragged gasps as she stared at the end of the spike protruding from her leg.

"Go to hell," she gritted. "I'm not telling you anything."

"Now that the rebellion has failed, what is Albadir's next move?" the guard asked.

"You have a lot higher opinion of me than they did. They didn't tell me anything."

The guard tsked at her and selected another spike. This one went into her shoulder. Tears stung her eyes and it was all she could do to keep from crying aloud.

"They apparently trusted you. Enough, even, to lead an army. Is such a thing possible? Why would they not share their plans with you, if they would trust you with the lives of so many?"

Sahara breathed against the pain that seared through her with every heartbeat. Warm blood trickled down her arm and chest, and more coursed over her thigh and puddled on the floor.

"You are stronger than most," he observed, selecting another spike. "Most cannot endure more than two."

Sahara spit in his face. He chuckled as he slid the next spike into her forearm. This time she did cry out, and she tried to wrest her hands free of the manacles, but every time she tensed her muscles, searing pain flared through her. He watched her squirm, then wiped the spittle from his cheek.

"You're a traitor," she said, forcing the words through her clenched teeth. "Whatever reckoning is coming, I hope death is cruel to you."

"See, that's the difference between us," the guard said, running his finger over another spike. "Your death will be cruel. And I don't have to hope for it." He smiled at her, showing his rotted teeth. "Thank you for telling me what I wanted to know."

"I didn't tell you anything!"

The guard pulled the spikes out slowly, one at a time. The pain of taking them out was so much worse than it had been when they went in, and Sahara's vision darkened and she bit down on her lips until she tasted blood. She would not give him the satisfaction of hearing her agony.

"Oh, but you did. You told me everything."

He tossed the spikes aside. They tinkled as they bounced on the stone floor. He gathered his tools of torture and slipped out of her cell.

"I didn't tell you anything!" she shouted after him. "I didn't..."

But horrible doubt ate at her. She pulled harder against her chains and bounced the metal chair until she toppled over. Her cheek slammed into the stone, and she melted into sobs.

What have I done?

FORTY

Jared rolled over and opened his eyes. For a moment, he thought he had only dreamed the strange interview with Childir. But then he remembered Sahara's voice in his head and Childir's assurance that there was nothing he could do to prevent her death.

He swung his legs over the edge of the bed and rubbed his hand through his hair. The sun was already bright against the softly billowing curtains, and he wondered vaguely if he'd missed breakfast. His stomach rumbled at the reminder, and he padded across the smooth floor to push open the curtains.

As the sunlight flooded into the room, all the questions that exhaustion had driven out last night crowded back into his mind.

"First food, then questions," he muttered to himself.

He dressed quickly and left his room. He took the stairs down into the courtyard and jogged across the green space with its cheerful fountain. He pushed through the heavy doors into the dining hall. It was utterly deserted.

"Where is everyone?" he grumbled.

He turned down a small hallway and shouldered open the door

to the kitchen. The stoves were cold, and the cooks were nowhere to be seen.

"Damn," he said. "I guess it's fruit for breakfast."

He left the kitchen by the back door and strolled out into the oasis garden. The *edulia* orchard lay down a gentle hill and stretched like a green ribbon next to the gurgling river. The water glittered in the strong mid-morning light until it was almost blinding, but the shade beneath the *edulia* trees on the bank was dense and cool.

Jared picked a few ripe, low-hanging fruits and sat with his back against a tree. Just as he was about to bite into one, someone dropped a hand on his shoulder. Jared jumped and swore under his breath.

The strange young man Brytnoth stood beside him, looking a bit sheepish.

"Brytnoth!" Jared said. "What are you doing here?"

"I didn't mean to startle you," he said with a grin.

Jared settled back against the tree and Brytnoth sat down beside him. "What do you want?" Jared asked, taking a bite of his breakfast.

"They say Sahara was an outworlder," he said. "But when I ask about her, everyone says I should talk to you."

Jared took a bite and chewed thoughtfully. "They do, do they?" he asked.

"Well, Rafe said so," Brytnoth said.

"Figures," Jared muttered. He nibbled the rest of the flesh off his fruit and then tossed the core into the grass.

"Where was she from?"

"Some planet called Amaryl. She didn't talk much about her past."

"How did she get here?"

"Drakkin prison transport. It went down in the desert and she walked away." He started on the second half of his breakfast and eyed Brytnoth. "Is that it?"

Brytnoth hesitated for so long that Jared began to wonder if he would ever speak at all. "We're alike, she and I," he said finally.

"Are you an assassin too? Because we sure could use another one like her."

Brytnoth frowned at him. "Are you being sarcastic?"

"No. I'm absolutely serious."

"I'm not an assassin." His scowl darkened and he finally met Jared's gaze with complete and open honesty. "I don't really remember who I am. My memory is...clouded. I woke up surrounded by sand...and I remember walking for ages...I was ready to lay down and die when I saw the city gates."

"How did you end up out in the middle of the desert?"

"I don't know. I think I spent most of my life on a freighter ship." He stared out across the dancing water of the river. "We were refugees. Refugees from...." His voice trailed off and he squeezed his eyes shut in concentration, but then he sighed and shook his head. "I don't remember."

"Why were you on that freighter? Did something happen to your homeworld?"

"I don't remember."

"You don't remember, or you *won't* remember?" asked Jared sharply. "What is your purpose here on Silesia?"

"I don't know!" Brytnoth cried, exasperation finally getting the better of him. "I don't know who I am, why I'm here, or what to do now!"

"What does all this have to do with Sahara?" Jared demanded.

"Nothing, I guess. I just wanted to hear about someone who lost everything and still survived."

"Not sure you want to follow her example there, brother," Jared said. "She survived by holding on to the one thing she had left."

"What was that?"

"Revenge." Jared squinted out over the rippling water.

"But that's not true," Brytnoth observed. "She wouldn't have offered her life for yours if vengeance had consumed her. Maybe that's what kept her alive, but she survived because she had Albadir." Then, carefully, "And you."

Jared glanced at him and his mouth twisted in a smile. "Sounds like it should be a fairy tale, right? And maybe it would be if it weren't for the Drakkin. They destroyed her world, and now they will destroy this one. You picked a hell of a time to visit."

Brytnoth nodded slowly. "That's how they operate," he said. "Sahara's homeworld... yours...mine—"

"I thought you didn't remember yours."

Brytnoth ignored him. "They arrive and drain the resources, eliminate the human population in extermination waves, and then..." He stopped and blew out his breath.

"Then what?"

"Then they load the remaining survivors onto a freighter and send them to drift in deep space until they die...or—" and he fixed Jared with an earnest stare— "until the ship runs out of fuel and crashes in the desert."

"Is that what happened to your people?" Jared asked, and Brytnoth nodded slowly. "And you think that's what's going to happen to us?"

Brytnoth shrugged. "It fits a pattern," he said. "It's possible."

Jared sat for a long time without moving. He didn't understand why the Drakkin would choose to exile a remnant instead of exterminating the whole population. It didn't make any sense...unless they thought it was the crueler way to achieve the same end. After all, people tearing each other to shreds in panic on a ship running out of fuel was so much more agonizing than just being mowed down in the streets.

"It makes no sense, Brytnoth," he said at last.

"I know."

They sat there for a long while in silence, and then Brytnoth angled to look at Jared. "Sahara offered her life in exchange for you and for the city, right?" he said.

"That's right." Jared clenched and unclenched his fist.

"Do you think her life will be enough?"

"Maybe. But I'm not planning on letting them kill her."

"You're going to stop the sacrifice?" Brytnoth asked. "How?"

"I have no idea." He got to his feet and extended his hand to Brytnoth. "Come on. There's someone you should meet."

Brytnoth nodded and grasped Jared's hand at the wrist. Jared pulled him up and they returned to the Great House together. Brytnoth was quiet the entire way, and Jared was grateful. He needed to get his thoughts together before they met Childir.

Jared led Brytnoth up the narrow stairs to the seer's chambers.

"Just tell him what you told me," he said.

Brytnoth nodded and Jared rapped on the door. The seer called out for them to enter, and Jared opened the door and led Brytnoth into the room. Childir looked up at them with interest, and then leaned back in his chair and folded his hands.

"And who is this new face?" he asked, fixing Brytnoth with an intense stare. "Another outworlder?"

"Yes. This is Brytnoth," Jared said.

"We seem to be collecting them these days," Childir observed drily. "Well, Brytnoth? What is your story?"

Brytnoth, his voice halting at first, told Childir what he had already told Jared. When he finished, Childir stroked his beard thoughtfully and regarded them with bright eyes.

"You didn't bring him here just to tell me a story, Jared," he said. "Nor, I think, to make up for not bringing Sahara to see me when she was still here."

"Do you think that what happened on his homeworld will happen here?" Jared asked.

Childir drummed the tips of his fingers together and pursed his lips. "Contrary to what you might believe," Childir said. "I don't know all future things with certainty."

Jared paused. *But you know some of them. Like the day that would be most favorable for an attack on the Drakkin fortress...*

"Will you take this information to Arnauld?" Childir asked.

"If there is a chance some of us might survive," Jared said, "I think he should know."

"But what would he be able to do about it, in the end? Will it really serve him?" He opened his hands, as if handing the question to Jared. "The Drakkin have accepted Sahara's blood in exchange for Albadir's security. It is enough."

Jared caught Brytnoth's eye. He was frowning.

"He is the ruler of the city," Brytnoth said. "He has the right to know what happened to my people. What could happen to his own people."

Childir ignored him. "Jared, what might such a revelation set in motion?"

Jared kept his face carefully neutral, but a horrible suspicion was forming itself in his mind. Brytnoth was right—Arnauld had a right to know the threat they faced. But there was a strange light in Childir's eyes, and every time he spoke, Jared felt something like the pull of a warm, invisible thread. The smell of *edulia* hung in the air, but there was another cloying heaviness that was starting to cloud his mind.

Something was very wrong.

Heart pounding, Jared forced himself to shrug. "I'm sure you're right," he said. "Why trouble him when everything is already settled?"

"That's right." Childir nodded slowly, and although he smiled, the fierce light in his eyes didn't fade. "That's the most reasonable thing to do. The best plan."

Jared stood abruptly and laid a hand on Brytnoth's shoulder. "Thank you for your counsel, my lord," he said to Childir.

"You've given me much to consider," said the sage, pressing his fingertips together.

Jared inclined his head and propelled Brytnoth out the door. As soon as it closed behind them, Jared jumped down the stairs three at a time. Brytnoth clattered down behind him. As soon as they reached the ground floor, Brytnoth caught Jared's arm.

"What the hell is the matter with you?" he asked. "What happened back there?"

"Not here."

Jared led Brytnoth back to his own chambers. As soon as they were inside, he bolted the door securely behind them. Brytnoth dropped into a chair as Jared paced in front of the fireplace like a caged beast.

"Damn!" Jared exploded finally.

"Would you tell me what's going on?" Brytnoth said. "What was all that? And what was that smell?"

"Oh, you smelled it too?" Jared said. "I think it was some kind of enchantment."

Brytnoth's face changed from irritation to shock. "Enchantment?"

Jared sighed and rubbed his hands over his face. "I never imagined it would be him." He swore again. "I must be blind."

"He's an enchanter?"

"Not really. But he understands the properties of things," Jared said with a frustrated sigh. "He's the sage of the city. Our holy man. He leads us in prayer, offers the sacrifices, reads the auguries and tells us the future."

Brytnoth nodded. "So why would he try to put us under some kind of spell?"

Jared barely heard him. He was talking to himself now, more than to Brytnoth. "He's consulted on everything...especially on matters of high and secret importance. Plans, for instance." He paused and turned to Brytnoth. "Battle plans."

"Like the plans for the attack on the Drakkin?"

"Yes. Exactly like those." Jared leaned on the table across from him. "They were ready for us, Brytnoth. Sahara and I didn't understand how they knew...but I think the word *betrayal* was in both our minds."

Brytnoth's face paled. "Oh..."

"He knows things," Jared said. "He knows about Sahara. About the city...all our strengths and weaknesses. All Arnauld's preparations. Nothing is hidden from him. And if he is working with the Drakkin..."

"You have to tell Arnauld," Brytnoth said, starting up. "He has to know."

Jared planted a hand in his chest. "Not so fast. We have to be careful. I'm not sure yet what he's capable of...or what he'll do with the information he has." He hesitated. "And I don't understand why he would betray us."

"We know he will do harm! Isn't that enough?"

"He wants Sahara to be sacrificed. That much is clear. The enchantment was to prevent us from taking any information to Arnauld that might sway him to interfere in that process."

Jared resumed his pacing and Brytnoth said nothing. Jared was glad of his silence. He raked his fingers through his hair, trying to collect his scattered thoughts. This betrayal cut him to the core. Childir had been his mentor—and more than that, he had been a father to Jared when his own father had been taken from him.

Maybe he arranged that too and then pretended to comfort me. The lying bastard.

All his anger hardened into a single shard of purpose. "I need some time to think," he said. "I'm going to the library. Find Rafe and meet me at the tavern tonight. Late."

Brytnoth rose and headed for the door. "We're going to go after her, aren't we?" he asked.

"Yes," Jared said. "Because if she dies, there will be nothing left to stop them."

FORTY-ONE

Jared leaned back in his chair and pressed the palms of his hands into his eyes. He'd been staring at manuscripts for so long that nothing made sense anymore.

"Brytnoth said I'd find you in here."

It was Rafe's voice, loud in the tomb-like silence of the library. Jared lifted his head and squinted toward the doorway. Rafe stood there, half blocking the late afternoon light.

"What are you doing?" Rafe asked, stepping into the gloom.

"Looking for something," he said.

Rafe took a seat at the table and Jared pushed three tomes, each of ponderous size, across the table at his friend. Rafe glanced at them, then the corner of his mouth twisted up in a half-smile.

"What am I supposed to do with those?"

"Well, there's this really remarkable thing called 'reading'," Jared said.

"Reading! That's what I have you for!" Rafe said. Then his grin disappeared. "Seriously, though. What are you looking for?"

"You know what they're planning to do with Sahara?" Jared asked.

"Vaguely. Brytnoth told me something about it--some ancient ritual of sacrifice?"

"The same sacrifice they demand to keep the sluice-gate open," Jared said. "And I'm looking for a way to save her."

"And you think the answer is in these books?" Rafe pulled one towards himself and stared at the open pages. Dense script filled the page and elaborate scroll-work crowded the margins. "How can you even read this? It makes me cross-eyed just to look at it!"

Jared grinned at him. "I'm actually not reading the text," he said. "That one's about methods of fertilizing the *edulia* orchards. I couldn't care less about that...but some of them would make you think twice about eating any of the fruit!" He tapped his finger on the margin. "Look at the illumination at the bottom of the page."

Rafe bent over and squinted. After a moment, his eyes widened and he sat up slowly. "Is that what I think it is?"

"I think so. Whoever illuminated this manuscript managed to get inside the Drakkin high temple and witness one of those ritual sacrifices. And he's preserved a record of it in this seemingly insignificant decorative flourish."

"I'll admit I never thought much of your obsession with these old books until this moment." Rafe rocked his chair back onto two legs and clasped his hands behind his head. "But what does this tell us?"

"If we're going to save Sahara, we have to understand the ritual. This picture here is actually the first in a series. The illuminator inscribed a cipher here." He pointed to the corner of the illustration, where a miniature open book lay on the ground, its leaves decorated with a strange figure.

"That scratch is a cipher?"

"Yes," Jace said. Rafe made a face and Jared grinned. "There are five illustrations in the series, and so far I've managed to track down the next two."

Rafe's eyes tracked to the massive shelves of books lining the walls. "We have to search through all of these?" he asked. "I hope the Drakkin are planning to wait five years to execute her."

Jared laughed. "No, Rafe. I've got a pretty good idea which section to search. These three volumes are all on agriculture, and they're in chronological order. The pictures occur in sequence."

"Great," said Rafe. "So where do we start?"

Jared moved to the center of one of the bookcases and pulled a book halfway off the shelf. "Here. And we go all the way down to the floor."

They pored over tomes for what felt like hours. Rafe ferried the books to and from the table, carefully replacing them in exactly the same order in which he found them. Jace scanned the pages for the final two illuminations.

Finally, Rafe replaced the last volume on the shelf and rubbed his eyes and face with dusty hands. "I never want to see another book for as long as I live," he said with a groan.

He stretched and joined Jared at the table. Jared scowled at the three manuscripts. "I don't understand," he said. "We didn't find them. We should have found them."

"Maybe there aren't any more," Rafe said. "Maybe he never finished what he started."

Jared blew out his breath and dragged the books closer to him. "Then we'll just have to go with what we have." Jared bent over the illustrations and squinted. "Why is it so bloody dark in here?" he asked.

"Because it's after sundown," called a new voice.

Jared and Rafe turned toward the doorway. Brytnoth sauntered into the chamber and pulled a lever on the wall. The power hummed to life and the lights flickered on. Jared and Rafe squinted at him as the sudden brightness hurt their eyes. Brytnoth grinned.

"You stood me up for dinner, so I thought I'd come to investigate." He looked them up and down. "Been dusting the shelves, have you?"

"Hey," said Rafe. "We've been working very, very hard. Not dusting."

"So I see." Brytnoth joined them at the table and leaned over to study the manuscripts. "Did you find something useful?"

"Maybe," said Jared. "And maybe not."

"Anything about Drakkin spies in Albadir?" Brytnoth asked.

Rafe swung around to face Jared. "What does he mean, spies? Who's spying?"

"Childir," Jared answered.

Rafe gaped at him. "You're not serious," he managed finally. "You can't possibly be serious." When Jared said nothing, Rafe blurted, "How do you know that?"

"Think about it, Rafe," Jared said. "He was the only one who knew our plans for the attack. Not even Arnauld knew the whole strategy. Sahara and I couldn't figure out how the enemy had anticipated our every move."

"Jared thinks Childir leaked the information to the Drakkin," Brytnoth added.

Rafe glanced at him, then turned back to Jared. "He has a real knack for stating the obvious, doesn't he?"

"Just trying to make sure you can keep up," Brytnoth said.

"Thanks," Rafe responded. "Look, Jared, I get that you're upset about what happened. But Childir is a Drakkin spy? That sounds crazy."

"Who else in the city has the knowledge or the skills to communicate with them?" Jared asked. "Or the opportunity?"

Rafe hesitated for a long moment, and the longer the silence stretched, the more tense Jared became.

"Jared," Rafe said finally, his voice very quiet. "You do."

Jared recoiled as if Rafe had punched him in the stomach. Brytnoth sucked in his breath.

"What?" Jared cried. "Rafe, no! Why would I ever betray—"

"I'm not accusing you," Rafe said softly. "I know you didn't rat us out. But I'm just warning you. If you try to bring down Childir, you better be damn sure you can prove it wasn't you."

Jared opened his mouth to say something, but then he stopped. Rafe was right. If he went to Arnauld with the accusation that Childir had betrayed them, Childir could defend himself simply by pointing out that Jared was the one who made all the trips alone to the western desert. Certainly, those trips had been taken under the guise of intelligence gathering…but it would be easy enough to turn them into meetings for information sharing.

And worst of all, everyone would assume that Childir was innocent. And who would ever dare to believe their holy man guilty of a crime like treason, unless he were trying to deflect suspicion from his own activities? Jared knew that there were plenty of lords who had reason to hate him because of the favor Arnauld had always shown him. And now, more than ever, when he had brought Sahara into the city and invited the Drakkin's vengeance, he couldn't trust that his reputation would be enough to protect him.

He rubbed a hand over his face and blew out his breath. "I hadn't thought of that."

"Well, you better start thinking about it," Rafe said. "And don't say a word against Childir until you can prove what you're saying."

Brytnoth clapped Jared on the shoulder. "Maybe that head of yours will work more efficiently if we feed it."

"That's the best idea I've heard all night," Rafe said. "Drinks and dinner on me."

They slid into a secluded booth at the tavern and Rafe summoned one of the barmaids. She was a sweet-looking young woman, and as she threaded her way toward them through the tables, her whole face lit up in a smile.

"What's your pleasure?" she asked, hovering next to him.

"All business tonight, Emma," he answered with a roguish grin. "Three of those meat pies this place is supposed to be famous for. And three tankards of ale."

Emma's shimmering dark eyes danced from Rafe to Brytnoth and then came to rest on Jared. Her face changed and she laid a hand on Rafe's arm.

"Rafe," she began, then bit her lip and stopped.

"What's the matter?" he asked.

She just shook her head and hurried away. Jared noticed that

Brytnoth followed her with his eyes until she disappeared into the kitchen. He jostled him with his elbow.

"She's already taken," he murmured, loud enough for Rafe to hear.

When Rafe scowled playfully at him, Brytnoth flushed and raked a hand through his hair until it stood on end. Jared and Rafe laughed.

"So, Rafe," Jared said. "Emma, is it?"

"She's Thormund Dell's daughter," Rafe said. "You remember him, don't you?"

"Of course I remember," Jared said, then explained to Brytnoth, "He's one of Arnauld's chief advisors. He used to be our ambassador to the Great City." Jared turned back to Rafe. "Strange, isn't it, that Thormund is letting his daughter wait tables in the tavern? Surely she could have any position she wanted in the Great House!"

"He's not pleased, but she was determined to make her own way."

"Why would she want work like this?" Brytnoth asked with a frown.

"It's the most varied society you can find in this place," he said. "There aren't very many ways to make your own way around here unless you're good at hiking through the desert and spying on the Drakkin."

Brytnoth shifted his gaze away from them. Jared followed it and saw Emma at the bar, chatting with two young men as she filled a trio of tankards with ale. When he glanced back at Brytnoth, he was surprised at the sadness in his eyes.

"Cheer up, Brytnoth," he said. "There are other young women in Albadir. Rafe hasn't claimed all of them."

"Not yet." Rafe grinned.

"It's not that. She...reminds me of someone, that's all."

"Your memory is coming back!" Jared said. "That's excellent!"

"In pieces." He blew out his breath. "And I think maybe I would rather it didn't. There's nothing there but misery and pain."

Rafe and Jared exchanged glances. "Who does she remind you of?" Rafe asked.

"My first love," Brytnoth said, his voice suddenly taut. "She was just the same—innocent, full of life. She loved people, loved making them laugh. On the freighter, we had a bar too, and for reasons I'll never understand, they assigned her the late shift. She was so excited. Said it would give her the chance to bring people joy." He slammed his fist down on the table as his voice caught in his throat.

"What happened to her?" Rafe asked gently after a long moment of silence.

"By the time I got there, it was too late," Brytnoth said. "Some of the men were getting claustrophobic. We'd been on that damned ship for so long. Too long. The men drank to forget why they were drinking, and by the time they were drunk enough to forget that, they'd forgotten everything else too. There were three of them that night." He took a deep breath. "It was too late for me to save her." He paused, then added, "They were a danger to the ship. So I killed them all, and blew their bodies out of the airlock."

Jared leaned back in his seat and blew out his breath. Rafe's mouth dropped open and for once, he couldn't find anything to say. Brytnoth buried his head in his hands.

"You can't understand," he said softly. "It was a living hell. No way out, no way through. Just drifting. They'd blasted our nav and comm systems to hell. Every day that passed, our life support resources were taxed a bit further. Gangs started forming, those last few days. It was my fault...because as soon as they realized we could get rid of people by blowing them out the airlocks, they figured out that less people meant more resources for the ones who remained on board. If we hadn't crashed in the desert, we'd have torn each other to pieces."

Rafe swung his gaze in Emma's direction and Jared saw him clench his hands into fists.

"Rafe, we think that's what the Drakkin have planned for Albadir," Jared said.

"No way in hell will I let it come to that," Rafe said. "Not while I'm still breathing."

The two young men at the bar suddenly turned in their direction. Their faces were red with drink, and one of them pointed at Jared. Emma seemed startled by whatever he said, because she turned away and hurried toward them with their order.

As she reached the table, Brytnoth raised his head. "There's still hope for Albadir," he said. "While there's life, there's hope, they say."

Emma placed the steaming pies on the table, but she kept glancing over her shoulder at the men. Rafe laid a hand on her arm to still her frantic movements.

"What's wrong?" Rafe asked, angling to see what was drawing her attention. "Are those idiots bothering you?"

"No," she said with a forced laugh. "Of course not. They're just —" She stopped and shifted her tray to her other hand. "Drunk."

"Why are they staring at me?" Jared asked.

Emma startled and tried to laugh again. "Oh, you know! They're not...I mean...they're just...they're harmless, mostly..."

Rafe caught her hand gently. "I know there's something going on," he said, his voice soft but firm. "Tell me."

"They think..." She took a deep breath. "They say Jared was responsible for their brother's death. Because the battle..." Her voice trailed off.

Jared's gaze locked with Rafe's. "Why do they say that?" he asked.

"I don't know," she said. "They're angry. They're drunk." She pulled her hand out of Rafe's. "I'd eat and go quickly...before they have any more to drink."

"Thanks," Rafe said.

"Be careful," Brytnoth said suddenly. "Please."

Emma knitted her brows at him and flashed him a smile. "That's sweet. But they mean me no harm. I'm the one pouring their drinks!"

"Just be careful," Brytnoth repeated.

Emma stared at him for a moment, as if she could sense the pain he was trying to hide. Impulsively, she reached out and covered his hand with one of her own. "Don't worry about me," she whispered.

With one last soft smile at Rafe, Emma whirled away and disappeared into the kitchen.

FORTY-TWO

After Emma's warning, Jared kept an eye on the two men at the bar.

"Did you know?" he asked Rafe.

Rafe jabbed his fork into his pie and stuffed his mouth with the flaky pastry laden with meat and juices. "Know what?"

"That men were talking against me," he said. "Accusing me. Is that why you warned me earlier in the library?"

Rafe finished chewing and carefully set his fork on his plate. "There's nothing being said in the Great House," he said. "But while you were gone, there was talk here in the tavern and in the streets. Some of those who lost family or friends in the battle said that you had been taken home where you belonged."

"I was a prisoner!" Jared protested. "The only reason I survived is because they—"

"Let you go?" finished Rafe. He met Jared's stunned gaze with a shrug. "And how do you think that little detail plays into their narrative?"

Jared's pulse jumped into a gallop and he glanced back at the men at the bar. They were staring in his direction, and now there was murder mingled with the drunkenness in their faces.

"I'm a dead man," he said softly. "I have to get out of Albadir."

"Isn't this exactly what Childir wants?" Brytnoth asked suddenly. "Sahara's going to be sacrificed, and you'll be torn apart by your own people. And meanwhile, he can continue to spin his own designs."

In that moment, everything became suddenly clear in Jared's mind. "That son of a bitch. He set me up. He told them to take me, and he told them to release me. And it's all so he can feed the people what they want: a traitor to blame. A scapegoat for all their problems. And if they take me out, there will be no hope of saving Sahara—and once she dies, there will be no one left from the Shell to stop them."

"When are they bringing Sahara back to Silesia for the ritual?" Rafe asked.

"I don't know," Jared answered. "That's what I was trying to find in those books."

"Funny way of trying to tell the future...looking a hundred years into the past," Brytnoth observed.

Two days from now.

Jared jumped and his fork clattered onto the stone floor. He stared at his friends' surprised faces, but they blurred out of focus.

"What's the matter with you?" asked Brytnoth, but his voice seemed to come from far away.

Jared squeezed his eyes shut as the pain burned through his mind. When he opened them again, the tavern was gone. Instead, he saw a squalid hovel next to the landing platform on K'ilenfir. A mangy three-headed dog was chained to the wall. Rain was falling, making soft puddles of oozy green and gray mud. In the hovel, there was a window with a single light.

Inside the hut, he saw a ramshackle cot draped with a dirty blanket. A table held a flask of old wine and a few hard biscuits. A candle guttered in a tarnished bowl.

Sahara sat on the other side of the table, staring straight at him with a focused, almost pained expression in her eyes.

Jared.

It was her voice in his head, and he tried to reach out to her, but found he couldn't move. *Sahara! Can you...see me?*

Yes. And you can see me?

Jared nodded. He drank in the sight of her, wishing desperately that he could touch her—to reassure her that this was real. There was a large purple bruise on her right cheek, and her wrists and ankles were weighed down with chains. Blood had soaked through the arm of the simple dress of coarse gray cloth that seemed something too big for her. She turned her head suddenly to glance out the window, as if some sound he couldn't hear had drawn her attention. Mud and blood were caked in her red curls.

What have they done to you? he asked.

Sahara turned back to him with a terrible smile, and Jared thought his heart would burst out of his chest. *They had questions.*

Did you answer? A cloud of doubt shadowed her face for a moment, and his entire body tensed. *It's okay. It's okay...just tell me where they're taking you.*

The old fortress...whatever that means. She shook her head. *They said something about the sacrifice happening on the night of the full moon...I'm sorry. That's all I know.*

The full moon is five days from now.

Sahara smiled at him again, but this time with a little of her old spunk. *Guess you better think fast.*

Jared's vision began to swim and a splitting pain throbbed in his head. *No, don't go. Don't go.* He tried to reach out a hand to her. *Sahara....*

Please... He couldn't see her, but he could still hear her voice, low and desperate. *Don't come for me. Don't risk—*

With a gasp, Jared came back to himself. He was drenched in sweat and his head hurt so badly that he could barely keep his eyes open. Vaguely, he could see his two friends staring at him.

"Jared," Rafe said. "Are you all right?"

Jared held up a shaking hand and took a long drink of ale. The throbbing in his head slowly subsided, and he managed a weak smile that didn't seem to do much to allay their worry.

"What happened to you?" Brytnoth asked.

"If I told you," Jared answered, "you'd think I was insane."

"Try us," said Rafe.

"You know that Sahara and I can communicate somehow in our thoughts," Jared said. "I don't know how to control it...it just comes suddenly, without any warning."

"That sounds awkward," Rafe said.

"I just saw her...spoke with her. She's being held in some mangy little hut near the landing pad on K'ilenfir. She said they're bringing her back to here, to the old fortress, in two days. The sacrifice will happen the night of the full moon."

"What's it like, being in someone else's thoughts?" Brytnoth asked.

"And why is it happening to you two?" Rafe put in at the same time. "You're not even from the same planet. Why would you be connected like that?"

"First of all, Brytnoth, it hurts like hell. Secondly, Rafe, I have no idea...and that's why I went to ask Childir—"

As soon as the words were out of his mouth, he froze. Then he swore viciously and slammed his fist on the table.

"So he knows about that too," Rafe said, lacing his fingers behind his head and leaning against the back of the booth. "Is there anything he *doesn't* know?"

"Whatever new information we learn has to be kept close," Jared said. "We don't know who we can trust."

"Well, well." This new voice surprised them all, and they looked up. The two men from the bar stood beside the table, their faces sour with drink and suspicion. The older of the two, a swarthy man with a jagged scar running down his neck, was clearly the leader. "Secrets, eh? What kind of secrets might those be?"

"Your seats are over there," Rafe said.

The swarthy man leaned on the table and it creaked under his weight. He thrust his pocked and scruffy face close to Jared's and sniffed.

"Yep," he said. "I can always smell 'em. Traitors."

Jared rotated his mug on the table, but his heart was galloping in his chest. "You're drunk, friend," he said. "Come back and see me when you're sober."

The man slammed his fist down on the table so hard that all the dishes clattered and everyone in the tavern turned to stare at them.

"Careful," Jared said, his voice quiet. "You might get yourself thrown out for causing a scene."

Emma swept up to the table at that moment, with a fat, pasty-faced man in tow. His grubby apron and the rag wrapped around his head made him look like a cross between a blacksmith and a washerwoman.

"Who's this, then?" asked Rafe with a lifted eyebrow.

"I thought you might want to give your compliments to the chef," Emma said brightly, with a smile too large and a laugh too loud. Then she turned to the drunkards and sidled herself between them and Jared's table. "It's almost closing time," she chirped. "Can I get you anything else before you go?"

The swarthy man straightened and he and his companion both folded their arms and squared their shoulders. The pasty-faced chef took one look at them and his flaccid cheeks started quivering.

"I think I best be cleaning up them dishes," he said. He reached for the plates on the table, but Emma planted her hand on his wrist and pinned him to the table.

"You in the habit of serving traitors?" the swarthy man demanded of the chef in a loud voice.

A murmur of surprise rippled through the room, and Jared saw the expressions of some of the men change from amusement to dark suspicion. The chef stammered something about serving everyone no matter their ability to pay.

"We didn't come here looking for trouble," Jared said, keeping his voice low.

"No, but trouble's found you anyway, ain't it?" The man thrust out his chest as if he could use it like a battering ram.

"Shut it and sit down!" called a smattering of voices from around the tavern. "Throw 'em out!" said others. Still others said nothing, but watched Jared with unfriendly eyes.

"I'd like to ask—that is, if it's not too much trouble—" the chef stammered.

"Perhaps you could take your conversation outside," Emma said brightly, gesturing at the door.

"Gladly," said the swarthy man.

Before anyone could react, the man elbowed Emma and the chef out of the way, grabbed Jared's collar and hauled him toward the door. Behind him, he heard Rafe shouting at the other man, and the sound of breaking dishes and the resounding crack of a table.

The swarthy man opened the door and flung Jared out into the street. He fell and rolled on the stone cobbles, and before he could get up, the man was there beside him. He planted his boot in Jared's stomach and Jared grunted as the pain shot through him like an explosion of little stars. He clutched his stomach with one hand and scrambled to his knees.

The man aimed another kick at Jared, but this time Jared was ready for him. He angled aside just in time and the man stumbled and slurred a string of curses. Jared got to his feet and brushed himself off. But just as he turned to leave, a dozen men emerged out of the shadows around him. Some had makeshift cudgels in their hands.

"What's this, Nat?" said one, a large, burly man with a club. "You catch our serpent?"

Jared backed slowly toward the tavern, but the group of men fanned out and cut him off. He took a breath and resigned himself to a fight. He suspected more than half of the men were drunk, but it was still twelve to one. Even though those odds wouldn't usually bother him, the searing pain in his head and his ribs made him doubt his ability to fight.

"I don't know what you think I've done," Jared said, deciding to try diplomacy. He held up his hands in a gesture of truce. "But I promise you, you've got the wrong man."

Nat took his place in the mob while the burly man advanced on Jared, clapping his club against his palm.

"No," he said. "We don't got the wrong man. He said it was you."

"Who said?"

The burly man's grin was feral. "You must think I'm stupid. He told us not to tell you anything—said you'd rat us all out to the Drakkin."

"I'm no traitor," Jared said. "How do you know he's not playing you for fools?"

"He said you'd say that." The man nodded once—a signal.

Someone kicked Jared's legs from behind and his knees buckled. He hit the ground hard, and before he could scramble up, another man, smelling of smoke and ale, pinioned his arms. Another seized him by the hair and dragged his head back to expose his throat.

The burly man handed his club to one of his minions and drew a long knife with a jagged blade.

Jared's heart hammered against his ribs. A thousand thoughts raced through his mind, jumbles of memories and fragments of words he wanted to say but couldn't.

The man advanced on him until the point of the blade was just inches from his throat.

I will not die here.

In a sudden flash of clarity, Jared saw the man's weaknesses: the feeble way he gripped the knife, the unbalanced stance. He wrenched his arms free and slapped the knife away. It clattered on the cobbles and the burly man shouted something Jared couldn't understand.

The man holding him by the hair lost his concentration for a split second, and Jared grabbed his arm, hauled him over his shoulder, and slammed him down into the pavement.

He scrambled to his feet and balled his fists. Slowly, he turned in a circle, keeping his balance light. He heard shouts from the direction of the tavern. As the man who'd held his arms charged at him, he planted his boot in the man's chest and sent him flying back through the circle of angry faces.

At that moment, Rafe and Brytnoth burst through the line, throwing punches right and left. As men fell under the rain of blows, Nat tried to run. Rafe chased after him, but Nat escaped into a dark alleyway before Rafe could bring him down.

Back in the center of the now-shattered circle, the burly man scrambled for his knife and grabbed the hilt. Jared planted his boot on the blade, pinning the knife and the man to the ground. He seized the man by the throat and tightened his fingers.

"Who told you I was a traitor?" Jared asked.

The man gasped for breath but still managed to sneer at him. Jared squeezed harder, and the man's face began to turn purple.

"Who told you?" he asked again.

The man swung feebly at Jared's arm, trying to break his hold.

"Jared!" Brytnoth shouted.

"Whoever it was," Jared hissed, "you tell him something for me. Tell him I know the truth. Tell him his reckoning is coming."

Jared released the man and tossed him away like a piece of garbage. The man crawled away from him, coughing and gasping. As soon as he'd gotten air back into his lungs, he scrambled up and took off after Nat. The rest of his crew lay groaning on the cobblestones, faces bloodied. Rafe kicked one who looked like he was recovering as he walked over to rejoin Jared and Brytnoth.

Jared picked up the knife. "I need to get off the streets," he said. "It's not safe for me here any longer."

FORTY-THREE

Jared led them swiftly through the darkened streets back to the library. As soon as they were all inside, he closed the heavy door and bolted it behind them. He flipped the switch to turn on the lights and then returned to the table where he'd spread out the old manuscripts.

"Now that word's got around that you're a traitor, they're going to come for you," Rafe said.

"I know. That's why I'm not staying."

"What are you going to do?" Brytnoth asked.

"Same thing I was always planning to do," he said, studying the drawings in the manuscripts. "I'm going after Sahara."

"You want some help with that?" Rafe asked.

Jared didn't answer, but instead shoved the book towards them across the table. The illustration was curiously worked, connected to the other marginalia on the page by gold-leafed scrollwork. The field was deep blue, and the five dark figures arrayed against it were barely visible. They were more shadow than light, and they appeared to be hooded.

On either side of the robed figures stretched an arched colonnade, punctuated at regular intervals with torches. In the center of the right-hand colonnade hung a massive golden gong, its mallet in an ivory stand.

"Nice," Rafe said. "Why do you care what's in these pages?"

"Because I think they can help us plan our attack," Jared answered.

He pulled the second manuscript toward him. It showed the same scene, but from a perspective behind the robed figures. The colonnade ended abruptly at the edge of what appeared to be a ledge or cliff of some sort. The illuminator had been at some pains to convey the threshold between inner court and outer ledge: marbled floor clashed against bare rock, the deep blue ceiling collided against the shimmering pinks and silvers of an evening sky. Stabbing upward into the softness of the sky, in the very center of the cliff edge, was a pillar.

Jared traced his finger down the pillar, then turned to the third illumination. This time, there were hands pinioned behind the pillar with a cruel chain. Masses of hair spilled over the victim's shoulders and whipped around the pillar.

"Are we really this desperate?" Rafe asked. "You have no other source of information?"

"Childir was my source," Jared said. "And I guess we all know how that worked out." He motioned for them to join him at the table and lined up the three books in order. "Let's go over what we know. This is some kind of designated sacrificial chamber on the edge of a cliff. It looks like five of the Drakkin are present for the ritual."

"Why is the victim chained to a pillar?" asked Rafe. "And why is it right on the edge of the cliff? There's no room for the executioner."

"Speaking of executioners," Brytnoth added, "no one but the victim is pictured in that third drawing."

"We're assuming that the executioner needs room to stand," Jared said slowly. He felt a chill creep through his veins as everything suddenly made sense. "But I don't think that's how it works."

He raised his eyes to meet Rafe's, and saw Rafe's face change as he understood Jared's line of reasoning.

"Damn," Rafe said. "You mean the dragon."

Brytnoth's face paled. "So now we're not just going to rescue Sahara, but we're supposed to fight the dragon too?"

"If we get to her before the dragon comes, maybe we won't have to fight that battle," Jared said.

Rafe shook his head. "The only way this ends—the only way we save Sahara and Albadir—is to kill the dragon."

"If this drawing is right, there are at least five Drakkin lords between us and Sahara...and that doesn't even count the guards," Brytnoth said. "And all of this is assuming we can even find the old fortress."

Jared paced the floor in frustration. "I'm not giving up," he said aloud.

"Nobody's asking you to," Rafe said.

"We don't have time to dig around in here for the answers," Brytnoth added. "And now that you think Childir can't be trusted..."

Jared stopped pacing and looked up at the ceiling and the golden symbol of the *lilia-dir*.

"Go back to the Great House and gather whatever things you might need for the journey," he said.

"What are you going to do?" Rafe asked, getting to his feet.

"I need to think," Jared said. "And I can't go back to the Great House...not yet."

Rafe clapped him on the shoulder and then nodded his head at Brytnoth. They left the library together, and Jared bolted the door behind them. Then he sank down on the floor, his back against the dusty shelves, and leaned his head on his knees.

FORTY-FOUR

When Jared finally left the library, it was almost the darkest hour of the night. The air was hazy with the dust whipped up by the sandstorms still raging outside the city walls, shrouding everything in a veil. If it hadn't been for the lamps that lit the streets at intervals, he wouldn't have been able to see his path clearly. He moved quickly, scanning the dim shadows to either side in case his assailants were waiting for him.

But nothing happened on the path through the orchard, and he relaxed as he entered the wide courtyard of the Great House. He paused by the fountain and leaned on its smooth side, letting the sound of flowing water refresh his fevered mind. Tiny droplets, tossed up by the cascades tumbling from the top tiers of the fountain, clung to his face and hands.

You've got it wrong, you know. About the Drakkin.

Jared's head snapped up. He could feel Sahara's presence, and he waited, breathless, for his vision to clear enough for him to see her.

"Sahara!" he said aloud. The sound of his own voice, husky as if he had been hours in the desert without water, startled him. He closed his eyes and reached out to her with his thoughts. *Sahara.*

You're wrong about them, Jared.

He opened his eyes again. Now, instead of the water in the fountain, he saw dingy walls, chains holding her hands and feet. Sahara's head was bowed, as if she were afraid to look at him. There was something wrong, and his pulse quickened.

What have they done to you? he asked her.

No time for that. Listen to me. I know you think you're coming to save me. But you can't. There's so much more at stake now than just my life...and if you do this, you risk destroying everything.

What are you talking about? What am I going to destroy?

Sahara's lashes flickered against her pale cheeks. He could just see the blood crusted on the right side of her face and matted in the hair above her ear.

He wished he could kneel in front of her, to wash her wounds and care for her as he had done all those weeks ago.

She raised her face and stared straight into his eyes. *They are coming for Albadir.*

Are you sure? he asked. *How do you know that's what they plan to do? Are you sure you're not –*

She cut him off with a sharp movement of her hand, rattling her chains. *And they don't bring the dragon.* She shivered a little, clenched her jaw, and continued. *It's not their pet or some kind of weapon they summon.*

Then what?

They <u>are</u> *the dragon, Jared.*

What? He frowned. *I don't understand.*

They are devoted to an ancient evil—and they have united themselves into a collective in its service. They have exchanged their individual identities for an unholy dark power...and when they exercise that power as the collective, they become the dragon.

Jared's mind whirled as he processed what she was telling him. *But if that's true...and the dragon could be destroyed...then we would destroy them all. The entire Drakkin collective.*

That's impossible. She shook her head at him. *It's over, Jared.*

Jared's heart hammered in his chest so that he could hardly breathe. *It's not over. Where there is life, there is hope.*

I couldn't leave without saying goodbye. Her eyes bored into his, and tears glittered in their depths.

Her voice was fading. The vision evaporated like mist.

He lurched forward, calling her name, and then tripped and fell on his hands and knees. He bowed his head, feeling the coolness of the stone against his hot skin. He let it seep into his fevered mind. He refused to let her go. He refused to believe that there was nothing more they could do. He would not let her give up.

And the tiniest seed of hope—that they could destroy the Drakkin once and for all, not just for Silesia, but for all worlds—blossomed in his chest.

He got up and slipped into the Great House. Noiselessly, he made his way through the corridors until he stood in front of Rafe's door. He rapped softly, checking around him to make sure no one had followed him.

When there was no answer, he rapped again, a little louder this time. Rafe finally opened the door, his hair mussed and deep sleep wrinkles on one side of his face.

"How you can sleep at a time like this?" Jared said.

"You said get ready for a journey, not pull an all-nighter."

"You're supposed to be packing supplies, you idiot."

Rafe sank down onto the low couch that faced the fireplace and rubbed a hand over his sleep-bleared eyes. "I delegated that to the new guy."

Jared sat down beside him. "Listen. We caught a break. Sahara told me what we werre missing. We've done some crazy things in the past, and you've never let me down...so I hope you're ready for this."

"What did she say?"

"If we bring down the dragon, we can end the Drakkin."

"You mean get rid of the five here on Silesia?"

"No. I mean the Drakkin. All of them. They're a collective. When they gather together, like they will on the night they sacrifice

Sahara, they'll take the form of a dragon. And if we kill it, we destroy them all."

"Wait. Stop." Rafe waved a hand at him. "Back up. The dragon is all of them? The whole council?"

"Yes. The whole council."

"You better be damn sure about this."

"I'm sure."

Rafe whistled and stared up at the ceiling. Jared watched him process the implications of the information, just as he had done.

"Can you even imagine life without the Drakkin?" He sat up with a sudden grin. "We can literally save the universe, Jared."

"My ego hadn't quite got that far yet," Jared said.

"Well, leave it all to me. I'll handle the dispatches."

"Before you start planning your hero party, we actually have to do the thing, Rafe."

"Right." He got up and pulled on his shirt and boots. "When do we leave?"

"There's one more thing we need before we go," Jared said. "But we're going to need Brytnoth."

For a moment, Rafe didn't move. When Jared raised his eyebrows, Rafe protested. "This is my room! Why can't you go get him?"

"I'm delegating."

Huffing under his breath, Rafe left. Jared stoked the fire and sat down on the sofa to wait.

He didn't have to sit there for long. When Rafe returned with Brytnoth, he told Jared that he'd filled Brytnoth in on the plan that would make them heroes of the universe. Brytnoth could hardly contain his excitement.

"There's something about the dragon that's tugging at my memory, but it won't come to me. So what's our plan?"

"Have you ever been to the Great City, Rafe?" Jared asked instead.

"Once, as a child. I don't remember much about it except that it was an enormous sprawling place—all tall white towers and streets like labyrinths. There were ships anchored near the mouth of the river and a space port. My father told me that our textiles and fabrics were prized by many other worlds." He smiled at the memory. "And the Temple of Bann was the most magnificent thing I've ever seen. My father took me there and presented me to the priests. They gave me a blessing or something, I think. Why do you ask?"

"I think that's where we need to go," Jared answered.

"Why? Everything's been destroyed."

"I think there's a cache of weapons buried somewhere. My guess would be the crypt beneath the Temple."

"Is this something else you found in those musty old books?" Rafe asked.

"No. I remember overhearing my father telling Arnauld about the shipment. I don't think I was supposed to know."

"Where did they come from?" Brytnoth asked.

"From Askalon."

Brytnoth started violently and his face paled. "Askalon!" He gripped his head and squeezed his eyes shut, as if the word hurt his mind. "Are you sure?"

"What's the matter with you?" Rafe asked. "This isn't a ghost story! It's a dragon story."

"It is a ghost story," Brytnoth said, his voice faint. "Askalon was my homeworld."

Jared and Rafe stared at him, and then Rafe whistled. Brytnoth dropped his head in his hands.

"This can't be coincidence," Rafe said. "You coming here, now, when everything hangs in the balance."

"My people must have smuggled the weapons off Askalon when the Drakkin arrived," Brytnoth said.

"If they were hidden in the Great City, wouldn't the Drakkin have found them?" Rafe asked. "They turned the place into ash and rubble."

Jared rubbed his sore jaw. "My father said there was a shipment, but he never said it was received." He laid a hand on Brytnoth's shoulder. "Try to remember. Were there weapons stowed away on that transport?"

Brytnoth raised his head slowly. "I...don't know."

"Could you find your way back to the site where your ship crashed?"

"Probably," he said, his voice strained. "Maybe."

Jared got to his feet. "That's good enough for me. Let's go."

FORTY-FIVE

Jared opened the door to step into the corridor and was faced with a dozen guards with Kirin at their head. They had weapons drawn and looked like they were ready for a fight. Jared raised his hands and stepped back in surprise.

"Arnauld wants a word with you," said Kirin, lowering his gun just slightly.

When Jared glanced over his shoulder at Rafe and Brytnoth, who were watching in stunned silence, Kirin nodded his head at them. "Don't worry about them. They'll be comfortable here under armed guard."

Kirin caught Jared's arm and pulled him out into the corridor. One of the guards closed Rafe's door, shutting his friends inside. Then four of them took up their posts in the hallway.

"Why are you doing this, Kirin?" Jared asked as Kirin propelled him down the hallway.

Kirin glanced at him. "Because, unlike you, I serve my city first."

When they reached Arnauld's chamber, Kirin rapped smartly on the door. Arnauld opened it, nodded to Kirin, and stood aside for Jared to enter.

"That will be all for now, Kirin," Arnauld said. "But don't go far."

He closed the door and motioned for Jared to make himself comfortable. As Jared took a seat, Arnauld poured himself a drink from a decanter on a silver tray.

"I would have come if you'd sent word," Jared said. "No need for all the ceremony."

Arnauld chuckled into his glass. "Ceremony. That's a nice way to think about it."

"Is this urgent?"

"Why? Do you have somewhere else to be?"

"Does heading off our annihilation count?"

"Don't make jokes, Jared. I'm really not in the mood." Arnauld sipped his drink and moved to stand near the windows. "And how exactly are you doing that, creeping around in the middle of the night?"

"We don't have time to wait for daylight."

"And what, may I ask, do you think is going to stop a Drakkin assault on the city?"

"Saving Sahara."

Arnauld grunted and drained his glass. "And you were planning to do this in secret, without my consent? Without considering what consequences you might invite for Albadir?"

"I have considered the consequences," Jared answered. "The Drakkin will destroy Albadir once Sahara is dead. Saving her is the only way to save the city."

"And how exactly were you planning to accomplish this?" Arnauld angled to face him.

"We're going to kill the dragon."

Arnauld laughed, a giant, rolling belly laugh that made the blood run hot in Jared's veins. "You must have been drinking," he said. "What in hell possessed you to come up with that?"

"We're going after the weapons cache from Askalon, and I think you know where it is." Jared met his gaze and held it. "And I also think, that if you stopped posturing long enough to listen to me, you'd be asking how you could help, instead of keeping me here and interrogating me."

Arnauld sobered. "When the Drakkin first appeared in this quadrant, Askalon was our foremost trading partner," Arnauld said. "We were working together to find a precious metal—it required us to initiate full-blown mining operations both here on Silesia and on Askalon. According to an ancient prophecy, that metal was the key to destroying the Drakkin in their dragon manifestation. The Crafters' Guild on Askalon discovered a trace vein of the metal and used it to forge those weapons. But somehow the Drakkin found out about it, and they descended on Askalon and destroyed it. Your father and I put out cryptic messages suggesting that the weapons had been brought here, and the Drakkin did not hesitate to pursue them. They destroyed the Great City looking for them. Then they took over our mining operations in the north, convinced that they would find what we had not."

Jared leaned back, pieces of the puzzle suddenly falling into place. "That's where they were sending Sahara," he said. "To work in those mines and help them search for that metal." Arnauld said nothing, and Jared frowned. "You let the Great City be destroyed to prevent them from finding those weapons because you know their power," he said. "So tell me where they are."

Arnauld shrugged again. "They had been secured on a freighter for transport when we lost all communication with Askalon."

"I was right," Jared breathed. He jumped to his feet. "I know where it is. The freighter."

"How do you know that?"

"Brytnoth is from Askalon. And the freighter that crashed in the desert—that's where the weapons are."

Everything about Arnauld seemed suddenly to tense, and he moved from the windows to carefully refill his glass. "They really did get you good," he said, gesturing to his own face.

Jared touched his swollen lip. "Well, it was a dozen to one," he said. "Or three, once Rafe and Brytnoth got there."

"Not what I heard."

"It doesn't matter," Jared said. Something was going very wrong with the direction of this conversation, and all the hopes that had welled up inside him a moment ago were fading fast. "I've been in fights before. And it won't be the last time." He tilted his head. "Why would anyone bother you with reports about a street brawl with a bunch of drunks?"

"It isn't nonsense. Not when it comes from a source I trust."

"Who? You mean Childir?"

Arnauld sipped his drink, but his eyes never left Jared's face. "Perhaps."

Jared closed his hand into a fist and said nothing. He was starting to sense where this was going to end up, and he felt like a drowning man caught in a current.

Arnauld took another sip. "And now here you are, asking about the cache. Using Sahara, and the city I love, to get the information you want so that you can report it."

"Is that really what you think?" Jared asked. "My lord, you know me. You've known me since I was a boy. I have been rash…I have even disobeyed you. But I have never lied to you or tried to deceive you. Childir is poisoning you against me."

Now Arnauld's face became dangerous. "I would be very careful what you say next, Jared."

"He ordered that hit on me," Jared said. "And there are rumors about me all of a sudden—evil rumors. The kind of rumors that get a man killed in back alleys. Where did those come from, if not from him?"

"You think I haven't heard those rumors?"

Jared met Arnauld's gaze. "And you believe them?"

Arnauld set down his glass on the table and laced his fingers behind his back. "I always thought that if I'd had a son, I would have wanted him to be like you."

He stopped and returned to the window. But as he passed Jared, a strange odor hung in the air, like the ghost of a heavy, spicy perfume. It was the same fragrance that Jared and Brytnoth had smelled in Childir's chambers.

He's under Childir's enchantment.

"Then treat me as a father would," Jared said. "Don't take a stranger's word over that of your own son. You know I am no traitor, Arnauld. In your heart you know it!"

Arnauld opened his hands in a gesture of helplessness. "Consider what I can see," he said. "What information I have. Consider all of that and then tell me you look innocent."

Jared cast about him desperately, trying to think of how he could reach Arnauld's mind through the smoke of the enchantment. "If you thought I was a Drakkin spy, you would have had me arrested already," he said. "You brought me here instead. You told me about the weapons. Think, Arnauld!"

"You're very good. Very convincing. But the evidence damns you, Jared. This is for your own protection, as much as for ours," he said. "I hope you understand."

As if on cue, the door burst open and Kirin led his armed guards into the room. Before Jared could react, they had him down on his stomach on the ground. Kirin put his knee in the small of Jared's back and shackled his arms.

"Arnauld!" Jared shouted, desperation and anger flooding through him. "You son of a bitch...listen to me! I'm not the traitor!"

Arnauld glanced down at him. "It's so easy to accuse! But who can trust you?" He shifted his gaze to Kirin. "Get him out of my sight. And bring in the other two. They're probably in on whatever scheme he has going."

"Yes, my lord." Kirin motioned for the soldiers to remove Jared from the room.

"And Kirin?" Arnauld called as the door swung shut. "Send a message to Childir. Tell him he was right."

"No!" Jared shouted. "Arnauld, don't! Don't tell him—"

The door closed and the soldiers propelled him down the corridor.

"Keep your mouth shut if you know what's good for you," Kirin said.

Jared glared at him but obeyed.

The prison rooms, which lay underneath the Great House, were barely used. The occasional drunkard was thrown in a cell to sleep off his stupor, or sometimes the guards would lock up a couple of rowdy teenagers to cool their tempers. Jared and Rafe had spent a night down here themselves not too many years ago, after picking a fight with the night watch.

The spiral stairs turned like a corkscrew into the well of darkness. The soldiers ahead of him switched on flashlights and he watched the beams angle around the curve and disappear. As they rounded the column, Jared saw that they had flipped the breaker to turn on the lights in the cell bay. It was empty.

Kirin shuffled him into the first cell on the left and slammed the metal gate behind him.

"Sit here and rot," he said, bashing his fist against the gate.

Kirin turned away and motioned for the rest of the guards to follow him. They left Jared alone, and then, to add insult to the injury, they switched off the breaker. Darkness swallowed him, and for a moment, it was all Jared could do to keep from panicking.

He sat down carefully, his back against the wall. The chill of stone was all that connected him to his senses and the physical reality of his world. He focused on breathing. In. Out. In. Out.

Steady, measured, tactical breathing. But the thought that they would just leave him down here kept pushing its way to the surface of his mind. He wondered if they would bring Rafe and Brytnoth and lock them up too, and he almost looked forward to it—at least he would have some company.

He wondered how much Arnauld would tell Childir—or how much Childir already suspected about Jared's plans. Like Arnauld, Childir had known Jared since he was a boy. And being a seer meant that he was more perceptive than most. The chances that he'd be able to anticipate Jared's every move were high. Jared leaned his head on his knees.

"Damn," he said aloud, and the darkness swallowed the word.

FORTY-SIX

He had no idea how long he slept, but a rustling sound brought him suddenly back into consciousness. He sat up and strained his ears, trying to identify the sound.

Footsteps. A woman's footsteps.

He frowned and strained his eyes, staring in the direction of the door. Slowly, he saw a soft, flickering light appear from the direction of the stairwell. He got to his feet, waiting, hardly daring to breathe.

The light came closer, and then he saw who carried it.

"Aliya!" he gasped as she hurried forward. The candle shook and guttered a bit in her hand.

"Hush," she whispered. "Hush."

Jared stepped back as Aliya produced a skeleton key and slipped it into the lock. She pulled the door open carefully, wincing as it squeaked on the hinges.

"You shouldn't be here," Jared said as he slipped out the door. "Why are you doing this?"

"Arnauld is not in possession of his senses. I didn't have time to warn him...to tell him that I had long suspected that Childir was no ally of ours. When I went to him last night, Childir had already put him under the influence of some kind of mind control drug."

"Do you know the antidote?" Jared asked.

Aliya shook her head. "I'm working on it, but I can't exactly ask him for supplies as I used to do. For now, it is enough to do the right thing by you. I overheard what you said to Arnauld. Go and search the freighter. But you have to hurry. Childir will warn the Drakkin, and if they get there before you—"

"Childir will know you helped me," Jared said.

"I can take care of myself," she responded with a lift of her chin. "Sahara took my place as the blood offering—this is the least I can do to repay that debt."

"They're coming for Albadir. Make what preparations you can."

Aliya's jaw tightened and she laid a hand on his arm. "Rafe and Brytnoth are waiting at Wes's house for you. May the All-Powerful guide you, and give my love to Sahara when you find her." Sadness misted her eyes for a moment. "Goodbye, Jared."

Jared kissed her gently on the cheek and then bolted for the stairs. Behind him, he heard Aliya close the cell door once more and lock it. He slowed his pace as he neared the top of the stairs, but he could hear nothing more.

As he emerged from the stairwell, he saw two guards lay asleep in a heap beside the stairwell, an empty wine flagon in one of their hands. Aliya's handiwork, he knew.

He jogged across the stone floor and slipped into the shadows of the colonnade. When he was sure there was no one in sight, he edged out the door and into the night.

Jared ran down the path through the gardens, reasoning that it was the least likely to be patrolled. Sweet-smelling flowers and herbs, delicately manicured shrubbery, and smooth lawns had once surrounded the magnificent structure of the Great House, but these had long been untended and now grew in a mazy tangle. A stone bench hulked under an arbor dripping with flowers and vines, and a gate hanging half off its hinges led from the barest semblance of horti-cultural order into sheer chaos.

Jared kept close to the shadows, pausing every few steps to listen. But he saw and heard nothing but the lazy chirping of the night birds and the low hum of the insects that lived in the moist earth.

He quickened his pace and Wes's house soon came in sight. He could just make out two dim shadows loitering under the trees that hung close to the low structure. As he got closer, they left the cover of the building and came forward to meet him, and he recognized Rafe and Brytnoth.

Rafe clasped him at the wrist and slapped his shoulder. "Glad you made it," he said. "Wes has our supplies."

"Childir knows everything," Jared said. "We have no time to lose."

They entered the house. A single candle burned low on the table and Wes hovered over it like a moth, a mug of steaming tea in his wrinkled hands. Three packs leaned against the table leg, with two crossbows and a knife belt.

"Get her back, Jared," Wes said. "She's a special one, that girl."

Jared nodded and they shouldered their packs. Rafe handed Jared the knife.

"You might need this," he said. "We could only find two cross-bows. I'm sorry."

Jared clasped Rafe's shoulder in thanks and strapped the belt around his waist. He checked the blade and then slipped it back into the sheath. Rafe and Brytnoth both readied their crossbows.

"Thank you," Jared said to Wes. "Watch yourself."

Wes lifted a hand in farewell and the three of them slipped out again into the night. The moon had sunk below the horizon, and the shadows were deep and still.

"Did you pack a light?" Jared whispered to Rafe.

A cold light sliced through the shadows in front of them, and a new voice said, "What, you haven't learned yet to see in the dark yet, Jared?"

Jared watched in horror as the light grew steadily brighter. Slowly, it illuminated the harsh features of Childir's face. He looked almost wraith-like, and the rest of his body was concealed by a dark cloak. The light came from a strangely-shaped crystal, which was suspended inside a lantern that dangled from Childir's bony hand.

"A fine night for a journey," Childir said. "Although, I must admit to being surprised, as I thought Arnauld had you safely tucked away in a prison cell. I should have known the fool couldn't follow a simple directive."

"It must be maddening to realize that there are some things you can't control," Jared said. His hand strayed to the hilt of the knife and he closed his fingers around it.

"It's only a matter of time before we control everything."

"We?" echoed Brytnoth. "Glad to see you've finally dropped the pretense of being a holy man."

Childir ignored him. "Sahara will be sacrificed as is our due right. Once the Chrysalis is destroyed and Albadir is gone, there is nothing more that can stand in our way. We will find what we have been seeking. You cannot stop us."

Jared glanced at Rafe and Brytnoth. Childir gathered himself, and it was as if the shadows wound themselves around him. Soon the only thing they could see was the bright crystal and the ghostly lines of his face. But they heard him murmuring under his breath, and Jared knew that he was summoning the Drakkin.

"Stop him!" he shouted.

Jared drew his knife and threw it. At the same moment, he heard the sharp whistle as Rafe and Brytnoth fired their crossbows.

Childir's voice gurgled to a halt as the knife and the bolts went home. For one agonizing moment, he stared into Jared's eyes. Then toppled and fell. The lantern shattered and the crystal bounced away into the shadows, its light extinguished.

Jared ran to Childir's body and took a knee. Rafe and Brytnoth stood over him, crossbows loaded and ready. As Jared felt Childir's throat for a pulse, he gripped Jared's wrist so hard that Jared almost cried out. His eyes burned into Jared's.

"You will never escape the darkness," he burbled through the blood that welled in his mouth. "It is waiting for you—the Taken will fill the void."

Then his hand went limp and the light in his eyes went out. Jared got heavily to his feet.

"What the hell does that mean?" Rafe asked, slinging his crossbow over his shoulder. "What darkness?"

Jared shook his head, but the seer's words needled him. "The crazy words of a dying man," he said, trying to brush away the fear. "Let's go."

"What about the body?" Brytnoth asked. "Are we just going to leave it here?"

Wes came forward and gripped Brytnoth's shoulder. "I will see to it," he said. "It is best done quietly."

Jared clasped his hand. "I won't ever forget this," he said.

Wes winked at him and stepped back, and Jared swung away and led his friends toward the desert. Just before they reached the walls, Rafe produced the glasses and triangular cloths that would protect them from the howling sands. They tied the cloths around their faces and settled the glasses over their eyes, and then Jared gripped the wall and started to climb. The others followed him slowly, and Jared heard Brytnoth mumbling curses under his breath.

One last effort brought Jared to the top of the wall, and he swung his leg over and sat there for a moment to catch his breath. Rafe and Brytnoth clambered up beside him and Rafe leaned over just a little to look down. The sands whirled so violently that they couldn't see the bottom.

"You sure about this?" he asked, his voice slightly muffled by the cloth.

Jared said nothing and lifted his gaze toward the horizon line. Once before, weeks ago now, he'd known without any doubt the direction he needed to go.

He had that same feeling now. He gripped the wall and began his descent. As the storm caught him and the wind howled in his ears, he clung to that certainty. There was nothing now but to take the next step, and then the next. As he reached the bottom, he waited until Rafe and Brytnoth were beside him. And then, holding hands so that they would not lose each other in the blinding storm, they headed west.

FORTY-SEVEN

The sandstorm spent itself in its last gasps just before dawn. As the haze began to settle and the rosy, golden light grew steadily brighter, Jared, Rafe and Brytnoth removed their face cloths and glasses. Jared took a deep breath, coughing a little as the still dusty air tickled his lungs. Jared could just make out the last few constellations in the still-dark western sky.

He called a halt so that they could put away their night gear. Rafe took a long drink from his canteen and then offered it to Jared. The water was cold and washed the dust out of his mouth. He shook his head and watched the sand from his hair rain onto the ground.

"I can't even remember a time when dust storms didn't blot out the night sky," Jared said to Brytnoth, gesturing to the stars.

"I'd rather look at them from down here than be out there among them," he said.

They munched some dried fruit and dense nut bread, but Jared kept a watchful eye on the eastern sky. He felt a strange prickling on his skin and turned to scan the sands around them.

"What?" Rafe asked, alerting on Jared's movement. "You see something?"

Jared shook his head. "Just a feeling," he said. "Like we're being watched. Stay sharp."

They shouldered their packs again and Jared led them steadily westward. As the miles unraveled in the warm sunshine, the adrenaline that had fueled him since the encounter with Childir began to subside, and as it faded, exhaustion took its place.

He hadn't realized until now how deeply Childir's betrayal had wounded him. For so many years, he had looked on Childir as a father...and even though he knew now that everything about him had been a lie, it didn't change the suffocating guilt he felt over the sage's death.

With a sigh, Jared gave up trying to reason his way out of grief. He let it sit on his skin, to be burned away by the sun.

He slowed his pace a bit and let Rafe and Brytnoth catch up to him.

"Damn," Rafe panted. "Do you walk that fast all the time?"

"Only when I'm out here, I guess," Jared answered with a grin. "And when I've got a lot on my mind."

He looked at Brytnoth and then saw something move over his shoulder—a dark speck of something on the golden sands.

He stopped and pushed Brytnoth aside. He squinted against the brightness of the sand, but there was no doubt—a Drakkin scout was coming straight for them, mounted on a beast unlike any Jared had ever seen.

Pulling his friends flat against the sands, Jared drew his knife. When Rafe frowned a question at him, Jared pointed. Rafe and Brytnoth readied their crossbows, and they fanned out, keeping the lowest possible profile in the undulating sands.

As the scout got closer to them, Jared heard his vicious, guttural shouts and the sound of a whip striking flesh. The beast—something like a horse, but with scales instead of hair and a squatter body—had its ears pinned back against its meaty skull, and its red nostrils flared in obvious fear. Whatever it was, Jared reasoned, it hadn't been bred for the desert.

He watched as the scout, plying the spiked crop until the flanks of his mount were dripping a dark blood onto the sands, managed to get it to lumber into something like a gallop. It tolerated this pace only a moment, its hide shuddering. Just when it was almost on top of Rafe's position, he stood up right in its path and fired his crossbow. The bolt struck the rider squarely in the chest, and the beast reared away in terror and flung the scout from the saddle.

The scout scrambled to his feet, the dark blood staining the bright sand. With a sharp whiz, another bolt lodged itself in the scout's shoulder, this one from Brytnoth's bow. The scout wavered, stumbled forward a few steps, and then dropped to his knees.

Jared sprang forward and forced Rafe to lower his crossbow before he took the kill shot. "Wait!" he cried, turning back just in time to see Brytnoth taking aim. "Hold fire!"

Brytnoth stopped and Jared plowed through the sand to the scout's side. He seized him by the matted black hair and jerked his head up.

"Where is the freighter from Askalon?" he demanded.

The scout gurgled something like a curse and a laugh. Jared slammed the scout's face into his knee, breaking his nose.

"Where is it?"

The scout pointed back the way he had come, and Jared drew his knife and slit the scout's throat. He shoved the body over and then waved his friends forward.

They ran through the sand in the shimmering heat, following the tracks the scout and his fleeing beast had left behind.

FORTY-EIGHT

Sahara shifted her feet beneath the chair. The rusted shackles dragged on the plank floor. Her face throbbed where the guard had backhanded her, and she rotated her jaw slowly. The pain made her eyes water.

The squalid hut reeked of damp and rot, and the chair beneath her squeaked threateningly as she shifted her weight, as if the wrong motion would splinter it into kindling. Sahara could hear guttural voices outside the door, and she wished they would just get this over with.

"Hey!" she shouted. The voices stopped, and Sahara felt a rush of grim satisfaction. "Hey!"

The brute guard slammed open the door, jostling the crude clay pitcher of water and the mug on the table.

"Shut up, you," he growled. He crossed the room in a couple of strides, baring a jagged knife as he came. He pressed it against her cheek. "They says not to kill you. But they didn't says nothing about cutting your tongue out of your head."

She glared up at the guard. "If you defile their sacrifice," she said, "I won't be the one hacked to pieces and left to rot."

The guard's squinty eyes narrowed in his lizard-like face, and he withdrew the knife. "Then sees you shut up," he said.

"How about you take off the cuffs. I'm thirsty."

The guard considered her for a moment, then grunted. "Likely story," he said. "They says you stay shackled."

"Then give me some water."

She lifted her chin and stared the beast in the face. He grunted again and poured some water into the mug and held it to her lips. She pulled a large mouthful of water and then spit it straight into his face.

He squealed and dropped the mug. He swiped at his face like the water burned his scales. He snarled a series of curses at her and Sahara laughed. The guard struck her across the face with his gauntleted hand, leaving a nasty gash on her other cheek.

She tsked at him. "What will your masters say when they see the state I'm in?" she said. "Do you think they'll be pleased with your handiwork?"

The guard hissed in her face, then left her, slamming the door behind him once again. Sahara blew out her breath and sniffed. The taste of water had made her realize how ravenously hungry she was.

She closed her eyes and tried to ignore the trickle of blood that was now working its way beneath her chin and down her neck. She pulled against the wrist shackles. A stab of pain raced like fire up her forearms and she gave it up with a low moan of pain.

When Marsyas had put her through the Shift all those months ago, she'd thought the transformation would be immediate. She'd thought, so wrongly, that the Shift was a single event. But she realized now that the Shift had only been the beginning—that her transformation was far from over. Every suffering, every challenge, every obstacle...it was another moment of change. Even as she sat there in the hovel, listening to the pouring rain and feeling the blood run down her face, trying to ignore the gnawing in her stomach and the ache in her arms, she was becoming something new.

She knew they feared her, and the realization that she might not yet be fully what she was meant to be made her feel powerful, in spite of her present weakness.

Thank you for showing me this path, Marsyas. She bowed her head and closed her eyes. *Thank you for teaching me to endure.*

Through the fog of hunger and pain, something began to take shape in her mind—a massive freighter, shattered in the middle of the desert. Converging on it from every direction were Drakkin troops. She frowned and concentrated. She was drawn to this place, but she couldn't yet see why.

And then, as if across a crowded room, she heard snatches of conversation. And then, at last, she made out the voice that made her lodge in her throat.

"If they've already found that cache, this trip is all for nothing," Jared was saying. *"If Childir warned them...if they know we're coming..."*

His voice faded out and Sahara leaned forward, as far forward as her chains would allow, as if that would help.

"We need a Plan B," said another voice.

Rafe's, of course.

She strained to hear, but the voices were lost in a deep rumble and something that sounded like an explosion.

"What's Plan B?" she asked out loud. Her voice startled her, and she came back to herself. The squalid hut, the chains, and her ravenous hunger.

The door opened and a pack of guards entered the hut. The one she'd spat on carried a nasty looking pliable baton in his right hand.

"Time to go," he said.

Two of the guards moved behind Sahara and unfastened her chains. She rose stiffly, her muscles protesting. She didn't move fast enough and the guard slashed the crop across the back of her thighs. Sahara bit her lips against a cry of agony, trying to channel all the pain into a tight knot of vicious anger. She staggered forward toward the door with the guard on her heels.

The ground outside the hut squelched under her bare feet and cold muddy water pooled up between her toes. The sky was a deep green in the weak light just before dark. Rain drove down like it would never stop, and before she'd gone ten paces, Sahara was soaked to the skin. Every time she stumbled, the guard would lash her legs with his crop. She could feel the warm ooze of blood seeping through her wet pants.

Up ahead, lights flashed through the gloom, and soon the rough claxon that warned of a ship's impending departure reached her. The guards drove her up a steep flight of slick metal steps and then across the expanse of the platform.

One way or another, she thought, shaking the water out of her eyes, *this will end. This will all end.*

The guards hustled her up the ramp of a transport ship. It was exactly like the one that had crashed in the Silesian desert with her on board all those weeks ago, but this time, it seemed, Sahara was the only passenger. The guards shackled her to chains hanging from the ceiling and left her there.

"Hey!" she called after them. "Don't I get drugs or something?"

The one with the crop returned to her side with a barking laugh. "You want oblivion?" he asked.

Sahara saw his grip tighten on the crop and her stomach knotted. "That's not what I—"

"I'll give you oblivion."

He raised the crop and slammed it against the base of her skull. Sahara sagged in her chains and the guards' laughter was swallowed in darkness.

FORTY-NINE

They could see the ship's wreckage long before they reached it. The shattered hull of the ship stretched hundreds of feet in the air, angled crazily into the sand like a crooked fence post. It was still smoldering, and they could smell the acrid stench of the smoke.

They stopped on the crest of a dune and studied the approach. There were no other Drakkin scouts in sight, but he spotted the beast nosing around in the shadows beneath the hull.

Rafe pointed at the section of the ship that was half-buried in the sand. "Structural integrity is doubtful at best," he said. "And if there was a core breach, we can forget surviving this stunt."

"Brytnoth walked out of this," Jared said. "He'd be dead by now if there was a core breach."

"True," Brytnoth agreed. He was pale, even in the hot sun, and Jared could see that he wasn't happy at the thought of going back inside that corpse of a ship.

Jared gripped his arm. "You can stay here," he said. "I understand."

"Like hell I'm staying here," Brytnoth fired back. "You'll never find your way through there without me."

They half-slid down the slope and jogged across the sand to the entry point Jared had spotted from their vantage point. They stepped inside the wreckage and Brytnoth shouldered ahead of Jared to take the lead.

The corridor was partially caved in and drifted with sand, and the punctured hull let in shattered shafts of sunlight. Jared was relieved to see that there were no bodies.

Rate seemed to be thinking along the same lines, because he said, almost under his breath, "No bodies."

Brytnoth glanced at him over his shoulder. "This wing had been abandoned months ago," he said. "And anyway, we froze all the bodies of our dead in cryostorage...just in case we ever got somewhere where they could be buried."

He led them down the corridor until they reached the section where the hull had split in two. They stopped and Jared studied the almost vertical slope of the floor that stretched away above them. Even if they had climbing gear—which they didn't—it would have been difficult enough. Without it, it would be almost impossible.

"Are we going up there?" Rafe asked. "Please say no."

"No," Brytnoth said.

He turned to the left and they picked their way through the wiring and ductwork that had spilled into the corridor from the shattered hull.

"How did you ever find your way out of here?" Rafe asked after they emerged through a gateway of razor sharp metal. A shaft that led straight down under the sands and up into the levels above them opened before them. There was no sign of the elevator.

"Over here," Brytnoth said.

Everything about him was mechanical—his voice, his movements. It made Jared wonder if there was something terrible ahead of them, something that he needed to numb himself against.

They edged around the lip of the shaft until they reached four severed cables. Brytnoth grabbed one and then swung himself over the shaft. His feet scrabbled on the edge, but then he gained his footing and let the cable swing back toward them.

"Are you kidding?" Rafe asked.

Jared handed the cable to him and pointed. Rafe took it and, after a moment of deep breathing, he followed Brytnoth across the chasm and sent the cable back to Jared.

Suddenly, an explosion rocked the ship. There was a deep groan, as if the metal had shuddered to life. Jared lost his balance and grabbed for the cable. He swung out over the shaft as the corridor behind him erupted in fire.

"Jared!" Rafe shouted.

Jared desperately tried to swing his legs to get enough momentum to carry him to the other side. The heat from the fire shimmered the metal of the corridor and the elevator shaft around him. Flames licked out into the shaft from the levels below him.

"Jared!" Rafe shouted again. "Come on! You can make it!"

Jared groaned. The muscles in his shoulders felt like they were going to tear themselves apart. He swung his legs again, but then his hands slipped. He caught himself just before he plummeted into the inferno below, but the metal cable cut into his palms. His right hand lost its grip and he dangled by one arm from the end of the cable.

He heard Brytnoth and Rafe shouting at each other, but he couldn't understand what they were saying.

He gritted his teeth. He had to get a better grip on the cable or he would fall. He could feel his left hand beginning to weaken from the strain. He roared against the pain and swung his right arm to catch hold of the cable again. Slowly, he hauled himself hand-over-hand up the cable until he could grip with his legs too. He hung there, feeling the heat of the flames below him intensify. He started to sweat. The weight from his pack was dragging him down, so he shrugged it off and let it fall into the flames below. Even without the burden, his grip was slipping.

"I can't hold it!" he shouted to Rafe.

Brytnoth was nowhere in sight, but Rafe was almost jumping on the edge of the shaft in his eagerness. He dumped his own pack next to Brytnoth's on the floor of the corridor and pointed to Jared's left.

"The other cable! Grab the other—!"

Jared gritted his teeth and turned his head to look. A longer, thinner cable dangled just out of his reach. Brytnoth was back now, and he was wielding a long piece of broken pipe like a staff. The flames licked out into the shaft behind Jared and the cable he hung from grew hot enough to burn his hands. He reached for the other cable, but it was too far. Brytnoth lay down on the platform and tried to push the cable toward him with the pipe, but it was still just out of reach of his fingertips.

"I can't reach!" Jared cried.

"Jump!" Rafe shouted.

Another explosion rocked the ship, setting Jared's cable swinging crazily. With a loud metallic twang, several of its strands snapped and he dropped a few feet closer to the hungry flames below.

The blast shook Brytnoth off the side of the shaft. The pipe and their packs spun away into the flames below, but Rafe grabbed him by the wrist just in time. As Rafe hauled Brytnoth back up onto the platform, Jared tried once again to increase his swing, and this time, he was able to get close enough to touch the other cable. The last few strands snapped and he jumped.

He caught the second cable, but his weight dragged him down and the metal bit into his hands. He roared with pain but hung on as his momentum carried him close to the side of the shaft. He climbed up the cable until he was level with the platform where Rafe and Brytnoth lay, hands extended, shouting at him to jump.

"Move!" he yelled at them.

They scrambled back as he swung one more time and then launched himself toward the platform.

For one ecstatic moment, he thought he would make it. He slammed hard into the side of the shaft, desperately hanging onto the edge of the platform with his bloodied hands. Just before he slipped and fell, Rafe and Brytnoth grabbed his arms and hauled him to safety.

They collapsed in a heap in the corridor. Jared's entire body was shaking, and he weakly patted Rafe's shoulder and then Brytnoth's arm with his lacerated hand.

"Thanks," he rasped.

Rafe just grinned at him, but he was clearly too exhausted to come up with anything witty to say. He sat up and tore a few strips off his sweat-soaked shirt. He gestured for Jared to give him his hands, and Jared obeyed. Rafe bound them securely and tied the ends.

"We can't stay here," Brytnoth said, his voice hoarse. "Not safe."

With great effort, they helped each other up and then Brytnoth led them down the corridor. This side of the ship wasn't in flames yet, but the acrid, hazy smoke followed them. It soon filled the corridor. Rafe stumbled beside Jared, coughing and trying to breathe into his elbow.

"Almost there," Brytnoth croaked.

They staggered on, and after another few moments, Jared saw a set of heavy blast doors through the smoke. They were wedged open with a few small pieces of pipe and some metal paneling, creating a gap just wide enough for them to squeeze through.

Brytnoth went first, and the pile of debris shifted beneath his weight. The doors groaned as the mechanism slipped.

Jared swore under his breath, but followed Brytnoth through the gap. He reached a hand to Rafe.

"Come on!" he shouted.

The doors groaned again and the makeshift blockade slipped a bit further. The opening was almost too narrow now for him to fit.

"Rafe!" Jared shouted again. "Come on!"

Rafe squeezed himself through the gap and fell at Jared's feet. The pipes snapped and the doors slid together. Only a few inches of space remained. Rafe got to his feet, giving Jared a wobbly smile as he brushed himself off.

"That was close," he said.

"Brace it or we're trapped in here!" Brytnoth shouted from the other side of the flight deck.

For a moment, Brytnoth's words didn't register, and Jared and Rafe just stared at each other. Then Brytnoth tossed Jared a length of pipe.

"Brace the door!" he shouted again.

Jared and Rafe sprang into motion. Jared shoved the pipe through the gap in the doors and Rafe sprinted to a heavy supply crate near the flight console and dragged it over to him. Jared strained against the pipe, trying to pry the doors open enough for Rafe to wedge the crate between them. Slowly, his effort paid off and Rafe jammed the box into the opening. Jared let go of the pipe and swiped his forehead with his sleeve.

"Good thinking," he said to Rafe.

He sat down on the crate and leaned over his knees to catch his breath. Jared looked around at the flight deck. It was like nothing he'd ever seen before. He himself had never been off-world, but his father had once taken him on board one of the transport ships docked at the space port in the Great City. It was nothing as sophisticated as this. Large, clear sheets of glass, most of them cracked, rose up out of the long, sleek control console that occupied the middle of the flight deck. At least a dozen stations lined the perimeter, each with their own smaller console.

Brytnoth leaned on the central console, head bowed.

"I think I found something," he called. "Look at this."

Jared and Rafe joined him and Brytnoth handed Jared a cracked tablet. The screen was frozen and the battery was almost dead, but Jared could just make out the words.

"What is this? A shipping manifest?" he asked.

"Let me see," Rafe said. Jared handed it over and Rafe studied it for a moment. "What the hell is 'Demon's Breath'?"

"I don't know," Brytnoth said.

"Is that the cache we're looking for?" Jared asked. Then, as the acrid smoke trickled through the gap in the blast doors, he frowned. "Was it some kind of poison gas, maybe? Like a chemical weapon?"

"I said I don't know!"

"Why would a disabled ship need a cargo manifest anyway?" Jared asked.

Rafe shook his head. "It wasn't disabled," Rafe said. "It was supposed to come here. Look at the delivery point for the cargo."

He gave the tabled back to Jared and pointed. There, next to the "Demon's Breath" entry, was the cargo destination: Silesia Labor Camps.

"This ship was coming here on purpose!" Jared said, rounding on Brytnoth. "What the hell were your people bringing here?"

He slammed the tablet onto the console. It struggled to life, and a weak hologram projection opened in its center. It was the image of a man, dressed like the ship's captain.

"Albadir station," the hologram said, the voice heavy with static and unnaturally slow from the lack of power. "Albadir station, hailing on all frequencies. Do you read?"

Jared and Rafe exchanged glances. "We abandoned that station months ago," Rafe said.

"Albadir station, this is the E5-2120 cargo freighter *Ardexa*, do you read?"

Another heavy fuzz of static.

"We have lost main engines and stabilizers are failing. Setting impact course for the Drakkin fortress. We have a ...of the Demon's Breath drug...sure it doesn't fall into...hands."

The hologram wavered. "The Triumvirate...to recover...weapons cache...cargo bay 4. Do you copy? Find...before they..."

The hologram faded and the console went dark.

"So this Demon's Breath is a drug," Rafe said. "What's it for?"

"If the Drakkin want it for the labor camps, I'm sure it's not medicinal," Jared said.

"Who are the Triumvirate?" Rafe asked Brytnoth. "Are they after our weapons too?"

"I don't know," Brytnoth answered. "But the cache is in Cargo Bay 4. Let's get what we came here for and get out before we have company."

FIFTY

Jared, Rafe, and Brytnoth stood at the edge of a giant hole in the floor of the corridor and looked down. The metal edges were curled and charred from fire damage, and exposed wiring dangled in the darkness like entrails. The stairs leading to the cargo bay were on the other side of the hole, but from the looks of things, they'd been blasted to hell.

"It's down there?" Jared asked. When Brytnoth nodded, he said, "You sure?"

"You got a light?" Rafe asked.

Brytnoth rummaged in his pack and produced a light stick. He cracked it and then he let it drop. It fell for an agonizingly long time before it finally bounced on the bottom. Rafe whistled and Jared took a deep breath. He got down on his stomach on the edge.

"What are you doing?" Brytnoth cried as Jared prepared to lower himself over the edge. "That drop will kill you!"

"Nah," said Rafe. "Break his legs, probably. But not kill him."

"What the hell good is he with broken legs?" Brytnoth demanded. "This is insane!"

"You got a better idea?" Jared asked. "Like a rope?" He waved a hand at the exposed wires opposite his face. "Because I am not using those."

Brytnoth said nothing, so Jared lowered himself over the edge. The metal bit into his already-wounded hand and he gritted his teeth against the pain. Just before he let go, he spotted a piece of flex piping hanging from the underside of the floor.

"Got something here," he said.

He let go of the floor with his bad hand and reached for the pipe. He got hold of it with his fingertips and hauled it toward himself. As soon as he had his legs around it, he let go and swung into the darkness.

He shimmied down as quickly as he could and dropped the last few feet to the bottom. He picked up the light stick and waved to his friends. One at a time, they followed his example, and as soon as they were all safely on the bottom, Jared held the light stick aloft.

They were in a wide corridor that ran straight in both directions, with no turns in sight. A faint sweet-spicy smell, like the odor of incense, hung in the air.

"What is that smell?" Rafe asked. "Is something burning?"

"This way," Brytnoth said.

He turned to the left and they jogged down the passage. After a short time, the corridor opened out into a massive space. Huge crates stacked precariously on each other loomed above them, looking like they would topple at any moment.

"If we get another explosion..." Rafe said, pointing at one particularly wobbly tower.

"Let's split up," Jared said. He handed the light stick to Rafe as Brytnoth took two more out of his pack and lit them. "Signal with your light if you find something."

Rafe opened his mouth to argue, but stopped and lifted a hand, listening intently. He looked up at the hold they'd come through and then Jared heard it too.

Harsh, guttural voices, coming from somewhere above them.

"Hide the lights!" Jared commanded in a harsh whisper.

Brytnoth grabbed them and shoved them all back into his pack, but the light illuminated it from within. They darted behind the closest tower of crates and flattened themselves against it.

After a few agonizing moments, the voices stopped just on the other side of the crates.

"This is a waste," one said. "They're not coming."

"They are coming," the other snapped. "Brezhed saw their tracks in the sand. And the one with the Sight doesn't lie...even if it takes a bit to make it squawk."

Jared frowned. *He must mean Childir. They must not know he's dead.*

"If he's got the Sight, why didn't he just tell us where the cache is?" the other said. "Why we got to dig around in this stinking hellhole?"

"We have to take them out," Rafe whispered in Jared's ear. "Before they find those weapons."

Jared nodded. He inched along the crate and angled to look around it. The scouts stood just feet away, their backs to Jared. He could see that they were both heavily armed, and one held a flashlight.

"What a mess," said the first scout. "Probably nothing's here anyway. It's all just stories."

"They could use them to destroy the dragon."

"Lies," the first scout said.

"Then why are we here, then?"

"Stupid," the first scout said with a harsh laugh. "Don't you know anything about setting traps?"

Rafe nudged Jared, and in the semi-darkness, Jared saw the glint of Rafe's crossbow. But his mind was reeling and he didn't know what to do.

Arnauld had been so sure. His father had been sure. The weapons were real. They had to be real. If they weren't...

We're finished.

Rafe nudged him again, harder this time. Brytnoth had his own crossbow ready now, and Jared drew his combat knife.

If we're dead anyway, we might as well take a few of them with us.

He took a breath, flipped the grip on his knife, and jumped out of the shadows.

FIFTY-ONE

It was over in a matter of moments. Rafe's crossbow bolt dropped the first scout, and Jared jumped the other and slit his throat before he had the chance to cry out.

The flashlight clattered to the ground and Rafe picked it up. Brytnoth pulled the light sticks out of his pack again and Jared wiped the blade of his knife on the scout's sleeve.

"Nice work," Rafe said. "Did Sahara teach you that trick?"

"No," he said. "That one was all mine."

"The weapons are real," Brytnoth said, his face ghastly in the greenish glow of the light sticks. "They have to be."

"Then let's find them...and fast," Rafe said. "If two of them got down here, more will be on their way."

Jared grabbed one of the scouts by the legs and dragged him around behind the crates. Rafe and Brytnoth followed with the other body and then they all returned to the hole.

"I'll stand guard," Brytnoth offered. "Get those weapons and let's get the hell out of here."

He tossed Jared a light stick and Jared and Rafe split up and raced down opposite sides of the cargo bay. As Jared ran, he scanned the crates for anything that might give a sign of the contents. Some were tattooed with graffiti, and others had no markings at all. He fought down his growing panic and tried to trust that somehow, against all odds, they'd find what they were looking for.

He stopped suddenly and hid his light in his jacket. From somewhere close, he heard voices and the tramp of heavy boots.

More scouts.

For a moment, he was afraid they had killed Brytnoth and his blood iced in his veins. But then he realized that the voices were coming from somewhere ahead of him. That could mean only one thing.

There's another way to get down here.

He edged forward. Up ahead, he saw the flare of light coming from a narrow aisle between the crates. He peeked around the corner and saw five scouts gathered around a nondescript crate—one that was in worse condition than the rest. But Jared saw the mark on the side of the crate: the three-petaled *lilia-dir*.

That's it.

"Smash it!" said one of the scouts. "Smash it open! Destroy it!"

He produced a nasty looking whip and cracked it over the head of the scout standing closest to the doors of the crate.

Rafe appeared close beside Jared. "Guess it's not lies after all," he whispered. "So what's the plan?"

Jared hesitated. This room was a death trap. He looked back over his shoulder, and an idea flashed into his mind.

It's crazy. But it's exactly what Sahara would do.

He caught Rafe's arm and pulled him back toward the place they'd left Brytnoth.

"We can't go in there like this, or we'll never make it out," he whispered. "We need a disguise."

Rafe pulled back and stopped. "Oh, no. No, no. This is not a good idea."

"Yes, it is a good idea!"

"You are officially insane," Rafe said.

"Would you listen to me? We need those weapons, but we also need to find out where they're keeping Sahara. Do you know the way to that temple fortress?"

"No."

"I didn't think so. And neither do I. So this way, they'll lead us right to her." Jared waited expectantly, and Rafe finally dropped his head with an exaggerated sigh.

"Fine," he said. "But if I get killed, I will come back and haunt you forever."

Jared grinned and they ran quietly back to where Brytnoth guarded their way out. As Rafe vanished behind the crates where they'd hid the bodies of the scouts, Jared explained the plan to Brytnoth.

"Rafe and I are going with the troop of Drakkin that are raiding the weapons cache right now," he said. "They'll get the weapons for us and lead us right to Sahara."

"We only dropped two scouts," Brytnoth said. "What do you want me to do?"

"As soon as everything is clear, head back to Albadir. Tell Arnauld to prepare for an imminent attack."

"Jared," Brytnoth protested. "How are you going to get the weapons away from the Drakkin? Not to mention infiltrating that fortress...this is suicide."

"One thing at a time," Jared said. "I'll think of something."

Brytnoth gripped his arm suddenly and so tightly that Jared winced. "End this, Jared. For all our sakes."

Jared nodded and they clasped hands. "Stay hidden," he said. "Don't let them find you."

Brytnoth switched off the flashlight and glided away into the shadows. Jared crept behind the crates and helped Rafe strip the scouts' bodies. Then they left their own packs near the bodies and put on the armor. The helmet and faceplate smelled so foul that Jared almost couldn't breathe.

"There are no words for how much I hate you right now," Rafe mumbled as he secured his own faceplate. Jared heard the muffled sound of a gag.

"You okay in there?" he asked. He heard Rafe take a deep breath.

"Yeah. I just really hate you right now."

FIFTY-TWO

Jared and Rafe slipped silently into the space between the containers and stood behind two Drakkin soldiers. The hulk with the nasty looking whip was supervising the others, who were straining to pry open the doors of the crate.

"Pull harder, you *gushva malaika!*" the captain shouted and lashed one with his whip.

The troop redoubled their efforts, and with a mighty groan, the doors opened. A soft light seeped out of the container, running over the threshold to pool on the floor at their feet. The Drakkin soldiers skipped back with shouts of fear.

"Keep away from the light!" the captain cried.

As the light slowly spread across the stone floor, chaos erupted in the aisle. The captain blocked the exit and plied his whip on anyone who came near him, so the soldiers stampeded around the edges, crawling on and over each other like rats in a flooded hole.

Jared and Rafe were jostled by the frenzy and tried to stand their ground. Jared's heart was hammering in his chest. The light was coming closer, and he didn't know what would happen if it reached them. Whatever the Drakkin were afraid of, it wouldn't have the same effect on Jared and Rafe, and they would be discovered before they had the chance to do anything.

As he watched, barely breathing, the light reached a narrow crevice in the floor and ran into it like a tiny river of molten gold. All around the crates, the light flowed into channels, forming an intricate lacework until it emptied into the cargo bay through a wider channel that ran right between the captain's legs.

As they realized that they wouldn't be destroyed, the Drakkin shuffled away from the walls and waited for orders.

"Bring the engine!" called the captain.

He stepped carefully aside to avoid the liquid light, and three of the soldiers vanished into the corridor. Moments later, they returned. One carried a large device that resembled a blacksmith's tongs. The other two lugged a large, dark metal crate between the two of them.

Jared and Rafe slipped along the container so that they could see inside. They watched as the soldiers with the crate set it down near the open container and unfastened its clasps. It was inlaid with some kind of matte metal panels that looked almost like pillows.

Inside the container itself lay a large stone chest that looked almost like a sarcophagus. The light was seeping out from beneath the lid, and two of the Drakkin had the unfortunate job of leveraging it off. It hit the floor of the container with a crash, and a flash of light made them stagger back. The soldier with the tongs edged forward and lowered them into the sarcophagus.

The silence was palpable as the Drakkin watched the process of extraction. Arms shaking from exertion and fear, the soldier pulled out a long, straight sword with an ivory hilt and a curiously worked silver sheath. He deposited it in the crate, and instantly some of the light in the container lessened. He pulled the tongs back, panting with effort, and plunged them inside the sarcophagus again.

This time, he produced a bow and a quiver full of arrows. After dropping these in the crate, he fished out a long throwing spear.

Rafe nudged Jared and nodded toward the crate. Jared knew

what he was thinking. They had to keep track of that crate no matter what happened.

As soon as the spear was inside the crate, the soldiers slammed the lid, and the light vanished.

"Move out," said the captain.

Jared and Rafe, blind in the shadows, felt the press of bodies around them, and they were all but carried out into the cargo bay. As the crowd swept them along toward the other entrance point, Jared saw the light growing brighter. And then, above the noise of tramping feet, he heard the whine of a dropship's engines.

He was glad the faceplate hid his sudden smile. His plan was going to work...and the Drakkin had no idea what was coming.

FIFTY-THREE

Sahara sat on a low stone bench, shackled hand and foot to an iron post driven into the marble floor about two feet away. There was a fiercely cold wind gusting through the high window in the outer wall of her prison chamber, but they had given her no blanket. She huddled as best she could into her clothes, but they were tattered now and crusted with blood.

In spite of it all, she leaned her head back against the stone and smiled.

She had skated on the edge of death for a long time, but the promise of it hung around her now like the chains that shackled her wrists and ankles. Her entire life was now circumscribed by a circle four feet in diameter, but she had never felt so free.

Jared hadn't listened to her...but she was glad of it. Together, Sahara promised herself, they would bring down this evil for good.

If he makes it in time.

She closed her eyes, and a vision swam into her consciousness.

The dark guts of a troop ship. Guttural laughter and foul language. A gauntleted hand gripping a leather strap.

She frowned, tried to see the face, but a plate covered it like a death mask. And then she saw the eyes.

Silver edged with shadow, like the desert in early dawn.

Jared? She reached out to him with her mind. *What are you—?*

But the door to her cell slammed open, shattering the vision before he had the chance to speak to her.

Two guards cloaked and hooded in shades of black entered through the gaping maw of the doorway and approached her. One carried a bowl of some thin gruel, which he set on the floor on the far side of the iron post.

"Time to feed, human filth," he said.

Sahara drew her knees tighter against her chest. "You're going to regret this."

"Oh, that's right. We forgot. You think you're getting rescued," the other guard sneered.

Sahara tried not to react to this, but they erupted in jagged chuckles. That, almost more than the mockery, made her suddenly afraid.

"Look at her pathetic face. She thought we didn't know," the first figure said. "She thought we were blind. She doesn't know what we can see."

Sahara swallowed hard, her mind racing. "And you don't know what I can see."

That seemed to rattle them, and the second guard struck her hard across the face. She clenched her jaw against the pain. Her ears rang, but she shook it off and glared at him.

"Eat that with your gruel, maggot!" he said. "Let that teach you to ape prophecy!"

Sahara lifted a hand to her cheek, rattling her chains. Still laughing, the guards disappeared into the darkness, and the door closed with a bone-jarring bang behind them.

She closed her eyes and took a deep breath. She didn't know what they meant about seeing. Could they read her thoughts, like Jared could?

Jared, she said within her mind, reaching out to him through the shadows. *What's happening? Where are you?*

This time, as the vision swirled around her once again, Jared's eyes crinkled at her from behind the mask.

We were going to surprise you. We'll be there soon. Be ready.

Her heart hammered in her chest. *Ready? Ready for what?*

The end, Jared said, and the vision swirled and dissipated like mist in sunshine.

Sahara stared down at her chains. She twisted her hands experimentally, but the cuffs were too tight. She blew out her breath in frustration, and then her gaze fell on the bowl of gruel.

She shuffled off the bench and knelt in front of it.

"I hope this works," she mumbled. "Because I'm starving."

Carefully, she tipped the bowl until the gruel spilled over the side and ran over her hands.

FIFTY-FOUR

The troop ship rattled around them like it would shake itself apart. Jared's grip on the strap tightened until he could barely feel his fingers. Beside him, he saw Rafe seize the strap nearest him too. Rafe glanced at him and Jared could read murder in his eyes.

"Oh, there are no words for how much I really hate you right now," Rafe mumbled.

"I know," Jared replied. He winked at his friend and then turned to look out the narrow window. Below, the desert stretched like a lifeless sea until it crashed against the feet of the mountains.

The ship banked suddenly, and Jared lost sight of the mountains. A claxon sounded, and the lights in the bay shifted to a livid green. Jared glanced over his shoulder, where the chest squatted at the back of the cargo bay, strapped down. Two soldiers stood guard on either side.

He faced the front of the ship again, his mind racing. If he and Rafe could convince those guards that they were supposed to rotate shifts, they might have a chance to steal the weapons before the sacrifice.

And if we can't convince them, we'll just have to do it the old-fashioned way.

The ship slowed and began its descent. Jared watched sheer walls of rock rise outside the ship. The landing pad was well-concealed, and he knew now more than ever that they never would have found this place in time.

A jolt shuddered the ship, and then the roar of engines died. At the front of the cabin, the captain stepped into the aisle with his whip. He barked out a series of what must have been orders as he came down the aisle, but he spoke in the Drakkin tongue. When he reached the rear of the cabin, he slammed his hand on a button and opened the hatch.

Jared didn't dare look at Rafe, and he hoped his friend would just follow his lead.

They scrambled out into the main aisle and moved with the soldiers toward the open hatch. When they reached the captain, he suddenly blocked their way with his whip. Jared's blood iced in his veins.

We're finished. He knows.

But the captain yelled something at them in the guttural Drakkin tongue and gestured at the chest. Jared caught himself, for a moment not daring to believe their luck. His hesitation earned them both lashes from the captain's whip.

Under the threat of more stripes, Jared and Rafe hurried to the chest and started loosening the straps that held it down. The two guards who had been stationed with the chest moved away and jogged down the ramp. The captain yelled something else in their direction, and then he, too, vanished down the ramp.

"Is this a trap?" Rafe whispered, his voice hoarse. "Or is this just crazy stupid good luck?"

Jared stared at the empty ramp. No one returned, and even the livid green lights inside the cabin switched to a small strip of white lighting that seemed to mean that the ship had powered down.

"I think it's crazy stupid good luck," Jared whispered.

"Help me," Rafe instructed, pointing at the last strap.

Jared worked the clasp and they removed the final restraint. They knelt there for a moment in front of the closed chest.

"Do we steal the weapons now?" Rafe asked, almost breathless.

"Not yet," he said. "We don't know what we're walking into. If we take them now, we can't conceal them. The chest gives us an excuse to wander around a bit."

Rafe nodded and got to his feet. "Let's go, then," he said. "You take that end."

Together, they hefted the chest and headed for the ramp. It was far heavier than Jared had imagined, and he could feel the tendons in his shoulders stretching beyond their natural limits.

"I thought I hated you before," Rafe said as they slowly edged down the ramp. "But this is real now."

The landing pad was almost deserted. As they entered the hangar that led into the mountainside, Jared saw a few soldiers standing in a knot under a sickly-looking light. They paid no attention to Rafe and Jared.

"I don't like this," Jared said softly to Rafe as soon as they were out of earshot. "Something's not right. Why would they just leave us with the chest? Isn't it more valuable than that?"

Rafe didn't answer, and Jared could hear his strained breathing. Jared looked around the hangar for somewhere they could set down the chest and spotted a small room on the far side. He angled his steps toward it.

The door stood ajar, and the light outside the room wasn't working. Jared shouldered the door open and they staggered inside. As carefully as they could, they set the chest on the floor.

"Damn," Rafe said, rubbing his shoulders. "I can barely feel my arms. What the hell is this thing made of?"

Jared shook his head. "This seems as good a place as any to leave it," he said. "We'll come back for it later."

"If it's still here later," Rafe pointed out. "I say we steal the weapons now. This place is practically deserted. No one will see us."

Jared nodded. "Okay. Open it up, Rafe."

Rafe undid the clasps and slowly lifted the lid. The weapons still shone with a muted glow, but when Rafe lifted out the spear, the glow faded and it became just an ordinary spear. He leaned the spear against the wall and took the bow and arrows. Jared reached in and took the sword.

For a long moment, he held it lengthwise across his hands. Then he leaned it against the chest and took off his cloak.

"Hide them under your clothes," he said. He strapped the sword over his shoulder and put the cloak on again, drawing the hood up over his head. Rafe followed suit with the bow and arrows. Once he had on his cloak, he kept the spear close to his side and drew the cloak tightly around him.

Jared closed the chest and fastened the clasps to make it look like it had never been opened.

"Let's find Sahara and kill us a dragon," he said.

FIFTY-FIVE

"Where is your savior now?"

Sahara looked up at the two guards. She held her chains in her hands between her thighs, and they didn't seem to have noticed that they were no longer binding her.

For a moment, she contemplated what it would take to snap their necks, but she decided it was too much of a risk.

"Go to hell," she said instead.

They laughed and one stepped closer to her. Sahara stiffened—hoping he wouldn't discover that she had escaped her chains.

It's going to be all right.

Her eyes flew open, and for a moment her heart lodged in her throat.

Jared!

Suddenly, the guard in front of her went rigid. Sahara watched the bright tip of a sword emerge from its chest, and then withdraw. The guard fell dead at her feet, only to reveal another guard standing just behind him, a long straight sword in his gauntleted hand.

Across the room, the other guard lay dead, an arrow protruding from its back. He too had been replaced by a guard with a bow.

Sahara jumped to her feet, and the chains clattered to the ground. She readied herself to fight. The sword she could handle...but avoiding the archer would be a challenge.

"Stop toying with me!" she shouted. "If you want to kill me, just do it!"

"Be quiet!" the guard with the sword said. "You want to bring the whole place down on us?"

Sahara caught herself and stared hard at the guard's face. His eyes, obsidian now, crinkled at her in a smile.

"Jared," she said, too stunned to move and almost too surprised to speak. Her gaze shifted to the other guard. "And—?"

"Rafe, of course," said the other guard, sweeping her a gallant bow.

"Why don't you ever listen to me?" Sahara asked, turning back to Jared. She took a few steps toward him, then stopped.

"I like surprising you," Jared said, a smile in his voice. He looked at the chains at Sahara's feet, then at her red and scraped wrists, and finally up into her face. "What did you do that for?" he asked. "We need them to march you out there!"

Sahara scowled at him. "You mean I have to put those back on? Do you know what I had to do to get them off? I used my dinner!"

Jared gestured with the sword. "Well, you have to put them back on."

"What kind of plan is this? Let's just get the hell out of here!"

"It's the kind of plan where we kill a dragon," Jared said. "This ends tonight."

"What are you going to do about them?" she gestured at the corpses of the guards. "I can put the chains back on, but you can't bring them back to life."

"Damn," Jared said. "I didn't think of that."

Sahara used what little was left of the gruel to help force her hands back into the manacles. Her left hand slid into the cuff easily enough, but her right got stuck. She winced in pain and pushed, but her hand wouldn't go through.

"Just a minute," Rafe said and disappeared out the door.

"Where's he going?" Jared said in exasperation. He saw Sahara struggling with her cuff and knelt down in front of her. He set the sword aside and took her hand in his. "Let me help," he said.

Sahara took a deep breath and released it in a slow hiss as he dragged on her hand. She couldn't help a cry of pain as the cuff finally slid over her wrist.

"I'm sorry," Jared said gently.

He touched her cheek with his hand as she sucked in a shaking breath. Her hand was chafed and bleeding, and it throbbed like something had broken. She lifted her eyes to his, and he removed the faceplate. Sahara couldn't help smiling at him, and then, so suddenly that it took her breath away, he leaned in and captured her mouth in a kiss.

Behind them, Rafe cleared his throat. Jared pulled away from Sahara and got to his feet. She managed another smile, though every vein in her body now felt like it was running with fire instead of blood.

"There's another cell across the corridor," Rafe said. "Let's hide the bodies in there."

Jared reattached his face plate and he and Rafe dragged the dead guards out of Sahara's cell. When they returned, it was only to say goodbye.

"We can't stay," Jared said. "Let them take you out to the pillar and we'll be waiting. Don't worry."

"Why would I worry?" Sahara said. "It's only a dragon."

Jared saluted her, and then he and Rafe left her alone, closing the door with a sharp clang behind them.

Sahara stared after them for a long moment, still feeling that kiss on her lips. Then she drew in a deep breath and exhaled. It was almost certain that none of them would survive the night, but she was glad of the company at the end.

The light outside her sliver of a window had faded completely to black when there was a noise at the door again.

No guards came to taunt her this time. Instead, a monstrous figure, twice the size of a normal Drakkin soldier, ducked through the door and stood in front of her. She sat up straighter.

You will not show fear.

She repeated Marsyas's words to herself over and over again, but it wasn't doing any good.

He flexed his massive razor-sharp claws.

"It is time," it said. Its voice was so deep that it seemed to shiver mortar from between the stones. He snapped a chain onto the collar around her neck. "Are you prepared for death?"

She lifted her eyes to stare him down. "Are you?"

FIFTY-SIX

Sahara walked slowly down the corridor, her chains dragging behind her. The creature held the chain that connected to the collar around her neck, and if she lagged too far behind, he gave it a vicious jerk that made her stumble.

They're waiting for me.

As her faith in her friends started to ebb her fear, she looked at the creature with a more critical eye. Everything had a weakness. She could find it.

"You think I can be taken," the creature said without turning around. "You look for my vulnerabilities."

Sahara startled so violently that her chains rattled. Could this creature read her thoughts? Did that mean he knew—

"How well we know," he said. "How well we know how you think. And even who you see when you speak within your mind." He swung his massive head around to look at her. "You do not know what you are becoming. But we know. How well we know."

Sahara swallowed hard, feeling the metal collar jump as her throat moved. She tried to stop herself from shaking, but the awful cold certainty of it iced her blood. It was over. They knew every-thing...and she had betrayed her friends.

Again.

"How can you know that?" she whispered. "You can't possibly know—"

"The void must be filled," he said. "A life for a life. A mind for a mind."

"I don't understand. What does that mean?"

The creature grinned at her over his shoulder. "Soon enough, Chrysalis, you will understand. It will not be long now."

"Your threats don't scare me," she said, hating that her voice made her a liar.

"It is not a threat. It is a promise." The creature hauled on the chain and drew her face close to his own. "Where will you run? If you escape, pretty one, where do you think you will run?"

The creature's foul breath drifted over her, and when he ran his tongue over his cracked lips, she wanted to vomit.

"Whatever you're going to do," she gritted, summoning every shred of courage she had left, "just do it."

The creature laughed a thunderous laugh and resumed his pace.

"All in perfect time," he said.

Sahara staggered behind him on buckling legs. She tried to tell herself that it was impossible. There was no way they could read her thoughts, or Jared's...or hear their conversations. How could that be possible?

But possible or not, she didn't dare try to warn Jared for fear that they would hear her.

They rounded a corner and the corridor changed. The dark stone walls were covered with hideous reliefs of sacrifice and transforma-tion. Shadowed wings and fire, the pillar and chains, and a river like blood running through steep cliffs. Sahara shivered.

"You think you understand us," the creature said. "You think the solution is so simple."

"You know what I think?" Sahara snapped. "I think you talk too damn much."

The creature's hideous laugh almost seemed to bring the images alive around her. "Your ignorance will be your undoing," it said. "We will take you, and what follows then?"

"You might find I'm hard to digest," Sahara said.

The creature turned and dragged her forward again. "We have devoured stronger ones than you," he said. "Like your father."

Sahara stiffened and fought helplessly against a floodtide of tears. They burned as they trickled down her bruised and lacerated face. As she swallowed the words she desperately wanted to say, the creature's lips curled back in a smile.

"It is too late for you," he said. "But it is perhaps not too late for the others."

"What others?" The question was out before she could stop herself. She tried to step back, but the creature pulled her closer still.

"The ones you think will save you." The creature's eyes bored into her, and she felt as though they could see through to her very soul.

"You care deeply about them," he said after a long silence. "For one in particular. Warn him. Tell him it is not too late for him. Go ahead. Call to him."

Sahara stood rigidly, feeling its breath on her face. She knew that if she reached out to Jared, they would find him. They would know where he was.

"No," Sahara said with a lift of her chin.

The creature gripped her shoulder, his claws piercing deep into her muscles. She cried out as he forced her onto her hands and knees. Then he dragged his claws out of her shoulder and seized her chin. The razor tips dug into her skin.

"Call to him," he said.

"Call to him yourself," she fired back. "If you can read our minds, you do it."

The creature withdrew his claws and slammed his hand across her face. "You will call to him before the end."

Sahara bowed her head to the ground. She felt dazed and sick, but the creature hauled her to her feet again and dragged her down the corridor.

Just ahead, she could vaguely see a long, shadowed chamber. The far wall on the cliff edge was missing, and the hulking shapes of mountains glowed red in the light of the setting sun.

As they crossed the threshold of the sacrificial chamber, Sahara saw a dark pillar rising out of the floor like a dire warning. Maybe it was the strange play of the sunset and shadows, but it looked like it was covered with blood.

The creature hauled Sahara to a small bench and fastened her chains to metal rings in the stone wall behind her.

"Prepare yourself," he said.

He lumbered away, leaving Sahara alone with the pillar of sacrifice and the bloody sunset.

FIFTY-SEVEN

Jared and Rafe crouched behind a low tumble of rock on the cliff edge, some fifty paces from the obsidian pillars of the sacrificial temple. The wind whipped around them, moaning through the crags like some undead thing.

"I don't like it," Rafe said. "Something doesn't smell right."

"You sure it's not just your faceplate?" Jared asked.

Rafe gave him a long-suffering look. "I'm sure."

Jared pulled off his own faceplate and rubbed his hand briskly over his face, as if he could wipe away the filth and stench he'd been breathing for hours.

"What are you doing?" Rafe asked.

"I need to breathe," Jared said. He stared across the cliff edge at the pillar.

"Do you think she's in there?" Rafe asked after a moment's silence.

"I don't know."

"Can you ask her?"

Jared hesitated for a moment, then decided there was no harm. He closed his eyes.

Sahara, he said, reaching out to her with his mind.

Slowly, the darkness in his mind yielded, and he could see the inner sanctum of the temple. Four torches, two on either side, shed their dancing light over the horrific murals of sacrifice and death that covered the walls. Dark and bloody forms crowded one upon another in a macabre dance, and weaving in and out of the haphazard mass crept the sinewy form of the dragon.

A long, low bench sat against the far wall, and there, huddled in the shadows, was Sahara. Suddenly, she lifted her face, and there was such horror in her eyes that it terrified him.

What's wrong? he asked.

No! she screamed, and flung up her hands as if to ward him off.

The force of her voice sent a searing pain through his head and he crumpled against the rock, the vision shattering within him.

For a moment, it was all he could do to keep himself conscious. Vaguely, he heard Rafe's voice, sounding like it came from very far away.

"Jared? Jared!"

There was something wrong. Something in his voice...

Jared dragged himself upright and opened his eyes.

A troop of Drakkin soldiers stood behind them, weapons raised. Jared recognized the captain as the leader of the troop that had confiscated the weapons cache on Brytnoth's ship. The captain's toothy grin was almost a snarl. Rafe raised his hands as he glanced at Jared.

"Please tell me you have a plan to get us out of this," he said.

"Get up," the captain barked.

Jared and Rafe got to their feet, and Jared took a quick head count. There were ten of them. While he didn't much like their odds, they might have a chance. He turned to Rafe, eyebrows lifted. Rafe's shoulders sagged just a bit.

"Oh, seriously?" Rafe said. "You really think that's a good idea?"

"Shut up," snapped the captain. "You're under arrest."

He reached out to grab Jared, but Jared ducked, drew his sword, and sent the captain's arm spinning into the abyss.

The captain roared in agony and fell to his knees. As the troops sprang forward to help him, Jared lopped the captain's head from his shoulders. His body toppled sideways and rolled slowly toward the brink. The Drakkin soldiers watched it disappear over the edge, and then they turned to Jared and Rafe with ferocious snarls.

Jared readied his sword and Rafe nocked an arrow.

"Who's next?" Jared said.

FIFTY-EIGHT

Sahara heard them coming before she saw them. The entire room seemed to shake under the slow, heavy tread—the tread of the executioner. Now that they had discovered where Jared and Rafe were, Sahara felt the chill of death closing around her heart. Keeping their location a secret had been their only chance of getting out of this alive. There was no way out for them now.

The footsteps stopped and she raised her head. It took so much energy. The monster had returned, and she wished they would just hurry up and put her out of this misery.

"Chrysalis," he said. "It is time."

Sahara held out her wrists. "I thought you'd never get here."

"Where is your knife now, Chrysalis?" he sneered. "And the ones you thought you would save—where are they? Do you know?" It gripped her chin in his claws. "Their halls are destroyed and they are starbound. They have you to thank for their desolation."

Sahara's throat tightened with tears but she choked them back. Even still, the executioner hissed in satisfaction and its slitted eyes closed, as if her pain brought it an ecstasy of pleasure.

"You feel it now," he said. "The burn of failure. The wells of grief. You know now that you will die for nothing. So much for your sacrifice."

He wrenched his hand away, slicing Sahara's chin with his claws. She closed her eyes. She had made so many promises...to her brother, that she would save him; to her father, that she would fight; to Marsyas, that she would never give up as long as she had breath.

And then, as if she heard Marsyas's voice in her head, the words came. *Use the Sight.*

Tears slid down her cheeks and she shook her head mutely.

Use the Sight.

She exhaled, long and slow.

And then she reached out into the shadows.

Everything around her became clear—and the creature in all his naked fear stood before her, all its vulnerabilities laid bare.

She opened her eyes and stared straight into the creature's eyes. He drew back as if he were suddenly uncertain, as if he could sense that she was no longer weak.

"Like I said," she said, "you talk too damn much."

The creature snarled at her and unfastened the chains from the rings in the wall. As he gathered them in his hands, she saw her chance.

She dove between its legs, jerking the chains through after her as hard as she could. The creature staggered, off-balance, as she rolled to her knees and gave a mighty pull. The creature collapsed in a heap and writhed to free himself from the net of chains.

Sahara vaulted onto his back and threw the chains around his neck. She dragged back as hard as she could. A grating, gurgling noise erupted from his throat, and his thrashing became desperate and erratic. Sahara clung tighter to the chains to save herself from being flung off his back and smashed to pieces. With a roar, she pulled harder.

Clawing at the chains around his neck, the creature reared suddenly and staggered madly for the cliff edge.

As they neared the pillar, three things seemed to happen all at once.

Screams of dying Drakkin mingled with the whiz of arrows and the clang of a sword against metal somewhere nearby.

Over the executioner's gurgling and the battle sounds, she heard a whooshing noise that echoed in the abyss and the cliffs that rose all around them.

And then, as the creature stumbled into a run and charged for the edge of the cliff, Sahara's blood froze in a rush of horror. She stared at the cuffs around her wrists, the chains she held in her hands.

Her hands were too swollen to pull them free.

FIFTY-NINE

THE CREATURE GALLOPED TOWARD THE EDGE OF THE CLIFF.
Sahara pulled at her hands, trying to slip them out of the cuffs that
held her wrists. They wouldn't budge, so she tried again to strangle
the creature and stop his mad rush before he killed them both.

Vaguely, she heard someone shouting. It sounded like Jared.

The zip and whine of an arrow made her duck, but the arrow
struck the creature in the side, just inches from her thigh. The creature's gurgling roar intensified, and he swung around to face the
direction of the bowshot. Crazed with blood rage, he charged.

She saw Rafe's stunned face, and she shouted at him to get clear.
She leaned back, twisting the chains and trying to tighten the noose.
He reached back and his claws raked across her back and arms. She
cried out in pain, but didn't loosen her grip.

Just before the creature barreled into Rafe, Jared jumped into his
path. She saw the flash of a bright blade in the blood-red light of the
sunset, and then the creature skewered itself.

Sahara slid sideways as the blade pushed through the scales on
the creature's back, dark with blood. Then Jared pulled it free, and
the creature groaned.

Slowly, he tilted sideways. Sahara realized her weight was pulling him over. He staggered one step, then two. She was dangling over the edge of the cliff when Jared and Rafe jumped forward and grabbed hold of the chains.

"Pull!" Jared shouted.

With a crash, the creature's lifeless body fell to the ground at the edge of the cliff. Sahara tumbled over his back and landed in a tangle of bloody chains.

For a moment, she lay there, staring up at the sky, not sure what exactly had happened, and not even convinced she wasn't dead. But then Rafe and Jared leaned over her, both battered and grimed with blood and dust but very much alive, and she sucked in a ragged breath.

Rafe grinned like a wild man. "Damn!" he said. "That was close!"

Jared knelt beside Sahara and helped her to sit up. Then he untangled the chains as best he could.

"Why did you call to me?" she asked, her voice thin and wobbly. "They know. They can hear us somehow." As he tilted her face to look at the cuts on her chin, she said, "And what took you so long?"

A warm, wide smile replaced Jared's look of concern. "Sorry," he said. "We were—delayed." He nodded his head in the direction of a tumble of rock and Sahara turned to look.

Several dead Drakkin soldiers had arrows protruding from various parts of their bodies, and the rest were a mess of severed limbs and heads. She shuddered.

Suddenly, the vague whooshing sound grew louder and they ducked, as if they expected something to spring on them.

"Take cover!" Jared shouted at Rafe.

Rafe sprang away from them, vaulted over several bodies, and dove behind the cairn. Sahara turned to Jared and held up her shackled wrists helplessly. He took her hands in his, staring at the cuffs for a breathless moment. Then he sprang up and raced for the cairn.

"Don't move!" he called over his shoulder.

"Like I'm going anywhere," she mumbled.

He disappeared behind the rock, and it was like he'd vanished from the universe. Tears of helpless frustration ran down her cheeks as she braced her feet against the dead creature and dragged against the cuffs.

It hurt so much. She choked down a sob as she tried again and again to free herself.

It was no use.

Suddenly, the deep-throated clang of a gong shredded the night air and shook the stone beneath her. It kept ringing, the vibrations building until the rocks danced beneath her. She tried to cover her ears, but then a wailing shriek rose above the noise of the gong and she turned to look back at the sacrificial chamber.

Dozens of cloaked figures slowly filled it, revolving around one another in a fluid death-dance. At every stroke of the gong, the shapes shivered into each other and then pulled apart again. Over and over again, they melted into each other and separated, but each time, the spaces between them grew smaller. At the final stroke of the gong, they trembled together and formed an amorphous shape like a mess of tar.

It writhed in upon itself, forming a shape like a giant, dark egg. And then, as the echoes of the gong continued to shake the mountainside, the surface split open.

Long, dark claws protruded from it, shining like shards of black glass. It shredded its outer skin in a bloody and violent birth, and Sahara watched a pair of leathery wings unfold from the sinuous body. And then it raised its heavy head and opened its eyes.

They were dark as snake's eyes and flat as discs. Sahara cowered behind the corpse of the executioner. Her entire body buzzed with fear, and she desperately tried to pull steadiness from the words that had gotten her through so many struggles.

But nothing could beat back the terror she felt when she thought those eyes would find her.

The dragon vaulted itself high above the cliff with a single thrust of its wings. Its scream caused a small avalanche behind her and the stone beneath her crumbled. She clawed her way to the other side of the executioner's body just before she was carried down with it. The whole time, she kept her eyes on the dragon high above her.

She saw it circle once, a ghastly blot against the red light of the sunset. Then it folded its wings and plunged toward the cliff.

It landed in front of the sacrificial pillar. Gurgling deep in its chest, it swung its head from side to side, as if it were searching for something. Its eyes, those horrible, terrible eyes, narrowed to slits. The glow of fire smoldering like coals rippled beneath its scales.

She barely dared to breathe. It must not find her. She shrank against the corpse as it took two giant, lumbering steps away from her.

Jared slipped to her side and hunkered down beside her.

"It's looking for me," she whispered, her voice catching on panic.

Jared pushed a spear shaft into her hands. She stared at it numbly and then looked up into his eyes.

"I can't," she whispered hoarsely.

He cupped her cheek in his hand. "Yes, you can." Then he drew the sword and readied himself.

"No!" she begged, almost inaudibly. "Don't...please..."

She seized his arm and the chains clattered together. The noise drew the dragon's attention. It reared and spun to face their position, and then it riveted on the executioner's body. With a gurgling roar, it slithered toward them.

Jared gripped Sahara's hand that held the spear and held her gaze. She couldn't look away, and she put her other hand over his.

"Do you trust me?" he asked.

She nodded mutely. Out of the corner of her eye, she saw the dragon rear its head. The flames that burned within its core swirled and gathered themselves. Her whole body shook so violently that she could barely hold the spear.

"I love you," he said.

Then he swung away from her to face the dragon.

SIXTY

Jared left Sahara and ran straight for the dragon. He didn't quite know what he was doing, but he didn't stop to think about it.

The dragon's gurgling was like a bellows, and it reared back and opened its massive jaws. Liquid fire dripped between its teeth and sizzled on the rock.

Jared heard the high whine of an arrow. It slammed into the dragon's scaly chest, and at first it seemed to vanish in the heat of its innards. But then the dragon's gurgling became an anguished scream. As Jared watched, a crack of light spread from the arrow wound, blistering the scales around it.

Another arrow found its mark, but now the dragon spun to face Rafe's position. It belched out a torrent of flames, scorching the cairn until it shimmered in the heat.

"Sahara!" Jared shouted over his shoulder. "Now!"

She scrambled up on top of the executioner's corpse and hefted the spear in her right hand. The chains hung around her like bloody garlands. As she readied the spear, he could feel her strength like a tide of light. With a guttural shout, she drew back and let the spear fly.

In spite of the chains that hampered her cast, her aim was true. The spear caught the dragon in the chest, and another, larger crack of light splintered the scales. The dragon's roar shook the mountainside. As the ground shook beneath them, Sahara lost her balance and fell off the corpse. Stones from the crags above tumbled down onto the cliffside. He saw Sahara curl herself into a ball, hands covering her head, as a shower of stones rattled down around her.

It was bringing the mountain down.

But then, like light breaking through the clouds, he saw it.

He could hardly breathe as the entire pattern of the dragon's scales, with all its weaknesses, unveiled itself in his mind.

Do you see? It was Sahara's voice, taut with effort. *Tell me you can see it.*

I see it.

Jared gripped the sword and sprang forward toward the dragon. The three cracks of light splintered across the dragon's chest and met in the center. Jared knew that was his target.

As he got close, the heat from the dragon's belly was like a furnace blast. Jared felt his skin prickling as if he were being singed. It lashed out at him with its claws and then tried to extinguish him with a blast of fire from its jaws. Jared dodged behind a rock just in time, but the heat took his breath away and nearly knocked him senseless.

As soon as he saw the dragon gather itself for another blast, he sprang from behind the cover of the stones and drove the sword up and into the ever-widening gap of light in the center of the dragon's chest.

It screamed in agony and the whole mountain shook again. The force of the quake knocked Jared off his feet and brought down another avalanche of stones and larger boulders. They bounced around him and he rolled just in time to avoid being flattened by a massive boulder. He scrambled away from the dying dragon on hands and knees.

He made it behind the cover of the executioner's corpse and gathered Sahara close in his arms. Huddled together, they watched as spurts of flame and gore erupted from the dragon's open mouth. Its scales contracted and pulsed with the final beats of its heart.

Then the light from the sword shattered the scales, and the dragon's body burst asunder. Liquid flame ran like blood on the stones, and for one awful moment, the two halves of its body balanced on the edge of the abyss.

The mountain trembled again and shivered the remains of the dragon into the darkness below.

SIXTY-ONE

For a long moment, Jared held Sahara's shaking body close and they stared up at the sky. The clouds of smoke and steam that had gathered over the cliff slowly dissipated, and the shadows gave way to the twinkling of a thousand thousand stars. Sahara huddled into him as if she couldn't get close enough to escape the horrors she had seen, and he wrapped her more tightly in his arms.

Then, suddenly, Rafe staggered over and dropped down next to them. Sahara sat up and threw her arms, chains and all, around his neck. He looked a bit singed, and when he shook his head, small tufts of hair drifted down into his lap.

"You made it," Jared said.gripping his friend's hand tightly.

Rafe stuck his finger in his ear and wiggled it. "What?" he said. "My ears are still ringing."

Sahara released him and Jared pulled her close again. She leaned her head against his chest and he kissed her forehead.

"It's done," he said. "It's over."

"Is it?" she whispered. She drew back just a little to look up into his face, but it was almost as if her eyes didn't see him. "It's so dark...it still feels so dark..."

"Let's go home," Jared said.

"I don't suppose we have the key for those, do we?" asked Rafe, gesturing to the manacles around Sahara's wrists.

"No," Jared said. "But maybe it does."

He motioned Sahara and Rafe aside and then rolled the corpse onto its back. Sahara shuddered at the sight of the face, bulbous from asphyxiation. Quickly, Jared searched the body and soon produced a ring of iron keys. One of them fitted the manacles, and as soon as they fell away, Sahara rubbed her sore wrists. Jared freed her ankles and then removed the collar around her neck.

"There," he said, caressing the bruises on her neck. "Better?"

She nodded, and heaved a shuddering sigh. "How do we get home?" She stared at the corpse, and then added, "He said...he said they were all dead."

"Who's dead?" Rafe asked.

"Albadir," she said, raising her eyes to his.

"Lying bastard," Rafe said. "Let's get that dropship and get out of here, Jared."

Sahara looked between them. "Can you fly?" she asked.

Rafe shrugged. "Guess we'll find out, won't we?"

Between them, they helped Sahara to her feet. Jared felt her weight sag in his arms.

"Can you walk?" he asked her. He watched her mull her answer, but before she could lie to him like she'd done the first time they'd met, he nodded to Rafe. "Let's carry her. We'll take turns."

The mountain shook again. They heard a rumble that quickly became a roar, and they looked up to see an avalanche of stones sliding down the mountainside. Jared gathered Sahara in his arms and they ran for the shelter of the sacrificial chamber. As they made it past the pillar, the cliff crumbled and crashed into the abyss.

"Damn," Rafe said. "That was way too close."

They didn't linger in the chamber. Rafe led them as quickly as they could go down the corridor. They'd wound their way far into the fortress when they reached an intersection in the corridor and Rafe stopped.

"I've got a really bad feeling about this," he said. "Like we could be ambushed at any moment. And now we have no weapons."

"Where do we go from here?" Rafe asked.

Sahara closed her eyes, and her face was lined with anguish. Her breaths were shaky, but steady.

"That way leads to the cell block," Sahara said, pointing to the left.

"Then it's the other way," Jared said. "I'll take the lead."

"I can walk now, I think," she said faintly. She hobbled a few steps and then stopped. "With help, I mean."

Rafe draped her arm over his shoulders and winked at her. As soon as they were ready, Jared led them down the corridor in the direction of the hangar.

The hallway grew steadily darker the further they got from the central fortress, and Jared felt a growing uneasiness. The air was oppressive and stale. And then he was sure he heard footsteps in the passageway behind them.

He stopped and looked back, trying to see through the shadows behind Rafe.

"What's the matter?" Rafe asked.

"I thought I heard something." He strained her ears, and then he heard it again. He glanced at Rafe. "They're hunting us."

He saw Sahara rivet on something over Rafe's shoulder. "They're here!" she cried. "Run!"

"Take her and go!" Rafe shouted.

Jared hoisted Sahara in his arms and sprinted for the end of the tunnel.

"No!" Sahara cried. "We can't leave him!"

Jared didn't answer. He heard Rafe's footsteps behind them, but when he glanced back, he couldn't see his friend in the shadows.

Suddenly, the corridor opened out and Jared felt a surge of relief.

"There it is!" Jared panted.

But as he barreled through the hangar, he spotted a dozen Drakkin soldiers sitting beneath a light, engaged in some kind of dice play. As soon as they saw Jared and Sahara, they scrambled for weapons.

"Rafe!" Sahara cried.

Jared looked back and saw Rafe sprinting behind them, legs and arms pumping. Another dozen Drakkin soldiers were right on his tail.

As Jared reached the ramp of the dropship, he set Sahara on her feet.

"Get inside!" he shouted.

She ignored him and grabbed a machine gun from the rack just inside the hangar door and slapped the magazine home. For one instant, their eyes locked and she nodded.

"Go. I'll cover Rafe."

He disappeared into the belly of the ship as Sahara took cover just inside the hatch.

SIXTY-TWO

The Drakkin were almost to the ramp when she opened
fire. She mowed six of them down before the others broke ranks to
take cover. Rafe dashed up the ramp and she fired again. But the
Drakkin returned fire and she ducked inside the hatch as a hail of
bullets pelted around them.

"Dammit Rafe, get up there!" she shouted over her shoulder.

"Already gone!" he called back.

She slammed her hand against the button to close the hatch. Two
Drakkin tried to get on board as the ramp lifted, but she dropped
them with a headshot. A moment later she felt the ship shudder to
life, and then the engines roared. The blast knocked the rest of the
Drakkin flat and then the ramp closed and sealed.

"Punch it, Rafe!" she shouted.

The engines roared, and the ship jolted her off her feet as it lifted
off. She scrambled up again and headed up the corridor to the bridge.

She stopped at the large gallery window. Dawn was just breaking, and the ground below was awash in gold. They were over the
desert again, and the air still shimmered with sand particles from the
night storms.

Then she caught her breath. Just below them lay the smoking ruins of Albadir.

"No," she whispered. She pressed her hand against the glass. "No..."

She rushed to the bridge, where Jared was helping Rafe to navigate the ship.

"Where should I set her down?" Rafe asked.

"Over there," Jared said, pointing to the long-unused platform near the city gates. As Rafe maneuvered the ship to a gentle touchdown, Jared asked, "You picking up anything on those sensors?"

"Nothing."

Rafe cut the engines, and for a moment, they just sat there, staring out the window at the blasted gates and smoldering ruins beyond. Memories tumbled through Sahara's mind—Wes's cottage, Aliya's gentle hands in the Halls of Healing, and even Kirin's irritating friendliness.

Everything she had most wanted to save was blasted to hell.

"This is all my fault," Sahara mumbled.

"It's not your fault," Jared said, but Sahara thought it sounded too automatic, and that hurt more than if he'd just agreed with her.

"Maybe there are survivors," Rafe said.

He and Jared unfastened their harnesses and left the flight deck together. Sahara trailed behind them. The platform shimmered in the early morning heat, and it burned Sahara's bare feet. They jogged down the stairs to the sands below, and she found no relief there.

It was so strange—to be hobbling towards the city in burned, bare feet and tattered clothes, just as she had done so many months ago.

It's no different now...except that it turns out they were right. I brought everything they feared down on them.

She battled down the tears and stumbled after Jared and Rafe. As they reached the gates, they stopped and Jared held up a hand.

"What is it?" she asked. The soles of her feet felt like they were on fire, and she shifted her weight as best she could to try to give them some relief.

"Look," Rafe said, pointing.

There were two huge, strange marks in front of them, almost completely covered by the sands. Sahara stared at them, and then, in a flash, she saw it all: the dark ship, the lines of people prodded and pushed aboard like animals, the Drakkin troops setting fire to the buildings.

"There was a ship here," she said. "That's why he said they were starbound."

"Who said that?" Jared asked.

"The executioner." She gripped Jared's arm, hoping he understood what this meant.

Where there is life, there's hope...

Jared stared at her for a moment. "You think they shipped them off somewhere?"

Sahara lifted her shoulders, and Jared's jaw tightened. He swung away toward the blasted gates. Rafe and Sahara followed on his heels.

The city was breathlessly quiet. The main street was pocked by deep holes and singed stone, and anything green and living had been utterly destroyed. Sahara shuddered as they passed the doorway where she'd met Del's mother. It was nothing but a heap of burned stone and ashes.

She fought hard against the voice in her head that said she had killed them all—that she might as well have held the flamethrowers herself.

This isn't your fault, came Jared's voice in her head. *We were marked for death long before you fell out of the sky.*

The Great House was still partly in flames when they arrived. Smoke billowed from the eastern wing, and Sahara could see tongues of fire licking at the windows on the second and third floors.

"Be careful," Jared cautioned as they stepped through the rubble that had once been the front doors. "The building could come down any second."

Sahara coughed, the smoke choking her lungs. There was no sign that fire had reached the central wing of the building yet, and she glanced down the wide corridor that led to the dining hall. Everything was empty and still.

They searched the first floor, but it was empty. Jared clattered up the stairs to Childir's chambers, and came back down almost immediately.

"Nothing," he said.

They made their way slowly through the western wing, stopping just long enough for Sahara to find new clothes and boots. As she pulled on the black battle dress pants and boots and tugged the black tank over her burned shoulders, she remembered how Aliya had tried so hard to guide her toward a gentler path—to heal, rather than destroy.

I'm so sorry I disappointed you, she said to the memory.

She ran her fingers through her hair, matted with sweat and blood, and pulled it all back into a tight ponytail. Then she rejoined the others in the corridor.

They swept the rest of the building, stopping just once more in the armory. It had been completely raided, and all the ammunition and weapons were gone. But when Sahara pulled open a drawer, she found that they had left the combat knives. She selected one and strapped the belt and sheath around her hips.

They returned to the dining hall. The building creaked and groaned all around them like an animal in its death throes.

"We should get back to the ship," Rafe said. "There's no one here."

"I know one place we haven't looked yet," Sahara said.

She led the way through the dining hall and into the kitchen beyond. On the right hand side was the doorway and stairs down, and they followed these down into the cool dark of the cellar.

As soon as they reached the bottom, she went to one of the shelves and shifted a large pot of honey. A small silver lever gleamed in the dim light. She pulled it, and the shelf slid sideways to reveal another set of stairs.

"What—?" Rafe said as Sahara clattered down the steps.

"Aliya showed me this place," she said over her shoulder. "Just in case."

The narrow corridor at the bottom ended in a wall of glass. A sophisticated keypad on the right blinked at them, and Sahara punched in the code. The light flashed yellow, and then the door slid open.

"Someone's been here," she said. "Someone else knew about this place."

"How do you know?" Jared asked.

"The light should be green."

"What the hell would Arnauld store down here?" Rafe asked.

"Come and see," she answered.

She led them through the door and gestured around. The room was clad in burnished metal, and soft lighting flickered on as soon as they stepped through the door. Long shelves lined the walls, some loaded with wine casks, others with chests and crates.

"It's an emergency supply bunker," Sahara said. "And it was designed especially for that." She pointed to a large case that hummed along the wall opposite the wine casks. It seemed to have its own regulator.

"What is it?" asked Jared.

"Medicine. Anaesthetics. Antibiotics. Vaccines." She shrugged. "Whatever we might need."

"But Albadir doesn't have supplies like that," Jared protested. "They ran out a long time ago!"

Sahara shook her head. "Lady Aliya stockpiled an emergency supply down here, just in case there was ever an outbreak or something that couldn't effectively be treated with herbs or other methods." She leaned in and lowered her voice. "And this also happens to be the perfect place to hide."

"You're right," said a voice behind them.

They spun around and Jared's face broke into a huge grin. Brytnoth came forward to meet them, and he and Jared embraced. Then he clasped hands with Rafe.

"Brytnoth!" Jared exclaimed. "You made it back."

Brytnoth took Sahara's hand and bowed over it, and she smiled at him quizzically. "We haven't met yet," he said. Then he turned and called out, "You can come out now, you two!"

SIXTY-THREE

Emma and Kirin slowly emerged from behind a row of casks and came forward. Emma's face was pale and dirty, but she lit up when she saw Rafe.

Kirin stood awkwardly, trying not to look at either Sahara or Jared.

"I thought you were dead!" Emma cried, her eyes welling with tears. She stumbled toward Rafe and he folded her in his arms. "When Brytnoth returned without you...I thought...."

"I tried to tell her you'd be just fine," Brytnoth said to Rafe. "But she was convinced I was lying."

Jared stepped toward Kirin. "I should execute you for treason," he said, his voice low and terrible.

Kirin raised his hands and Emma stepped between them. "He said he didn't know better! He said he was sorry!"

"You're sorry?" Jared asked Kirin. "You think that makes up for what you did to me—what you almost did to us all?"

"Lady Aliya—she found me. She forgave me, and told me to come down here with Emma." He shifted his gaze to Sahara. "She said you'd know to look here, if you came back."

Emma edged around Rafe and stared at Sahara as though she'd never seen her before. The color rose into her face and then faded just as suddenly.

"You're the one they were going to sacrifice to the dragon," she said. "The one who took Aliya's place."

"Yes." Sahara's breath caught in her throat. "Did she—?"

Emma shook her head sadly. "I don't know."

From somewhere overhead, there was a crash, and the acrid smell of smoke began to fill the room. Rafe took Emma by the hand and they hurried for the door. Sahara went to the chest in the corner and opened it.

"Grab some provisions on the way out," she said. "I'll meet you outside."

They raced up the steps and she focused on packing a medkit. There was a small pouch inside the chest for just that purpose, and she loaded it with everything she thought they might need. As she zipped the pouch closed, another crash from upstairs made her jump. She closed the chest again and ran for the stairs.

A billowing inferno of fire met her. For a moment, she was too blinded by heat and smoke to realize that her only escape route was cut off. Coughing, she retreated to the bunker and strapped the medkit securely to her belt. Then she tore a wide strip off her shirt and soaked it in one of the barrels of water in the bunker. She wrapped it around her mouth and nose and hair.

She took a deep breath, and plunged into the smoke.

The roaring disoriented her so badly that she could barely make it up the stairs on all fours. Bits of burning wood fell all around her, and she heard the sound of falling masonry somewhere close. She made it into the pantry and fumbled her way to the door. Just as she reached it, the ceiling caved in. She dove through the door and kicked it shut behind her.

For a moment, she lay there, coughing and trying to catch her breath. Then she saw flames licking underneath the door and she scrambled to her feet. She sprinted for the doors that led out to the courtyard.

She burst out of the Great House to find the others waiting beside the dried-out fountain. As soon as he saw her, Jared hurried forward and helped unwind the cloth from around her head.

"Are you all right?" he asked. "What happened?"

The roaring behind them intensified, and Rafe looked at the Great House. Then he waved frantically at the others.

"Run!" he shouted. "It's coming down!"

They bolted for the street and they didn't stop running until they reached the city gates. Then Kirin caught Jared's arm and pulled him up short. Sahara stopped beside him, and the others returned to gather around.

"What are we supposed to do now?" Kirin asked.

"We have to get out of here," Sahara said. "There are Drakkin soldiers still in that fortress. They'll come after us."

"I thought you destroyed them all!" Brytnoth said.

"We took out the Council," Jared said. "We cut the head off the serpent...but the body's still thrashing a bit."

"You mean they'll come back?" Emma said, hovering close to Rafe.

"Where are we supposed to go?" Kirin pressed. "There's nothing left."

"Our people are out there somewhere," Sahara said, pointing toward the brilliant blue sky. "They're still alive...but they won't be for long unless we find them."

"You're suggesting a rescue mission?" Kirin asked.

"Yes."

For a moment, they all looked at one another. Sahara's heart hammered in her chest, and she hoped they would agree with her. She'd failed her brother...she would not fail the people of Albadir.

"I vote yes," Brytnoth said. "I would do anything to save your people from suffering what mine did."

"And it's better than rattling around on a dead planet, I guess," Kirin agreed.

Sahara smiled. "Let's go."

Jared and Sahara led the way up the steps of the platform to the ship, and then he caught her hand to hold her back as the others boarded.

"There's so much I want to say," he said softly. "So many things I want you to know."

She closed her fingers around his and he laid his hand against her cheek. She closed her eyes, feeling the warmth of his touch radiate all through her.

"Hey!" Brytnoth said, leaning out of the hatch. "You coming?"

The moment shattered like glass. Sahara's eyes flew open and she pulled away from Jared. He glared at Brytnoth.

"I wasn't interrupting something, was I?" he asked.

"No," Sahara said.

She pushed past him and heard Jared following her. The klaxon sounded as Jared slammed his hand on the button to close the hatch. Then he edged past them with a look in Sahara's direction that scorched her to the core.

She turned away from Brytnoth's inquisitive eyes and checked to make sure their gear was secured. Everything was stashed in a cargo net, and she adjusted the strap. She could feel Brytnoth watching her, and she wished he would just go away.

"How many times are you going to redo that strap?" he asked finally.

Sahara glanced up to see him standing right beside her. "As many times as it takes for you to leave," she said.

He laughed, even though she hadn't meant to be funny. But he left her alone in the hold, and she took a moment to collect herself before following him up to the flight deck.

Rafe was once more in the pilot's seat, and he flipped a series of switches to bring the engines online. Jared sat in the co-pilot's seat beside him, strapping in.

"We all set?" Rafe asked Sahara as she took her seat next to Emma.

"Ready," she said.

Rafe did a final check of the instruments and then glanced at Jared. "Where to?"

"Are we really heading into deep space on this piece of crap Drakkin ship and no clue where to look for our people?" Kirin asked.

"That would be a stupid plan," Jared said.

"Wait—that's not the plan?" Rafe asked.

"No. Not enough fuel in her cells to get us much beyond K'ilenfir. If we're planning to go beyond that, we're going to need another ship."

Emma gripped the armrests of her seat until her knuckles were white. "Where are we supposed to get another ship?"

Jared turned to wink at Sahara, and she grinned. "I've got a plan."

"What plan?" Rafe asked.

"We need a deep-space vessel, so we're going to K'ilenfir to take one," Jared said.

"Great. Sounds like suicide," Kirin muttered.

"Outstanding," Rafe said. "Everybody ready to die?" He glanced over his shoulder at them. "Good. Then let's do this."

He fired the engines and they lifted off the ground. The blasted ruins of Albadir sank slowly out of view, and then he gunned the engines and they were slammed back into their seats.

With a dizzying rush, Sahara watched the desert world shrink below them through the flames that licked around the windows.

Then, just as suddenly, they were out in the black, and Jared set their course for the tiny Drakkin prison moon of K'ilenfir.

TEASER
ASKALON'S RECKONING

Stationed next to the door, Sahara was the first one to hear the erratic *slap-slap, slap* of feet plunging through the puddle-ridden mud track that snaked its way through the jungle. The sound was growing louder by the second.

"Someone's coming," she hissed to the small group huddled around the table behind her.

She slipped into position behind the door, knives out and at the ready. In her black battle dress, she was all but invisible in the flickering shadows within the miserable hut.

Jared, Rafe, and Brytnoth were on their feet behind her, weapons drawn, eyes fixed on the door. Emma scrambled onto the solitary cot at the back of the room, hugging her knees to her chest. Sahara glanced at the young barmaid, saw her face pale with fear. Then Rafe pinched out the candle on the table and darkness swallowed them.

In the breathless seconds that followed, they all listened to the runner, his frantic pace slowing as he approached the squat wooden structure.

Sahara slid to the window and peered out. The rain cascaded from the drooping thatch eaves and obscured the path, but she could just make out a darker figure against the hazy greens and grays of the jungle beyond. Silently, her mouth a grim line, she slipped back to her place beside the chinked plank door. Jared moved up close beside her.

"Is it him?" he whispered in her ear.

"Can't tell."

Tap, tap-tap, tap. The stranger's knuckles rapped the warped planks of the door.

"It's him," Rafe said from the darkness behind her.

The flickering light of the candle danced out across the room as Jared handed his crossbow to Brytnoth and flung open the door.

Kirin stood there, rain running down his face, his clothes in shreds. A long, ugly gash split the length of his thigh, weeping blood down his pant leg.

"They're coming," he gasped, staggering forward. "They know."

———

Continue the adventure in *Askalon's Reckoning...*

WANT EVEN MORE ADVENTURE?

You already know that Sahara is an extraordinary and fearless warrior. But that's not how her story begins.

I can't wait for you to discover Sahara's origin story in *The Shift — A Silesia Story*...and best of all, it's yours for free!

Tap the cover or head to shannonblakebooks.com to pick up your copy today!

AUTHOR'S NOTE

Dear reader,

From the bottom of my heart, thank you. Thank you for coming along on this adventure with me, and for the gift of your attention and your time. It truly means the world to me.

I'd like to ask you for one more gift for me and for your fellow readers. You know how much a good review can help you decide which adventure to choose next, so please help other readers by sharing your rating and review on your favorite store and on Goodreads.

You can find all of my books on Amazon at amazon.com/author/shannonblakebooks.

See you on our next adventure!

Shannon

ALSO BY SHANNON BLAKE

ABOUT THE AUTHOR

Shannon has been dreaming up stories and writing them down for almost as long as she can remember. She's insatiably curious and loves science fiction for giving her the excuse to research the most random things — and for giving her the freedom to explore galaxies.

In addition to penning novels, Shannon is an award-winning screenwriter managed by Art/Work Entertainment in Hollywood. She loves giving back to the writing community through coaching and teaching, and she also works as a ghostwriter and creative entrepreneur.

When she's not writing, she loves running, dancing, obstacle course racing, and hanging out with her family and friends. And she has never been known to turn down chocolate or a chai latte.

You can find more about her upcoming projects and author appearances at shannonblakebooks.com or follow her on Instagram @shannonblakebooks.